"You're the boss," Blake said. At least, for now.

He saw Jo's eyes widen as if she'd heard his unspoken words.

"You don't have a problem with my taking charge?" she asked.

His shoulders lifted. "Why should I? I'm a sensitive New Age kind of guy."

"Yeah, right."

Feigning hurt feelings, Blake's eyebrows rose. "You don't believe me."

"I believe you'll let me lead when it suits you," Jo responded.

Keeping the grin off his face, he said, "I might surprise you."

The skeptical look she gave him only made him want her more. He would take the greatest delight in breaching her journalistic facade to connect with the woman beneath. She'd be all softness, all warmth and all passion. She was an all-or-nothing kind of lady, *his* kind.

Dear Reader,

We keep raising the bar here at Silhouette Intimate Moments, and our authors keep responding by writing books that excite, amaze and compel. If you don't believe me, just take a look RaeAnne Thayne's *Nothing To Lose,* the second of THE SEARCHERS, her ongoing miniseries about looking for family—and finding love.

Valerie Parv forces a new set of characters to live up to the CODE OF THE OUTBACK in her latest, which matches a sexy crocodile hunter with a journalist in danger and hopes they'll *Live To Tell.* Kylie Brant's contribution to FAMILY SECRETS: THE NEXT GENERATION puts her couple *In Sight of the Enemy,* a position that's made even scarier because her heroine is pregnant—with the hero's child! Suzanne McMinn's amnesiac hero had *Her Man To Remember,* and boy, does *he* remember *her*—because she's the wife he'd thought was dead! Lori Wilde's heroine is *Racing Against the Clock* when she shows up in Dr. Tyler Fresno's E.R., and now his heart is racing, too. Finally, cross your fingers that there will be a *Safe Passage* for the hero and heroine of Loreth Anne White's latest, in which an agent's "baby-sitting" assignment turns out to be unexpectedly dangerous—and passionate.

Enjoy them all, then come back next month for more of the most excitingly romantic reading around—only in Silhouette Intimate Moments.

Yours,

Leslie J. Wainger
Executive Editor

Please address questions and book requests to:
Silhouette Reader Service
U.S.: 3010 Walden Ave., P.O. Box 1325, Buffalo, NY 14269
Canadian: P.O. Box 609, Fort Erie, Ont. L2A 5X3

Live To Tell

VALERIE PARV

Silhouette®

INTIMATE MOMENTS™

Published by Silhouette Books

America's Publisher of Contemporary Romance

SILHOUETTE BOOKS

ISBN 0-373-27392-4

LIVE TO TELL

Books by Valerie Parv

Silhouette Intimate Moments

Interrupted Lullaby #1095
Royal Spy #1154
††*Operation: Monarch* #1268
**Heir to Danger #1312
**Live To Tell #1322

Silhouette Romance

The Leopard Tree #507
The Billionaire's Baby Chase #1270
Baby Wishes and Bachelor Kisses #1313
**The Monarch's Son* #1459
**The Prince's Bride-To-Be* #1465
**The Princess's Proposal* #1471
Booties and the Beast #1501
Code Name: Prince #1516
†*Crowns and a Cradle* #1621
†*The Baron & the Bodyguard* #1627
†*The Marquis and the Mother-To-Be* #1633
††*The Viscount & the Virgin* #1691
††*The Princess & the Masked Man* #1695
††*The Prince & the Marriage Pact* #1699

*The Carramer Crown
†The Carramer Legacy
††The Carramer Trust
**Code of the Outback

VALERIE PARV

With 20 million copies of her books sold, including three Waldenbooks bestsellers, it's no wonder Valerie Parv is known as Australia's queen of romance and is the recognized media spokesperson for all things romantic. Valerie is married to her own romantic hero, Paul, a former crocodile hunter in Australia's tropical north.

These days he's a cartoonist and the two live in the country's capital city of Canberra, where both are volunteer zoo guides, sharing their love of animals with visitors from all over the world. Valerie continues to write her page-turning novels because they affirm her belief in love and happy endings. As she says, "Love gives you wings, romance helps you fly." Keep up with Valerie's latest releases at www.silromanceauthors.com.

For Tracey and Steve, a truly inspirational couple

Chapter 1

The disturbing sensation of being watched nagged at Jo Francis. She felt her features tighten as she watched Nigel approach the creek. "This isn't a good idea. Blake warned us not to camp closer than fifty yards from the creek, and not to get fresh water from the same place every day."

Nigel shot her a disparaging look. "I'm getting mighty tired of hearing, 'Blake said...' every time I want to do something. Maybe you'd rather have him sharing this crazy stunt with you instead of me."

The words of denial Jo knew he expected from her stalled in her throat. In some ways, she would rather have Blake with her, but not for the reasons Nigel suspected. Living in the Kimberley, one of the world's last great wildernesses in the far northwest of Western Australia, was proving to be a far greater challenge than she had anticipated, and they'd only been in the outback for three days.

How was she supposed to survive for a month in such a

hostile environment, when Nigel thought he knew more than a man who owned the local crocodile farm and had grown up on this land? The bush shelter they were supposed to be moving into tomorrow was barely started because Nigel insisted on doing things his way. Now he was going beyond stubborn all the way to reckless.

"Please be careful," she implored.

"Blake Stirton isn't the only man who can handle this stuff," Nigel threw at her over his shoulder. "Your editor has more faith in me than you do."

Hearing the censure in his voice, Jo regretted letting Nigel talk his way into sharing this assignment. Nigel was the marketing director at *Australian Scene Weekly*'s advertising agency and they'd dated until he'd gotten too serious for Jo's comfort. She knew he was hoping to win her back during the trip, but she was equally determined to convince him that their relationship was over.

Maybe she was out of her mind for thinking she could survive in the wilderness with only the minimum of modern-day amenities, she berated herself silently. Like Nigel Wylie, she'd lived in the city for all of her twenty-six years and had gone camping only on family outings. She'd enjoyed them, but had always been happy to get back to civilization.

Under the harsh outback sun, her fair complexion was a liability, and she was beginning to wish she'd had her long, streaky blond hair cut short before leaving Perth. Even tied in a ponytail, it felt uncomfortably hot and heavy between her shoulder blades.

Her editor, Karen Prentiss, had come up with the idea of sending her feature writer on a survival mission soon after hearing about the discovery of some ancient cave paintings on a cattle property called Diamond Downs in the wilds of the Kimberley region of Western Australia. According to Jo's research, the property owner, Des Logan, and his late wife had a daughter, Judy, and fostered four sons after they discovered they couldn't have any more children of their own. The boys were all from problem backgrounds, but Des had managed to straighten them out over time and each was now successful in a different field.

Blake, the oldest of the Logan foster sons, had briefed her and Nigel on what to expect during their stay at Diamond Downs. He owned Sawtooth Park, a crocodile breeding and education center outside Halls Creek, a few miles away.

Thinking of the enormous crocodiles he'd shown them during their orientation, Jo shivered. The scaly throwbacks to the dinosaur era both fascinated and terrified her. She'd taken to heart Blake's warnings about respecting the wild crocodiles who inhabited the rivers and creeks of Diamond Downs, more than Nigel had done, it seemed.

A fresh prickle of unease lifted the fine hairs on the back of her neck as she watched him steady himself by grasping the branch of a freshwater mangrove, so he could lean over the still water to fill his canteen. They had fresh water at camp, but Nigel insisted it was colder straight from the creek.

The surroundings were idyllic. Around her, majestic pandanus, paperbarks and eucalypti created a cool oasis. The air was fragrant with the sweet scents of the mangroves, tropical orchids, gardenias and grevilleas. An outcrop of large granite slabs protruded into the water, forming a natural jetty. Blake had pointed out a series of worn cavities in the surface of the rocks where, over centuries, the aboriginal people had crushed grass seeds into paste for food.

He had also warned them that death lurked beneath the deceptively tranquil, lily-strewn water.

Her sense of unease grew. "Please, watch out for—"

"Crocodile!" Nigel shouted at the same moment.

In a blur of movement, an olive-colored torpedo surged out of the water, wolflike dagger teeth snapping shut around Nigel's canteen with the force of a steel trap. She barely had time to glimpse a great dragon head with horned eyebrows and blazing yellow eyes, before the prehistoric creature sank back into the creek, its powerful serrated tail churning the water to foam.

For a horrified instant, she thought Nigel had been dragged in, as well, until she saw him swing himself into the tangled branches. His grip on the tree must have saved him. "Get away from there," she screamed.

"What the flaming hell do you think I'm doing?" He pulled himself hand over hand back to shore, while she kept a wary eye on the water. The crocodile was nowhere to be seen, but she could sense its fearsome presence lurking in the depths.

Then Nigel was back on land, sheet-white and shaking, rubbing the back of his neck where the strap from the canteen had etched a furrow. The torn leather dangling from his neck told its own story. Angrily, he jerked the strap off and dashed it to the ground. "Blasted man-eater ought to be shot."

He spun back in the direction of their camp where Blake had supplied them with a .303 rifle for protection. She grabbed Nigel's arm, barely halting his progress. "You can't shoot it. Crocodiles are a protected species."

"Not if they attack humans," he spat at her.

"It didn't attack. You invaded its territory," she said, as shaken by the near miss as he was. "If you injure it instead of killing it, you could make matters worse."

His scathing look raked her. "Worse than nearly being dragged under and eaten alive?"

She refrained from repeating Blake's lesson that crocodiles didn't eat their prey alive. They rolled you over and over until you drowned, then stowed you in an underwater lair to be eaten once you'd softened sufficiently. The very thought made her sick. She had a feeling Nigel wouldn't welcome the reminder right now. If he hadn't had such a firm grip on the tree...

"I'm glad you're okay," she said softly.

His stare remained wintry. "Are you?"

"Of course I am."

"Because you care about me, or because you want to get your story?"

"No story is worth a life."

"No? Then tell your boss what she can do with this assignment."

She gestured impatiently. "You know why I can't."

"Because you need Karen to use her influence with her husband. Isn't there another way to keep Lauren's home open that doesn't involve risking both our necks?"

"None that Karen was prepared to share with me," Jo said, too shaken to hide her bitterness. Ever since the editor heard about Diamond Downs, she'd had a bee in her bonnet about setting a feature there. Jo would have been happy simply to interview the Logan family, but for some reason, Karen wouldn't hear of it. "Too predictable for *Scene Weekly*. Our readers expect an inside story, a sense of being there," she'd told Jo. That's when she'd hatched the idea of having Jo live off the land for a month and report on the experience diary-style in each issue.

Nor was Karen above using Jo's worry about Lauren to gain Jo's cooperation. "This is the way the world works," she'd said with a shrug. "You want me to do something for you, you do something for me."

Karen's husband, Ron, was the developer whose company wanted to develop the land where Lauren's home, Hawthorn Lodge, stood. Jo had been Lauren's surrogate big sister, watching her grow from a shy, introverted girl with a learning disability to the charming young woman she was now. Much of that progress was due to the sheltered environment Lauren shared with seven young people like herself and one understanding set of house parents. Karen knew as well as Jo that Lauren would be lost out in the world, even if Jo took her in. When the home had been extensively remodeled the previous year, Lauren had stopped speaking for over two months, until she adjusted to the changes. Jo hated to think how Lauren might respond if forced to move to a new location.

Nigel read the truth in Jo's eyes. "You're not giving up, are you, not even after what just happened?"

Jo wished she could give him the answer she knew he

wanted, but she couldn't. "It was as much our fault as the crocodile's. We can learn from this and move on," she said.

"That's the first true thing you've said since we got here. We can learn from this and move on."

Something in his voice made her blood chill. "I mean together."

"No, you mean I can learn to do things your way by your rules, as usual."

"You're putting words into my mouth."

"I'm stating facts. Nearly getting eaten makes you see things with crystal clarity. I wanted to do this because I care for you, Jo. I want you to feel the same way about me. But it won't happen as long as every waking minute is taken up with staying alive."

"What are you saying?"

"I want you to give this up."

At the pleading note in his voice, she wavered. Maybe she didn't have much sense, but giving up wasn't on her agenda. "I'm sorry you feel that way," she said, meaning it.

"You can't do this by yourself."

"The Logans are there if I need help."

"Meaning Blake Stirton, I suppose."

"Meaning the Logan family. This has nothing to do with Blake."

Nigel pushed his way toward their camp as if he had difficulty making his limbs obey him. Shock was probably setting in, but he wasn't about to let her sympathize with him, she saw from his shuttered expression. "Nothing to do with Blake," he sneered. "So I imagined the way you hung on to his every word?"

"Of course you didn't. Our survival depends on listening to his advice," she snapped, tired of defending herself. If Nigel had paid more attention to Blake's briefing instead of being jealous of the other man, they might not be having this discussion now.

Nigel dragged a pack out of the tent. "Well, not anymore. You can go or stay as you choose. I've made my decision."

He began to stuff clothes and possessions into the pack, making it clear he was serious. She hadn't doubted it. Nigel always did what he said he'd do. She'd been frankly astonished when he'd volunteered to take part in this experiment. *Spontaneous* wasn't in his vocabulary.

She had to try one last time. "You don't have to leave. I know you had a bad scare and you're entitled to be rattled."

He leveled a searing look at her. "Rattled doesn't begin to describe how it feels to stare death in the face. I'm getting out of here while I still can."

"I can't exactly blame you," she admitted. "I'm sorry I got you into this in the first place."

He stopped packing long enough to smile fleetingly at her. "I'm sorry, too. I thought we might get back some of the romance we used to have, but it isn't going to happen, is it?"

"I told you it was over between us long ago," she reminded him.

He straightened. "You didn't tell me you were hoping to find some he-man who can swing through trees on a vine and catch your dinner with his bare hands. I'm a bloody good businessman, but that will never be enough for you, will it?"

She couldn't argue with his assessment of himself. They'd met through the magazine, and she'd been attracted by his good looks and the rapid-fire way his mind worked. "I thought this was about a crocodile attacking you. How did it get to be about us?" she asked.

"You must have known how much I wanted things to work out between us."

She let a sigh whisper past her lips. "I hoped you would learn something about your own strengths, as well. Isn't that why people undertake these survival-type challenges?"

"I've learned all I needed to. Not only that I don't want to be around man-eating crocodiles, but that I don't want to be molded into something I'm not."

"I never tried to mold you into anything."

"No? Then why didn't you listen when I said I thought this project was a bad idea?"

He was right. She hadn't listened. She'd been too fixated on satisfying Karen. At least that had been the reason Jo had given herself. Now she wondered if Nigel wasn't right. Saving Lauren's home had been Jo's justification for agreeing to undertake the assignment, but she wasn't the reason Jo was here. At least not the whole reason. "I'll miss your help," she conceded.

He didn't relent. "You know where to find me if you change your mind." His tone said he wouldn't hold out much hope.

The snap of a dry twig outside brought her head up. "Someone's out there."

His head swung around. "What now, rampaging buffalo?"

"It sounded more like a footstep." Perhaps Blake had come to check on their progress. The flood of relief accompanying this thought was something she'd have to think about later.

Right now, she wanted to check on the source of the noise. She flung the tent flap aside and strode out.

"Jo, wait for me. You don't know what's out there."

She got outside in time to see a man disappearing into the bushes. From force of journalistic habit, she noted that he had dark skin, a stocky build and was about her height. He was dressed like the stockmen who worked the cattle on Diamond Downs. "Odd that he didn't stop to say hello," she said to Nigel, who'd followed her outside. Everyone they'd met so far had gone out of their way to be friendly.

"He could be from a tribe that doesn't belong here," Nigel suggested. "Or maybe he's wary of strangers."

"He must have seen or heard the croc attack. Wonder why he didn't show himself before or try to help."

"The crocodile could hold some cultural significance for him. We could speculate all day and be none the wiser."

"You're right." Shock at Nigel's near miss was taking a toll on her, too. The thought of someone spying on them didn't help. Suddenly, she became aware that she would be on her own once Nigel left. Bile rose in her throat, threatening to choke her. She had to fight the urge to pack up and go with him.

He seemed to sense her ambivalence. "Sure you don't want to come with me?"

No, she wasn't sure, but she shook her head. "I can't."

Can't or won't? his expression asked. Just as well he didn't voice the question, because she didn't know what her answer would have been.

"I'll get one of the men at the Logan homestead to drive me to town and bring the rental car back here for you," he said.

Impulsively, she wrapped her arms around his neck, stung when he made no move to respond. What did she expect? "Thanks for giving it your best shot," she said.

His mouth found hers, hot and hard, the way he knew she liked to be kissed. Normally the touch would have ignited her passion; now, there was only deep regret for what might have been. She kissed him back out of that regret.

A cough made her spring back. "Hope I'm not interrupting anything."

The laconic tone made her blood boil. "How long have you been standing there?"

"Long enough to be sure the crocodile didn't snap off anything vital," Blake drawled. Another man followed Blake into the clearing. For a moment, she thought it was the man who'd been watching them from the bushes until she realized that this man was taller and had a lighter complexion. The only thing Blake and his companion had in common with the spy was the khaki shirt, pants and battered Akubra hat that seemed to be the uniform for outback males. She couldn't help noticing how ruggedly appealing it looked on Blake.

"One of the stockmen was across the river when he heard a commotion and saw the crocodile attacking. Evidently, it was greatly exaggerated." Blake spoke softly to his companion. The other man nodded and moved off toward the water hole. Looking for the crocodile, she assumed. She was about to mention the man she'd glimpsed moments after the event, but Nigel spoke first.

"There was an attack all right, Stirton." Nigel's tone was the classic one of alpha male meeting another of his kind in his territory. The fact that he'd been about to relinquish that territory didn't matter for the moment. Instinct won out.

Jo resisted the urge to step between them, struck again by how much at home Blake was in this environment. He could take care of himself. "Nigel was getting water from the creek when a crocodile lunged out of the water at him," she said.

"Luckily it only snapped off my canteen, not my head," Nigel contributed.

Blake frowned. "From the look of you, it was a close call. If you want my advice…"

Nigel gestured dismissively. "Thanks, but no thanks."

Jo felt the beginnings of a headache. "Nigel, please. Blake's only trying to help."

"If he wants to help, he or his stockman will grab the rifle and blast that man-eating monster out of the water before someone gets killed."

She saw Blake's jaw tighten. Nigel was reacting out of shock and she could hardly blame him, but attacking a man who'd come to help them wasn't the answer.

"The crocodile isn't responsible for human stupidity," Blake said. "And Andy Wandarra is a tribal elder, so you'll show some respect."

She winced, wishing he had chosen his words more tactfully. She had a feeling tact wasn't Blake Stirton's strong suit.

Nigel wasn't a small man but Blake was half a head taller, with a cowboy's rangy build, most of which looked to be solid muscle. He stood with his feet apart, at home in the bush, although she imagined he'd look equally good wearing black tie in a ballroom. Longish hair the color of antique brass, turned up slightly at the collar, gave him a bad-boy aura. His warm hazel eyes were deep-set and creases radiating from them suggested he spent a lot of time staring across vast distances. Right now, his gaze was narrowed on Nigel, and what she saw in his expression wasn't approval.

She hoped Nigel's adrenaline-charged state wouldn't drive him to challenge Blake physically. No amount of loyalty to Nigel could convince her he was a match for Blake in a fight.

Nigel balled his hands into fists. "When the truth about this experience comes out, we'll see who your readers think is stupid, won't we, Jo?"

Blake fixed her with a glare that could have melted stone. She was proud of not quailing beneath his scrutiny, but it took some effort. "We were warned not to get water from the same place every day," she said with scrupulous fairness.

A glimmer of something like surprise flashed in Blake's hazel gaze. She didn't like the answering shiver that shook her.

"Crocs are cunning creatures. They wait and watch until they judge they can grab an easy meal," Blake said in a tone that suggested that this explanation was part of a much-repeated lecture. "You might get away with it the first or second time, but try it a third and you're history."

He illustrated the point by extending his arms and crashing his hands together like the jaws of a crocodile, and she saw Nigel flinch.

Instinctively, she moved closer to offer the comfort of her nearness, but he remained coldly aloof. His pride was stung, she thought in amazement. Not only by his brush with death, but by the fact that Blake was right and he was wrong.

"Are you okay?" she asked, pitching her voice low.

Wrong question, she saw as Nigel's jaw hardened. "I'm fine for someone who was almost eaten."

"Maybe you should see a doctor," Blake suggested. "One of our people can drive you to Halls Creek."

"There's nothing wrong with me that the sight of a dead crocodile won't fix. If you can't handle it, I'll do something about it myself."

Nigel turned toward the tent but in a move so fast she barely registered it, Blake put himself between Nigel and the equipment. "There are penalties for killing protected species out here."

Halted in his tracks, Nigel curled his lip into a sneer. "Oh, yeah. Your brother is a ranger, isn't he? Between you, you've got the Kimberley sewn up. If one Logan doesn't get me, the other will. Oh, I forgot. You're not Logans, either of you. You're a bunch of mongrels Des Logan took in and tried to civilize, without much success evidently."

Blake didn't move. "You're going the right way to get yourself thrown off this land, Wylie."

"He doesn't mean it. It's the shock of the attack."

Both men turned hard glares on her, but Jo wasn't about to back down. This was her show, whether Nigel accepted it or not. She needed this assignment. From her research into Des Logan's situation, he suffered from a heart complaint and was having trouble keeping Diamond Downs going. The discovery of the ancient rock art on the land had started to bring in tourist dollars, but he also needed the substantial fee her magazine was paying to use the site.

Without quite knowing how she knew, she saw the knowledge reflected in Blake's gaze. He shifted his attention to her. The ferocity of it sent shafts of heat through her, surprisingly difficult to ignore. "I'll overlook the personal insults this time." His tone made it clear there would be no second chance. "I still think this is a damn fool stunt. If you were really surviving, you wouldn't have so many frills. You have no business coming to the outback for the titillation of a few magazine readers."

She anchored her palms on her hips. "A moment ago, you mentioned respect. Yet you're not willing to accord us the same privilege even though those magazine readers you dismiss so readily number in the thousands. And my editor is paying your foster father a lot of money for us to be here, correct?"

"Correct."

She ignored the grudging tone. It was enough that he accepted her right to be here. "Our inexperience in the outback is the whole point of the exercise—to see how well we cope, also correct?"

He nodded tautly. "True enough."

"Then I don't see a problem. This isn't your land. You might have grown up here, but you live at your crocodile farm, don't you?"

"While we're playing twenty questions, I have one for you."

He was entitled. "Go ahead."

"Why the hell is this so important to you? Surely there are other subjects you can write about without risking your neck?"

Not subjects her editor was passionate about, she thought. She still wasn't sure why Karen had been so determined to send her on this assignment. Jo knew why she herself wanted to be here, but Blake didn't need to know. "I have my reasons," she said evenly.

Blake jerked his head toward Nigel, standing at Jo's shoulder, fuming but, for the moment, having the sense to keep quiet. "And your friend here?"

"I'm here because I refused to let her carry out this crazy assignment alone," he supplied.

So much for keeping quiet. "Our motivations are none of Blake's business," she demurred, not wanting to argue with Nigel in front of the crocodile man. "Part of the deal is for Blake to teach us how to survive in the outback, not to interfere."

The reminder didn't sit well with Blake, she saw, as his gaze darkened. He must feel strongly loyal to his foster father to have agreed to be part of a scheme he plainly opposed. "There's not much point in me giving you advice unless you have enough sense to take it."

The gibe was clearly aimed at Nigel and she felt him bristle at her side. "You can stop worrying, Stirton. I've had it up to here with this insane project. When you turned up, I was packing to leave."

"It didn't look like that to me."

Blake's reminder that Nigel had been kissing her when he'd arrived brought heat surging into her cheeks. "Again, none of your business," she insisted. "Nigel, I know the attack was a shock, but you can't mean to throw in the towel? It's only been three days." Two, if she didn't count the orientation day spent with Blake.

"Three days when I've been bitten to death by mosquitoes, sunburned gathering materials to build a stupid shelter when there's a perfectly good tent standing there and had my life threatened by a man-eater that Stirton thinks has more right to live than I do."

Blake's mouth thinned. "The crocodile was only defending its territory."

Was something similar going on between him and Nigel? "Why did you recommend we set up camp here if you knew it was dangerous?" she asked.

"I didn't know," he said surprising her. "We've had no problems with crocodiles in this area for years. I don't know why it happened now."

"So you admit you don't know everything," Nigel gibed, ignoring the warning pressure of the hand she placed on his arm.

"I never said I did," Blake responded mildly, but his hazel eyes flashed fire. "I assume after what's happened, you're both leaving?"

She moved a few feet away from Nigel in what she recognized was a symbolic gesture. "You assume wrong. Until the agreed-upon month is up, I'm not going anywhere."

Nigel flashed her a look of disbelief. Had his packing been an attempt to manipulate her into going with him? "You can't stay here alone," he said, reinforcing her suspicion.

Blake settled his hands on his hips. "She can't stay here at all. This wasn't part of the deal between Des and the magazine."

She folded her arms. "As I recall, neither were you, except as technical consultant."

Blake's eyes flashed fire. "What does that have to do with anything?"

"You have no authority to throw me out if I choose to remain."

"Des Logan does, and he will if I recommend it for your safety."

"For my safety or for your convenience? From the moment I arrived, you've made it clear you don't want me here."

"Surviving in the outback is not a game."

She nodded. "It won't be reported as such. My editor wants me to faithfully record our experiences for our readers."

"To achieve what, exactly?"

"If even one person is stranded in the outback and applies something they've learned from my articles, the series will have served a purpose."

Nigel pulled the straps of his backpack tight and looked around the camp. "Are you two going to argue the point all day? I have everything of mine. The rest of the gear belongs to the magazine. Can I get a ride to Halls Creek with you, Stirton? I don't want to leave Jo without a vehicle."

"You don't have to leave at all," she said. "Why not give yourself a little more time before you decide?"

"I have decided. I only agreed because I thought this wouldn't last more than a couple of days, then you'd see sense and we could get back to civilization."

Her mouth dropped. "You expected me to fail?"

Blake gave a humorless smile. "Charming."

Nigel shot him a look of irritation. "Of course not. Damn it, Jo, the only reason I agreed to be part of this is because I care about you. It's important to you, so it was important to me until I found myself staring death in the face." He jerked his thumb toward the now-tranquil creek. "We don't belong in that monster's territory, and I'm getting out while I still can."

She shuddered involuntarily, having no comeback. If the same thing had happened to her, would she feel like bailing, too? But it hadn't and she couldn't give up now, even though the memory of the crocodile leaping out of the water would haunt her for a long time. "I'm sorry."

Nigel's hand rested on his backpack. "Me, too. Look, I'll stay if you agree to my condition."

Her hopes rose but with them, a quiver of uncertainty as she guessed what he was about to say. "Nigel, don't. And besides, I don't need a caretaker," she said, annoyed that both men seemed determined to cast her in the role of a dependent. She was the youngest in her family, and her two older brothers had tried to do the same. Had she jumped at this assignment as much to prove them all wrong as for any other reason? At the same time, she knew there was more to her reluctance to accept Nigel's proposal, but this wasn't the right time for self-analysis. "I'll be fine on my own," she insisted.

"You won't be on your own," Blake intervened. He actually sounded pleased that she hadn't accepted Nigel's offer. Was that because he hoped it would get rid of her sooner? She couldn't imagine that his interest was in the least personal. "I may not be able to insist that you leave, but I can stick around and make sure you get through this in one piece," he said.

"Even if I don't want your protection?"

"It isn't a suggestion."

She gave vent to a sigh of frustration. "I can hardly throw you off your family's land, but you'd better not get in my way. I'm the one supposed to be learning to survive out here."

"You'll learn all right. I don't intend to make things easy for you."

If anything, he was going to make her task more difficult, she thought, and not only when it came to outback survival. He attracted her far more than she wanted him to. After her experience with Nigel she didn't plan on getting hot and bothered over any other man for some time to come.

Aware that hot and bothered barely covered the way her blood pressure soared every time Blake came near her, she looked from one man to the other. Talk about a rock and a hard place. Nigel's face was set in an expression that she knew only too well—it meant he wouldn't change his mind. And Blake didn't strike her as the type to back down, either. What was it about the outback that turned men into Neanderthals? "Seems like I don't have a choice," she demurred.

"None at all if you want to stay. So you'd better get your things together."

"Why, if I'm not going anywhere?"

"Until Andy and I find out why that croc attacked, you're not staying here alone. I have to meet my brother at the airport, so we can drop Wylie off at the same time. Then I'll come back with you and make sure everything's secure here."

"Sounds reasonable," she conceded.

His expression didn't alter. "I'm glad you approve." His tone said he didn't care one way or the other.

Before she could think of a suitable response, Andy Wandarra emerged from the bushes. "I found fresh tracks along the river bank. This was buried not far from the tracks. I disturbed a wild pig digging it up." He held up a handful of bloody entrails.

The rancid smell assaulted her senses and she recoiled. "I thought you said crocodiles drag their food into the water?"

Andy threw the mess into the creek where it sank leaving only bubbles. "They do. Whoever made the tracks must have dropped it."

Nigel swore colorfully. "I assume that wasn't the remains of the intruder's lunch."

"More like the crocodile's. If someone has been feeding the croc from the landing, it would explain the attack."

Nigel moved closer to her side. "The only person we know who wants us out of here is you, Stirton."

"He wouldn't," she protested, appalled at the suggestion.

Nigel made a slashing motion. "How can you be sure? You don't know him, yet you're prepared to put your life in his hands. I only hope you know what you're doing."

"She'll be safe with me, because I intend to get to the bottom of this," Blake vowed. He turned to Jo. "Did you see or hear anything around the time the crocodile attacked?"

"I caught a glimpse of a man hanging around in the bushes."

Blake nodded. "Did you see what he looked like?"

"Like Andy," she said. "When the two of you arrived I thought he was the same man, but the other man was younger and his skin was a darker color."

Andy and Blake traded looks. "Eddy Gilgai?" Andy said.

Blake nodded. "If it's Eddy, that means Max Horvath is involved in this."

"They're employees of your father's, I suppose," Nigel said.

Blake gave him a withering look. "Max Horvath is a neighbor who has designs on Diamond Downs. Max hired Eddy after Des sacked him for misconduct."

She didn't try to hide her confusion. "How would feeding a crocodile help your neighbor get his hands on your father's land?"

"Crocs don't have much in the way of brains but they're creatures of habit. You can train them to expect food at the same place and time. If Eddy taught this one to come in close to the landing, he could have had only one motive. He hoped to send you packing."

"Fine with me," Nigel said. "For you, too, if you have any sense, Jo."

He was probably right, but instinct wouldn't let her turn her back on what was shaping up to be quite a story. She couldn't wait to learn more about the neighborhood feud from Blake and his family.

"Don't power up your laptop yet," Blake said, as if sensing her interest. "This doesn't concern you."

"If it's meant to scare me away from Diamond Downs, it does."

"We're only guessing that was the explanation for the attack. Wylie could simply have been in the wrong place at the wrong time."

"But your theory fits the facts as you know them," she said. "It also explains some of the disturbances I've heard around the river since we set up camp here."

Blake's interest sharpened. "You didn't mention any disturbances."

"I don't know what's normal for the outback. For all I know, the sounds in the bushes could have been dingoes or one of those wild pigs."

"Or someone setting me up to be eaten by a crocodile," Nigel added. "Why the devil didn't you say something sooner, Jo?"

"I'm sorry I didn't, but it doesn't help now. It's more important to find out if your Max Horvath is behind this, and stop him before somebody gets hurt."

Blake shook his head. "Don't you get it? That someone could be you. I'm putting both of you on the next plane back to Perth."

She and Nigel spoke at the same moment.

"Good idea."

"The hell you are."

"You can throw me off Diamond Downs, but you can't make me leave the Kimberley until I'm ready," she asserted.

Blake's expression conceded reluctant defeat. "Then you're better off where I can keep an eye on you. If you carry on with your assignment as if we don't suspect anything, Horvath might get cocky and give himself away."

"And both of you could wind up dead."

"We won't. Blake knows what he's doing." At least she hoped he did.

Blake picked up Nigel's pack. "We'll take your car back to town. Andy, you take the jeep and see if you can find any more signs. We'll meet back at the homestead later."

The other man grinned. "Tom will be dying of curiosity by then."

"Tom's my brother and Andy's honorary clan brother," Blake elaborated. "His engagement party's tonight."

He must be the ranger who was marrying the princess, she assumed. Quite a family. "Do I get to meet him?"

Blake pushed his Akubra hat back on his head. "According to Des, under your editor's rules, you're only supposed to come to the homestead in a life-and-death emergency. I guess a crocodile attack qualifies. If you happen to be there for the party, it can't be helped. Until we know more, I don't want you staying out here on your own."

Nigel shifted impatiently and she nodded, feeling the familiar surge of excitement that told her she was on to a big story. Far bigger than Karen, her editor, had guessed when she dreamed up this assignment. "You're on."

Chapter 2

Are you crazy? Blake asked himself as he drove to Halls Creek. Nigel sat stony-faced in the back seat clutching his pack. Jo was in front beside Blake, staring thoughtfully out the window. Blake couldn't force Jo to leave, but what could she do if he dumped her in town and refused to return her to Diamond Downs? Once he knew the facts, Des would back Blake's position. So why didn't he?

Because from the moment she'd turned up at his croc farm expecting him to teach her how to survive in the bush, she'd caught his attention. What red-blooded man wouldn't be attracted to someone who moved as enticingly as she did? Neither athlete nor vamp. More like a woman with a mission. She had a compact, curvy shape that raised Blake's temperature on sight, and her unusual blue-green eyes reminded him of the semiprecious gem New Zealanders called greenstone. The last few days in the open air had kissed her milky skin with roses. His fingers itched to release her streaky blond hair from its ponytail for the pleasure of watching the breeze catch the strands.

Her refusal to be scared away by the crocodile had earned his grudging admiration, although he believed her confidence was misplaced. She didn't belong in the outback. The whole idea of a survival-type scenario was bull. But he couldn't deny that his foster father needed the fee her magazine was paying. Some money was coming in from visitor interest in the recently discovered rock art on the land, but there was a long way to go before tourism replaced the dwindling income from raising cattle.

Blake, his foster brothers and Des's daughter Judy helped as much as they could, but she was a bush pilot with people depending on her. Tom had responsibilities as the shire ranger. And Blake had the croc farm to run. None of them could give Diamond Downs as much money, time and attention as it needed. Yet Des wouldn't consider selling up. The land was in his blood and he wanted to leave it for Judy and her kids, and theirs after that.

The other fly in the ointment was Max Horvath's greed.

What a piece of work he was. He'd been an unpleasant child, taunting Blake and his brothers about their lack of pedigree. Max had been thirteen when his parents' marriage ended and his mother took him to live in the city. He'd come back for vacations and had developed a huge crush on Judy. Too softhearted to reject him out of hand, Judy had gone on occasional dates with Max, only breaking off the relationship when Max became serious. Now Blake wondered if her rejection of Max's marriage proposal had sown the seeds for this dangerous feud.

Unbeknownst to the boys, Des Logan had borrowed heavily from Clive Horvath, Max's father and Des's best friend, to keep the station going. After Clive was killed suddenly in a riding accident, Max had inherited their place and the mortgage Clive had intended to tear up. His son wasn't so forgiving. Since taking over, Max had been pressuring Des to repay the debt or forfeit Diamond Downs to him.

Blake thought he knew which option Max preferred. According to family folklore, Des's grandfather had found a fabulously rich diamond mine on his land. The location had been lost when he vanished without a trace. The belief that Des's ancestor's spirit guarded the site had kept the indigenous people from revealing what they knew about the mine's location. As boys, Blake and his siblings had tried without success to find the mine, eventually giving up and deciding there was no substance to the legend.

Max wasn't so easily convinced and had made no secret of wanting to find the mine. First, he had to claim ownership of Diamond Downs, and that wasn't going to happen while Blake had breath in his body to prevent it.

He steered the car into the airport parking lot, cut the engine and swiveled toward Nigel. "Your stop, Wylie."

The other man ignored him and looked at Jo. "Last chance to change your mind."

Against his better judgment, Blake decided to do the gentlemanly thing. "I'll give you two a few minutes to say your farewells."

He stepped out of the car and closed the door. He tried not to listen but overheard when Jo's voice rose in protest. Evidently she was still resisting Wylie's entreaties to return to Perth with him. After a couple of minutes, the other man slammed out of the car and headed for the terminal without a backward glance. Jo got out more slowly, her gaze troubled.

Blake couldn't help himself. "Is the love affair still on?"

"I'm not in love with Nigel, not that it's any concern of yours."

Blake was surprised by the sunburst of satisfaction blooming through him. If she'd been his woman, nothing could have made him walk away. He resisted the childish urge to yell "and stay out" after Wylie, instead switching his focus back to Jo.

As his gaze collided with hers, he felt a slam of sexual awareness unlike anything he'd experienced in a long time. His breath whooshed out and he felt his knees flex, if not exactly buckle. Suddenly, working with her didn't seem like such a bright idea. He might not have liked Wylie, but at least he'd served as a buffer zone between them.

Now there was only the two of them and a lot of time alone in the bush ahead.

"What now?" she asked, sounding strained.

He shrugged off the urge to hold her and soothe away some of the strain. "Now we meet Cade's flight."

"Cade Thatcher, your youngest foster brother," she supplied.

His brows winged upward. "You've done your homework."

"A good journalist does," she said. "And despite what you think of me, I am a good journalist."

"I never said you weren't. Only that you're a novice in the outback. From what I've read of your articles, they're well researched and written."

She hadn't expected the endorsement, he saw from the surprised look she gave him. The pleasure lighting her gaze sparked an answering surge in him. He was really going to have to watch himself around her.

Between the scars he carried from his past love life, and his foster father's troubles, Blake didn't need any more complications in his life right now. That certainty sharpened his tone as he said, "Let's get inside out of the heat."

Heat was on Jo's mind, too, but not in the way Blake meant, she decided as they approached the terminal. Through the glass, she saw Nigel standing at the check-in desk. He saw her but he didn't react. His parting words had convinced her he accepted it was over between them. Shouldn't she feel upset instead of relieved, as if a weight had been lifted from her shoulders?

Later would do to examine that, she decided as a tall, raven-haired man spotted Blake and strode out of the terminal to meet them. He was almost rail-thin and moved with the unconscious grace of a man at home in his body, as he gave Blake a back-thumping greeting. "About time you got here."

"Jo Francis, meet my no-manners foster brother, Cade Thatcher."

Cade's smile broadened. "Jo Francis? You're a writer with *Australian Scene Weekly*, aren't you?"

She nodded, finally placing him. "And you're the wildlife photographer."

"I was."

He didn't say what he was doing now, and she didn't feel she could ask at first meeting. Blake grabbed the other man's well-worn leather bag. "Car's this way."

In the parking lot, Cade regarded the vehicle with interest. "What happened to your Jeep?"

Blake put Cade's bag into the back seat, then held the front passenger door for Jo. "This is Jo's rental car. Andy's using the Jeep. Jo's staying on Diamond Downs on a writing assignment for the next month."

Cade climbed into the back. "Are you coming to Tom's wake tonight, Jo?"

"I thought it was an engagement party." Then she caught on and smiled. "Looks like it."

Cade nodded. "The more, the merrier. I haven't met the bride yet, but I hear she's beautiful and royal to boot. She should soon straighten Tom out." Then he grew serious. "How's Des?"

Blake steered the car onto the highway. "Not good. He's moved up the waiting list for a transplant but the way things are at home, he's not keen on having the operation even if a donor heart becomes available."

Cade rested his forearms on the seat back between her and Blake. "Can't say I blame him. He values his independence."

A trait he'd passed on to his foster sons and natural daughter, she'd already noticed. She couldn't imagine Blake willingly depending on anyone. "Is Max Horvath the reason Des doesn't want to be away from Diamond Downs?"

Cade's fingers drummed a tattoo on the seat back. "You've heard about him?"

She nodded and Blake said, "We think Max put Eddy Gilgai up to feeding a big croc to lure it closer to Jo's camp. Earlier today, it attacked the man she was with."

"Is he okay?"

"He wasn't harmed, but he's on his way back to Perth right now."

A taut smile ghosted over Cade's features. "Do you plan on following him?"

"I'm staying," she said, her tone daring either man to argue. "My assignment is to report on what it's like to survive in the outback, not to turn tail at the first sign of danger."

"Brave lady," Cade murmured, sounding impressed. "You must tell me more about this assignment. Maybe I can help."

Blake's irritation flared into full-blown jealousy. "I've agreed to show Jo the ropes. She doesn't need two guides."

Cade withdrew to the back seat, symbolically conceding the turf to his older brother. Amusement rang in his voice as he said, "I knew I should have caught an earlier flight."

"I still have to clear the change with my editor," Jo said, sensing the unspoken communication between the two men. Annoyed because she also sensed it concerned her, she sharpened her tone. "Blake may have too much experience to make the story work."

"I don't have anything like his experience," Cade said coyly.

Blake's fingers tightened around the steering wheel. "We're talking about bush craft."

"What did you think I meant?"

Enough was enough. "Will you two either cut it out, or let me in on the joke?"

"No," both men said with one voice.

"I'm glad you agree on something." She pulled out her cell phone and speed-dialed Karen's number. The editor's secretary put her straight through. As if dictating a story, Jo reported the day's events and Nigel's abrupt departure. She was aware of Blake and Cade silently absorbing her account.

The editor expressed horror at the near miss with the crocodile, but said nothing about Jo aborting the assignment.

When she reached the part about Blake offering to help out in Nigel's place, Jo found herself crossing her fingers. Not that she wanted to work with the crocodile man. She just didn't want to be pulled off a story that instinct told her had the potential to grow far beyond the original assignment.

"You're sure it's Blake Stirton you'll be working with?" Karen asked.

Jo's glance flickered to him. He controlled the car with easy movements, and his fingers had relaxed on the wheel, but his posture suggested a tension that made her curious. "Is there a problem?"

The vehicle swerved very slightly. Blake may have been dodging a rough patch in the road, rather than reacting to her words. She couldn't tell. "Would you like to talk to him yourself?" she asked Karen on impulse.

"No. Don't put him on." As if realizing how strange she sounded, Karen moderated her tone. "I'll take your word that you can work with him on this. The deal will be the same as we agreed with Nigel Wylie."

"Great. I'll tell him. Thanks." Confusion had reduced Jo's speech to monosyllables. The editor had reacted like a scalded cat at the prospect of speaking with Blake. What was going on here?

She flipped the phone shut and replaced it in her bag. "My boss is happy for you to help me complete the assignment."

Blake looked doubtful. "She said that?"

"Not in so many words. But she didn't pull the plug on the story." She shimmied sideways as far as her seat belt allowed and addressed Blake. "Have you ever met Karen Prentiss?"

A frown furrowed his brow. "Not as far as I know. Why?"

"When I offered to let her talk to you, she reacted as if I'd arranged a personal introduction with the devil."

"Maybe she's the mother of one of your old flames, Blake. Your sinful reputation precedes you," Cade suggested unhelpfully.

Jo caught her lower lip between her teeth, not enjoying the

tightening in her stomach that went with picturing Blake and his old flames. "Karen doesn't have children. After a few drinks at last year's office Christmas party, she told me she and Ron couldn't have any."

Cade grinned. "Then she must be jealous of you teaming up with a world-famous crocodile expert."

"World-famous in the Kimberley," Blake said ruefully. "You probably caught her at an awkward time, that's all."

She let a sigh escape, wondering why the idea of working with Blake held so much appeal. "You could be right." But the puzzle nagged at her all the way back to Diamond Downs. Karen wasn't usually the hysterical type. Something about Blake's involvement in the project had shocked her even more than hearing about the crocodile attack. Jo wished she knew the reason.

Chapter 3

Half the people in the region had to be at the engagement party, Jo decided, surveying the rows of trestle tables groaning with food, much of it contributed by the guests themselves in the best outback tradition. Festooned around the homestead, ribbons of fairy lights competed with the impossibly starry night. Until coming to the Kimberley, she'd never known so many stars could be visible from Earth. They spilled across the inky blackness like countless diamonds on a jeweler's cloth, seeming close enough to touch.

"It's a beautiful night, isn't it?" came a softly accented voice.

Lost in wonder, she hadn't heard the other woman approach. She immediately recognized Tom McCullough's fiancée, Princess Shara Najran. On arriving at Diamond Downs, Jo had met Tom and his royal bride-to-be who were not long back from visiting her father, King Awad of Q'aresh to obtain his blessing on their marriage.

Any family would be lucky to have Tom in their midst, Jo had decided. He was as easygoing and charming as he was good-looking. In contrast to Blake's intensity, she thought, her gaze automatically seeking him out and finding him a little apart from the crowd, leaning against the veranda railing. Nobody would call him easygoing. From the little she knew of him already, he expected a lot from people, but even more from himself. Charming didn't fit, either. Her writer's mind sought out a more appropriate word, finally coming up with *compelling*. He was the kind of man she instinctively knew would complicate her life, but who nevertheless attracted her like iron filings to a magnet.

When their eyes met, she recoiled, as if she'd been punched. The feeling was so blatantly sexual that her breath stalled in her throat and she had a hard time wrenching her attention back to the princess.

Shara's generous smile emphasized her pearly teeth and lovely café au lait skin. She was dressed in what looked like a traditional Eastern costume of cream silk trousers, caught at the ankles by gold embroidery, and a billowing blouse cinched at the waist by a gold circlet, with more embroidery at the wrists.

Beside her, Jo felt positively plain in the uncrushable teal linen pants and matching sleeveless vest she'd insisted on changing into at camp before letting Blake deliver her to the homestead. Although her assignment hadn't allowed for socializing, she had brought this suit for traveling and felt it fitted the occasion better than jeans and a T-shirt, although there was a scattering of both among the party guests.

"It's a lovely night," she agreed. "Thank you for letting me share your engagement party, Shara."

Jo felt odd calling the princess by her first name, but Shara had insisted when they first met, saying she'd had enough of titles in her own country to last a lifetime. "My pleasure," Shara said. "Are you recovered from your close call with the crocodile this morning?"

Jo suppressed a shiver. "It was terrifying, especially for Nigel, but thank goodness he wasn't hurt.

"I'm relieved to hear it, although I understand he decided to return home as a result."

Jo nodded. "I can't say I blame him, can you?"

Shara smiled. "Perhaps not. I'm relieved that the crocodile didn't drive you away, as well."

Tom came up carrying a tray of drinks. The waves of love carried on the look he and Shara exchanged pierced Jo with unaccustomed longing. What must it feel like to know you were so totally loved?

Shara retrieved a glass of wine for Jo and one of mineral water for herself, her fingers trailing over Tom's gripping the tray. The two of them looked as if they couldn't wait to be by themselves. When he moved away, the princess's gaze lingered on him.

"You must love him very much," Jo observed.

Shara took a sip of her mineral water. "Is it so obvious?"

"Only to every eye in the gathering." Smiling, Jo raised her glass. "May you and Tom always feel the way you do tonight." She drank to the sentiment, then remembered the backgrounder she'd read on the family. "I understand it was you who discovered the ancient cave paintings that are helping to put Diamond Downs on the map."

Shara lowered her lashes. "The Uru civilization is a passion of mine. Tom and Blake actually found the cave when they were children."

"But you recognized the paintings on the walls as the work of the Uru and caused an international sensation. After the wire service picked up the story, my editor couldn't wait to send me up here to do a feature."

Shara's interest piqued. "Is your editor a fan of ancient history?"

Jo shook her head. "Oddly enough, she hates history. But when she read about Des Logan and his special family, Karen was determined I should come to the Kimberley. She was the one who dreamed up the survival scenario."

The only thing that would have surprised Jo more was if Karen had announced she was undertaking the assignment herself. Her editor was the archetypal city girl, surgically attached to her cell phone and PDA. Jo could have sworn her boss had been itching to go, but had stopped herself for some reason. She had made Jo promise to report every detail of her experiences, holding nothing back. The request had almost offended Jo, and she'd reminded Karen that she knew how to do her job.

The princess made a face. "When you arrived you told me you have a list of tasks to undertake and report on your progress. How will you manage alone?

"I've already started on the shelter." If gathering a heap of raw materials could be termed starting. She'd probably have made more progress if Nigel hadn't insisted he knew how the job should be tackled. "Blake has offered me some guidance," she added.

Shara smiled. "You're very brave."

"Not brave, persistent. I hate giving up on a challenge."

Shara gave her a conspiratorial look. "You may find Blake a greater challenge than dealing with the outback."

Jo felt warmth seep into her face. "I don't have to deal with him. All he's doing is helping me complete the assignment, nothing more."

Shara excused herself to mingle with the other guests. Jo was grateful to have a few minutes to herself. She hoped the others didn't all think she was interested in Blake. He was a means to an end, that was all.

Wasn't he?

Blake rested his forearms on the homestead veranda railing and watched Jo move gracefully among the guests. Every time she turned that high-voltage smile on one of the male guests and the man melted into a puddle at her feet, Blake wanted to head over there and drag her away. An odd impulse, considering he was avoiding romantic entanglements for the time being.

After Rhonda Saffire, he'd believed it would be a long time before a woman interested him again. Rhonda had worked as a receptionist at Sawtooth Park and their relationship had meandered along for a few months without any real sparks, until they'd gradually stopped seeing each other. Then she'd come to tell him she was pregnant and that he was the father. Not physically impossible, just unlikely, considering he usually took the proper precautions. On the one occasion when he'd slipped up, she'd told him she was protected. She also knew that Blake's experience of being unwanted until Des Logan took him in meant he wasn't going to let any child of his grow up without a father.

They'd have made it all the way to the altar if a friend of Blake's hadn't tipped him off that he'd been drinking with a man who claimed *he* was the father of Rhonda's child. When Blake confronted the man, he'd confessed that he loved Rhonda but was scared of taking on a family. Given the choice between answering to Blake and facing his responsibilities, the man had chosen the latter course. Surprise, surprise, thought Blake.

Later, a radiant Rhonda had shown him her engagement ring and apologized for lying to him. She admitted that she'd turned to him in panic after the real father of her child had let her down. Her fiancé hadn't told her what had changed his mind, Blake gathered. To his surprise, he'd felt disappointed, having discovered he liked the idea of fatherhood a great deal. He missed that more than he missed Rhonda.

Romance might not be high on his agenda for now, but it didn't mean he was dead from the waist down. Or that he couldn't appreciate Jo's lithe, feminine movements and the enticing way her long hair rippled when she tossed her head.

She was talking to Shara and he saw her laughing about something; then she looked up and saw him watching her. He felt the connection as a jolt of current stronger than one he'd received after accidentally touching an electric fence at the park. This also shocked him to the toes of his boots, but there was no cutoff switch, no way to short-circuit her effect.

He could practically follow the sizzling bolt of energy as it arced between them. Her reaction came a split second later, as she rocked back on her heels, her eyes going wide with amazement until she dragged her gaze away.

Blake had heard all the old chestnuts about eyes meeting across crowded rooms, but this was the first time he'd experienced the effect. The prospect of showing her around the outback suddenly seemed less like a favor to Des, and more of a no-holds-barred challenge.

At least Blake could protect Jo from some of the dangers of the outback. Had she gone to the creek instead of Wylie, she might not have been strong enough to stop the crocodile from pulling her into the water.

At the idea, he went cold from head to foot. Not long ago, an American model had been taken along Prince Regent Sound in the Kimberley, making headlines around the world. Blake had no business thinking of Gilgai's actions as anything but a crime. In some countries, it was illegal to feed wild crocodiles. It should be in Australia, he thought. Then both Gilgai and his puppet master, Max Horvath, could be arrested for attempted murder. Since they couldn't, Blake would have to make sure they didn't harm Jo on his watch. From what he'd seen of her, she wasn't the type to welcome a protector, but for himself, he found the prospect thoroughly appealing.

Midnight had come and gone by the time the party started to wind down. "Ready to go back to your camp?" Blake asked Jo as she sipped coffee and watched some of the guests dancing to recorded music. The dancers' movements were slow and desultory, and in some cases downright stumbling, thanks to the effects of a much-depleted bar.

She suppressed a yawn. "I should have called it a night long ago, but it seemed a shame to break up the party." She didn't add that she was reluctant to exchange the cozy atmosphere of the homestead for an isolated camp where danger lurked around every corner. She'd told Blake she was seeing the assignment through, and she wouldn't back down now.

He glanced around. "Some of this mob will still be here for breakfast. In the outback, you stay or go according to your own schedule."

She placed her coffee cup on a table, stood up and stretched. "How come you're so bright-eyed and bushy tailed?"

He winked, sending a jolt to her insides. Probably the result of too much late-night caffeine, she decided. "Years of staying out all night catching crocodiles," he said.

She shuddered at the thought of meeting one of the prehistoric monsters in the dark on their own territory. "Sooner you than me."

The Jeep stood waiting on the edge of the lighted circle. "Would you like to drive?" he asked.

Her tired smile told him she appreciated the choice, but she shook her head. "I haven't driven one of these before."

"In daylight, I'll give you lessons. Or we can take your rental car if you prefer."

"I'll leave it here as we agreed. Your vehicle is better equipped for this terrain." And she was almost out on her feet, so she'd probably run them off the dirt roads into a creek, whatever they were driving.

She was blearily aware of joining Blake in making their farewells, and then they were driving away from the homestead into the star-studded blackness. The Jeep rocked in sync with the corrugated road and she was soon nodding.

"Are you asleep?" he asked when she had been silent for some time.

She forced her heavy lids open and lifted her hair off her nape with two hands. "Are we there yet?"

He laughed, the luxuriant sound resonating through her. "You sound about thirteen."

Her tone was husky as she said, "You're half-right."

"You're twenty-six?"

"Twenty-seven next month. I was speaking figuratively."

"You'll have to tell me what day and we'll celebrate."

"Most men don't bother remembering such details."

"I'm not most men."

Tell me something I don't know, she thought. Out loud, she asked, "So when's yours?"

"I don't know."

She gave a start. "How can you not know your birthday?"

"It's a long story."

She straightened. "You started this, and we don't have anything else to do right now." Nothing they should be doing, at least. What the late hour and the isolation suggested, she was better off not thinking about.

His voice reached her out of the darkness. "To know your birthday, you need to know where and when you were born."

The Jeep tilted forward as it topped the rise. "I get it. You don't know because you were left on a stranger's doorstep when you were only a couple of weeks old," she said, quoting her research. Thirty years ago, his story had been front-page news.

"If you know so much, why ask me?"

Recoiling from the resentment in his voice, she said, "I wasn't sure if your mother ever got in touch with you again." Her research hadn't been able to confirm that detail.

"If she tried, I wasn't there to meet her." The harshness in his tone rejected any possibility.

"By then, I suppose you'd moved to the outback?"

Blake gave a hollow laugh. "Eventually. After my first foster parents found out they were having their own child and I became surplus to their requirements. I decided if I was that unlovable, I may as well act the part, getting myself chucked out of a succession of foster homes."

She swore colorfully, earning an answering murmur from him. "My thoughts exactly. Then I came up against Des and Fran Logan, who refused to give up on me."

His voice held no trace of self-pity so although her heart ached for him, she felt bound to match his steadiness. "Des is a good man." He'd made Blake into a good man, too, when the outcome could so easily have been different.

"Now it's your turn," Blake said.

She shifted uncomfortably. Turnabout was fair play, but she hated talking about herself. It was probably why she'd become a journalist—so she could probe other people's histories without revealing too much of her own. "Not much to tell. Father and mother, both doctors, currently working on a research project in Vanuatu. Two older brothers, one a computer whiz kid, the other a money market expert. They're married with kids, but they still think it's their mission in life to protect me from absolutely everything." They'd been horrified when she told them about this assignment and had tried to talk her out of coming; they backed off only when they saw her resolve hardening instead of weakening.

"Because you were abducted from a public event when you were six," Blake put in.

She strove to keep the aversion out of her voice. "How did you find out?"

"Like you, I believe in doing my homework. I wanted to know why a city girl would voluntarily maroon herself in the outback for a month."

"It's my job," she said, sounding defensive despite her best efforts. "Your research must have told you I was with my abductor for all of five hours before the police found me and took me home. The poor old woman had dementia and thought I was her little girl, who had to be in her thirties by then. While I was with her, we watched cartoons and she fed me ice cream. I thought it was pretty cool."

"The way I thought being left on a doorstep was cool," he commented.

"Maybe I do want to show my family they don't need to protect me all my life. So what?"

Blake drove into the camp and cut the engine. The sound was immediately replaced with the buzz and rustle of nocturnal life. He let his hands slide off the wheel and turned to her. "First rule of handling a new species—find out what makes them tick."

A sensation of raw need coiled through her, urgently pushed away. "For the record, I'm not a new species, and there's going to be no handling involved." The very idea made her throat feel dry and her hands go damp. Blake's unexpected substitution for Nigel had thrown her, she told herself. Yet Nigel's words had never made her heart beat this fast.

Thinking of what Blake might do with more than words drained the last of her strength. If she hadn't been sitting in the car, she'd have sunk to the ground. Lifting her into his arms, Blake would have found her mouth, and the needs she'd been tamping down all evening would have flared into fiery passion.

She blinked hard, struggling back to full wakefulness. What was she doing, imagining herself in Blake's arms? Just because she hadn't found Mr. Right yet didn't mean she was ready to fall into the arms of the first man who came along, even if he was a walking, talking female fantasy.

The fantasy unfastened his seat belt and reached into the back to retrieve his holdall and tropical sleeping bag. He'd collected both from Sawtooth Park after meeting Cade at the airport. At first, the prospect of his company had reassured her; now, she wondered if having him around was such a smart idea, given the way he made her feel.

"Out here, city girl is an introduced species," he continued. "You're checking out the new environment and uncertainty is making you defensive. You've spotted a promising male and you're instinctively making overtures to attract his attention, but you're uncertain if it's the right thing to do."

Was he reading her mind now? Her fingers froze on the seat belt release.

"Puh-lease. Next thing you'll have us sending out mating signals."

"What do you think we've been doing all evening? Humans are no different from animals. We dress up our mating rituals in fancy clothes and expensive restaurants, but the objective is the same—survival of the species."

Because he was uncomfortably close to being right, she took refuge in sarcasm. "Good grief, I've walked onto the set of the Nature Channel."

"We live on it. All humans do." His tone warmed. "You felt the pull between us the second we met."

A pulse jumped in her neck. "In your dreams."

"That, too," he said without missing a beat.

She got out of the car but kept a hand on it as if braced for flight. "I suppose having driven off your rival, you're now staking out the female?"

"You're getting the idea."

Anger swirled through her, although some of it was at his perceptiveness, she recognized. She *had* picked up the signals flashing between them, and her responses were as primitive as his animal analogy suggested. Arousal stronger than anything she'd ever felt. Annoyance that he could read her so easily and completely.

And fear.

Blake Stirton was exciting but dangerous. He saw life in far more basic terms than she did. Thinking she should be scarred by her childhood experience, for example, when it was no more than a glitch on her life's radar screen. Assuming because the sparks were there, she intended to act on them.

He was wrong on all counts. The outback might be his world, but hers was the city, with its nonstop excitement and shops where you had more than one choice of everything. The crocodile hunter and his habitat were an assignment, nothing more.

He came around to her side of the car and she tensed, but

he brushed past on the way to the tent. One tent. Why hadn't she asked him to set up another so they wouldn't have to share? At least there were two cots, and he'd brought his own sleeping bag. Zipped up in hers, she'd have more to worry about than arousal. Like how to go to the bathroom without getting eaten by a crocodile.

And how to be around Blake for a month without falling for the crocodile hunter and becoming *his* prey.

Chapter Four

The phrase *sleeping with the enemy* kept popping into Jo's head as she washed herself with water from a bucket behind the tent. The night was hot and sticky, and she'd give a lot for a proper shower before bed. A swim would have been wonderful but after this morning's experience, she wasn't going anywhere near the creek.

And Blake wasn't the enemy. He was a lifesaver; his presence made it possible for her to stay and write her series. So why did she have such confusing feelings about him?

She finished swabbing her face and neck, wrung out the damp cloth and pressed it against the back of her neck. He was only trying to scare her away with his talk of mating signals between them. If she was sending any such things, surely she would know.

"Bathroom's all yours," she said, carrying the empty bucket around to the front of the tent for him to refill with clean water from their supply.

She stopped in her tracks. He had stripped down to khaki shorts and boots and nothing else. In the flickering light of the lantern, his flexing muscles gleamed as if oiled as he set the camp to rights for the night.

She watched, fascinated in spite of herself. Nigel had been happy to leave things where they dropped and had teased her for trying to keep order, calling her Miss Efficiency.

Now she was watching Mr. Efficiency as he began to get the campfire ready for next morning. "You don't have to do that. I'll do it tomorrow," she said, her conscience nagging. He was supposed to be assisting her, not doing the job for her. Not that he was tough to watch, she thought.

"Old habits die hard," he said mildly. "Leaving things lying around camp is asking for trouble in the outback."

"Nigel didn't think so."

Blake lifted his head. "Missing him already?"

"What do you think?" she asked, avoiding answering his question.

He finished hooking the billycan over an arrangement of sticks he'd placed across the fire then speared her with an unnervingly direct look. "I think you haven't given him a thought since he flounced off at the airport."

Since she couldn't defend herself, she felt bound to defend Nigel. "He didn't flounce. He left because he was almost taken by a man-eating crocodile."

"Hardly a man-eater," Blake corrected.

His lack of feeling was as infuriating as her own overabundance of it. "The beast leaped out of the river and attacked him. In my book, that makes it a man-eater. Or don't you count near misses? Perhaps you'd prefer to see actual blood."

Blake straightened. "You're overreacting. That crocodile has lived in this river system for fifteen years without bothering anyone. Ask the indigenous people. They've swum in this creek for years."

"Maybe it only eats nonindigenous people," she responded.

"And maybe someone has been feeding it from the landing, luring it in." His gaze narrowed. "Crocodiles only rec-ognize food and nonfood. To them, there's no difference be-tween a piece of meat and the hand holding it. All this animal has learned is that anything a human holds out from the rock landing is food."

Her palms felt icy and she rubbed them together although the night was warm. "You think Eddy Gilgai deliberately taught the crocodile to feed close by so it would attack hu-mans?"

"His presence in the area, coupled with the rotten remains Andy found, make the theory seem likely. The difficulty will be in proving anything."

"Did Andy find any more clues after we left for the air-port?"

"Plenty of tracks, but nothing that would hold up in court."

"If he had found something, would you still be here?"

In the flickering lamplight, his eyes gleamed. "Why don't you ask me outright why I decided to stay?"

Annoyance rippled through her, although she wasn't sure if it was at him for being so smug or at herself for caring what he thought. "I know why you stayed. You think I'm an incompetent city type who can't be let loose on her own in the bush. If I get into trouble, it looks bad for Diamond Downs."

His wide shoulders lifted and fell. "You said it, I didn't."

"You're wrong about me," she snapped. "I was a news re-porter before I joined the magazine. I've investigated crime, drugs, you name it, without falling apart. I'd already started building a shelter before you showed up."

His gaze went to the bush building materials she'd piled on the camp fringe. "So I see."

"I wasn't counting on a crocodile trying to eat my partner."

"From the look of things, your partner wasn't much help anyway."

"We'd barely settled in."

Blake braced an arm against the tent frame. "This isn't a holiday camp. If it was a real survival test, you wouldn't have the luxury of settling in. You'd get moving and do what you must to keep yourself alive."

She tried not to be distracted by muscles she couldn't remember seeing outside a gym and rarely enough inside it. His body had been sculpted by hard use rather than vanity, she thought. With his build, he'd make a great male model, although she couldn't imagine Blake being willing to pose for hours. "I intend to survive," she assured him.

His gaze leveled. "I think you will."

She brushed aside the glow his approval brought. "I won't have much choice, since I'll be on my own after tomorrow." She was grateful that he'd interrupted his routine to help her tonight, but she couldn't monopolize his time indefinitely.

No matter how appealing the idea, a traitorous inner voice insisted.

"Anxious for me to leave, Jo?"

"Yes. I mean no. Yes and no."

He leaned closer, the warmth of his body enveloping her in a masculine glow. "Make up your mind."

"This project is my responsibility. You have the crocodile park to run and your foster father to worry about."

"I can keep a better eye on Des from here than from the park. And my deputy is accustomed to running the show when I'm away rounding up rogue crocodiles. He can consult with me by phone if he needs to."

Her throat felt dry. "You can't be planning to stick around for the whole month?"

"Depends." He lifted a hand and brushed his finger lightly down the side of her face. Whispers of need coiled through her, hot and urgent, until she almost leaned into his hand.

Shaken by the strength of the temptation, she stiffened her spine. "On what?"

"On what you want."

She found her voice with an effort. "I want to prove I can survive out here, so anything you can teach me is welcome."

"Oh, I think we have plenty to teach each other."

"I was talking about bush survival."

"That, as well. Have you heard of the code of the outback?"
She shook her head.

"My brothers and I dreamed it up when we were boys. The code says you don't give up and you don't back down. You also stand by your mates."

"Is that what you're doing?"

"All of it. There is something between us, Jo. You felt it the moment we met. Under the code, we don't back away from what we feel, and we don't give up if what we feel is right. What I feel for you is very, very right."

"This isn't why I came to the Kimberley." Why she had come, she couldn't readily answer, but it couldn't have been for *this*.

"Maybe not, but it's why you're staying."

He made it sound like forever, which was impossible. He was right about the attraction. It wasn't going to go away. Neither was he, she understood. Which left her where? Previously, when men had disturbed her emotional balance, she'd ended the relationship. But she couldn't dismiss Blake while she needed his help with the assignment.

Things had been fine between her and Nigel until he'd told her how important she'd become to him, she thought. Instead of being flattered, she'd started to pull away, not wanting to have to live up to his expectations. So what did she want from a man? Spending this time in the outback, she hoped to find some answers.

She stuck her hands into her pockets. "If we're going to work together, we need some ground rules. And I don't mean that code of yours."

"It works for me, but go ahead."

She began to tick points off on her fingers. "First, you don't mollycoddle me. I need to make my own mistakes and learn from them."

"I guess bringing coffee to you in your sleeping bag in the morning is out?"

He sounded almost disappointed and she shook off the

urge to smile. "Be serious. I'll get up when you do and pull my own weight in everything." If it killed her, she thought. Remembering the crocodile, she wondered if she should have stuck with Blake's code of the outback while she was ahead.

"Sounds reasonable so far," he agreed. "Anything else?"

This was the tricky part. "This is my show. I'm in charge."

The muscle she saw working along his jaw told her he didn't like the condition. He was probably used to being the leader, calling the shots. Well, not this time. The silence stretched as he thought.

"I can live with it," he conceded, his easy tone belying his tense body language. "With one exception."

She watched him warily. "What?"

"If I see you doing something that could get you injured or killed, I'll step in and take over with no arguments from you. Agreed?"

The condition was reassuring and she nodded her acquiescence. "In that event, I'd be a fool to argue. Do we shake hands on the deal, or what?"

"Or what," he said.

Releasing his hold on the tent, he stepped closer and his hands closed around her shoulders, pulling her against him. She should have expected this. He'd warned her he was attracted to her. And heaven knew, she was attracted to him. Still, she was unprepared for the onslaught of sensations as his lips found hers. Her mind reeled.

The mouth that she'd dismissed as hard and uncompromising was anything but, she discovered when his lips teased hers apart. His were firm and sensuous, tormenting her with featherlight forays to the corners, then claiming her whole mouth as if to share air. Not an unpleasant act, she discovered, breathing in the masculine scent and taste of him as her reason threatened to slip.

She was out of her element, exhausted. How else could she explain her sudden bout of weakness, as if her limbs had turned molten? Desire bubbled up, making nonsense of her claim to be in charge. The night didn't help, dizzying her with a thousand pinpoints of starlight so that she had to cling to Blake as her world spun.

His breathing sounded fast and shallow. His fingers massaging her shoulders made her shift restlessly, as if to steer his hands to more intimate places. Eyes closing, she dropped her head back and allowed him access to her exposed throat. His lips lingered on the pulse she could feel fluttering like a trapped bird.

Somehow, she managed to find her voice. "Blake, this isn't a good idea."

His cheek nuzzled hers, the beginnings of a beard rasping against her softness. The contrast felt wonderful. "You make it sound as if we have a choice," he murmured.

Strange how hard it was to argue. "There's always a choice."

He kissed the hollow at the base of her throat. "Between?"

A moan struggled to break free. The fog in her mind resisted logical thought, but she made a valiant effort. "What we're doing and—not doing it."

He was planting kisses along her collarbone, pushing aside her top to worship her sun-kissed flesh. Shivers rippled. Needs clawed. Trying to blame the late hour, the alien surroundings or the stresses of the day seemed pointless. The only reason she was in Blake's arms was because she'd fantasized about it all evening. He was right about the lack of choice. The only question had been when she would find herself in his arms. Never in her wildest dreams had she thought it would be so soon.

Too soon. She felt as if she were falling into a bottomless pit, but couldn't seem to stop herself. "We barely know each other," she tried.

He traced a finger down the cleft between her breasts, her answering shiver almost ending the argument there and then. "I thought we were about to remedy that."

She twisted away, the effort almost too much. "You're assuming I want to."

His smile deepened and desire glinted in his eyes, echoing

her own. "I know you want to. But until you're ready to acknowledge the truth of it, I can wait."

"For how long?"

"As long as it takes."

She shook her head. "No woman likes to be predictable."

"That's the wonder of you, Jo. You're not in the least predictable."

Except in this, she thought, astonished to be having the discussion with Blake at all. It had nothing to do with kissing or lovemaking. This was Shakespeare's "marriage of true minds" and Blake was taking her to that place of unbelievable intimacy at a speed that terrified her. She didn't want to feel this way about any man.

There was no logic to feeling threatened by closeness, but the fear had haunted her for as long as she could remember. She assumed she was afraid of losing someone she loved, although that didn't explain the sense that being special to someone was somehow dangerous. She'd tried getting help to fight the fear, but so far, nothing had worked.

"It's late," she said before she said anything more revealing.

He looked up at the sky. "Actually, it's early. Do you want to sleep, or watch the sun come up over the plains?"

If she had any sense, she would crawl into her sleeping bag and hope for oblivion. But she sensed that Blake would be in her mind no matter what she did. In her dreams, if she managed to fall asleep. Strangely, she felt wide-awake now. "As long as you don't expect me to function too well later, I'd like to watch the sun come up," she said. "I need to finish that shelter today."

"There's more to the outback than survival," he pointed out. "There's savagery no city person can imagine, and beauty almost beyond bearing."

Her wide-eyed look met his. "I didn't know you were a poet, too."

"You can't live in the outback without becoming poetic. Not if you have any soul at all."

He had one, she didn't doubt. She had been on the verge of misjudging him, she realized. Writing him off as a muscle man who was happiest chasing through the bush with a gun slung across his shoulders. She hadn't allowed for all the times he would need to be still, to read the signs around him and make sense of what had happened or would happen. The patience to wait sometimes for days until a crocodile lost its fear of the unknown and approached a trap he'd set for it, so it could be moved without harm to safer territory.

All this and a mouth that threatened to command her soul, she thought. What had she gotten herself into?

The experience was all Blake had promised and more.

While she'd changed her shoes and grabbed a jacket, he had put on his own shirt and collected a torch from the car.

The torch was almost superfluous, the starlight illuminating the path to a grassy hilltop overlooking a spiderweb of rivers and creeks on one side and the immense plains on the other, ringed by mountains that would have looked at home on the moon. On her own, she would have been terrified of meeting a hunting dingo or wild buffalo, and the distant coughing sound that Blake told her was a crocodile would have frozen her blood. With him at her side, the sounds exhilarated more than they frightened.

Instinctively she dropped her voice, not wanting to intrude on the timeless landscape. "It would have been a sin to sleep through such beauty."

His heated gaze told her they wouldn't have been sleeping, and she shivered. The predawn chill seeping into her bones made her glad of the jacket. Nor did she object when Blake's arm slid around her shoulders, and he brought her closer to him. She told herself the sudden fast beating of her heart was due to the spike in her body temperature. Nothing to do with being in his arms.

Dawn came as a spill of dusky coral across the cobalt sky. One by one, the stars winked out, replaced by a glow that slowly stained the darkness with orange and pink threaded with turquoise. Her breath caught as orange fire lit up the sky. The sunrise as she had never seen it before. No wonder early civilizations had convinced themselves that the sun was a god, prostrating themselves before it in awe.

She turned toward the first rays, letting them steal the chill from her face. "Do you make a habit of this?" *Do you bring many women up here to watch the sunrise?*

"When I'm out catching a croc, I work more by night than by day, so I'm often around to see the sun come up," he said, answering only the question she'd asked. His arm tightened around her. "You're a big improvement on a team of unshaven, unwashed men."

Laughter bubbled up. "Is that supposed to be a compliment?"

"It's meant to be."

At least they weren't other women, she thought on a glow of satisfaction she didn't want to feel but couldn't seem to dispel. She settled her back more comfortably against him and found herself watching him as much as the sunrise. His head and shoulders were silhouetted against the sky as he leaned against the outcrop, totally at ease.

What was he thinking? she wondered. Of the sunrise or her? Annoyed with herself, she swung her gaze back to the vast plains, distracting herself by trying to identify the birds flying in to feed off the lush grasses and the insect life thronging the waterways. There were parrots and magpie geese and wild ducks, long-legged jabirus and clouds of budgerigars flocking to the water below their vantage point. A lone wedge-tailed eagle soared on thermal currents high above.

Thinking of the concrete canyons where she normally spent her days, she felt an instinctive tug of resistance. How could she be happy shut away indoors when so much beauty and freedom were here for the taking?

She felt rather than saw Blake tense. "What is it?"

He made a shushing sound and pulled her to the ground with him. From his pocket, he took out a pair of compact binoculars and trained them on a distant cluster of paperbark trees.

She dropped her voice to a whisper, although no one could possibly hear them. "What do you see?"

He handed her the glasses. "Movement at twelve o'clock."

Positioning herself to face the direction he indicated, she adjusted the powerful glasses to her vision. A lone man in khaki clothing jumped into focus. He had a sack slung over his shoulder and was retreating into the trees. "It's the man I saw watching our camp," she murmured. If he'd been visiting the creek again, his intentions—whatever they were— had been thwarted because she was up and about instead of sleeping.

Blake nodded confirmation. "Eddy Gilgai. Take a good look so you'll know him if you see him hanging around again."

She did so, then lowered the glasses. "You sound as if you expect to see more of him."

"If Max put him up to this, we will. Max isn't the type to give up easily."

"Shouldn't we try to catch Eddy now?"

"That stand of trees is farther away than it looks. By the time I get there, he'll have melted into the bush. One of his clan could track him but I doubt that I could. And besides even if we did catch him, we couldn't prove he was up to no good."

"Even though Des asked him to leave?"

"Visiting his relatives isn't a crime, and that's what he'd claim to be doing."

"If feeding a wild crocodile isn't illegal and you can't arrest him for trespassing, how will you pin anything on him?"

His mouth tightened. "Tom's the lawman. I have my own methods."

Not entirely orthodox, she deduced. "I don't think I want to know."

"No reason you should. None of this need concern you, provided you stay well clear of the creek."

A vision of a prehistoric killer rearing out of the water

made her shiver. "Don't worry, I intend to." She wasn't sure about taking the rest of his advice.

His dark gaze told her he suspected what she was thinking. "I'll be around to make sure you do."

"I don't need a minder."

"No? Then show me the direction that takes us back to camp."

She stood up and looked around. "Should be easy enough. We climbed up here from that side." A network of creeks bordered their location. And all the clumps of trees looked alike. Surely there should be a glimpse of the tent from here? A faint track gave her more confidence. "That way," she said, pointing.

He looked amused. "The trail does lead to a camp, but it's about three times as far away as yours and only used at cattle mustering time."

"Smart-ass," she muttered under her breath. Then remembered her resolution and folded her arms. "Okay, Crocodile Man, how do I work it out?"

In a fluid movement, he uncoiled from the ground and picked up a stick. Pushing it vertically into the ground, he placed a stone at the end of the shadow cast by the stick. "Now we wait twenty minutes."

She was intrigued. "For what?"

"Patience," he counseled.

Easy for him to say. She wasn't known for patience. She wondered if he knew it and was testing her. She decided not to give him the satisfaction of being right and schooled herself to remain still, although her awareness of him grew to agonizing proportions.

He stood statue-still, his gaze on the far horizon. How could he be so at ease when her muscles twitched with the need for movement? The twenty minutes seemed like an eternity.

When her watch indicated the time had passed, although he hadn't even glanced at his watch, he placed another stone at the slightly changed angle of shadow cast by the stick, then drew a line from the first stone to well beyond the second.

"This line runs west-east." He turned her until the shadow stick was behind her and she was standing with her left foot halfway between the stones and her right foot on the line the same distance again past the second stone.

Warmth flooded through her from his touch, and her concentration wavered. His breath was hot on her cheek, his smell invitingly masculine. She dragged in a steadying breath. "Now what?"

"Now you're looking north, in the direction of the camp." Hunkering down he drew a line at her feet bisecting the first line, indicating north-south, she assumed.

When she said so, he nodded. "This is how you make an earth compass."

Trying not to focus on the luxuriant spill of his hair, or give in to the temptation to run her fingers through it—an entirely new temptation for her—her brows knit. "How would this help us at night?" They had climbed the hill before dawn.

He stood up, standing a fraction too close to her for comfort. "The earth compass works in moonlight, too. Once you decide in which direction to travel, you stand on the compass and face the way you intend moving. Look for a bright star, or better still, a group of stars in that direction and move toward them."

Follow your star, she thought. Was there a message here? "Won't the trees get in your line of sight?" she asked, annoyed at the husky way her voice came out.

He nodded. "Good thinking. You don't choose stars that are right on the horizon, or you'll lose sight of them behind the trees. You also need to remember that stars move east to west at about fifteen degrees an hour, the same as the sun. I'll show you how to measure degrees using your hand span."

He took her hand and the world lurched again. Much more of his touch and she would be in his arms again, not answerable for the consequences. She tugged free, feeling heat flood into her face. "Show me later. I think we should get back to camp and make sure Eddy hasn't disturbed anything."

Blake saw the telltale color stain her cheeks and felt an inner swell of satisfaction. She would be his before this adventure was over. She might not be sure if she wanted him, but he had no doubts. What happened after that was up to fate, although he had ideas about that, too.

"You're the boss," he said. *For now, at least.*

He saw her eyes widen as if she'd picked up his thought. "You don't have a problem with that?"

His shoulders lifted. "Why should I? I'm a sensitive new-age kind of guy."

"Yeah, right."

Feigning hurt feelings, he stuck out his lower lip. "You don't believe me."

"I believe you'll let me lead as long as it suits you."

Keeping the grin off his face, he said, "I might surprise you."

The skeptical look she gave him only made him want her more. He'd take the greatest delight in breeching that tough journalistic facade to connect with the woman beneath. She'd be all softness, all warmth, all passion. An all-or-nothing kind of lady. His kind.

But first he'd have to win her trust and make her want him as much as he wanted her. Then he'd see who led and who followed.

He couldn't stop himself. He brushed his thumb along her jawline and saw her shudder. Dark, potent desire leaped into her gaze and he watched her master it with an effort. Or thought she had. She would never know how tempted he was to show her how thin her veneer of control really was. He knew because his own wasn't much better. The awareness was in his gruff tone as he said, "Let's get back to camp."

Chapter 5

Blake's survey of their campsite showed no signs of disturbance, although he frowned when he spotted fresh footprints near the perimeter. "Unfortunately, they don't tell us anything except that someone was here."

"And we already know that," she said, setting the ingredients for the bush bread called damper out on a folding table.

In the middle of starting the fire, Blake paused. "Don't take this too lightly. What Eddy's doing has more than nuisance value. If I had my way, feeding wild crocodiles would be illegal in Australia."

She mixed flour and water, plunged elbow-deep into the sticky mix and began to knead. "It's already illegal in countries like the United States, but it's popular with tourists."

"Who have no idea of the risks involved," he said. "Teaching crocodiles to jump creates an association between people and food. When they do what they've been trained to do and eat someone, the same people training them will be baying for their blood."

She kept kneading, sprinkling extra flour over the ball of dough as she worked. "I'm starting to feel sorry for the crocodiles."

The fire flared to life and he stood up, dusting off his hands, a hunter in his element, performing the most primeval of tasks. "I'll make an outback woman of you yet."

A twinge shot through her as sharp as a knife thrust. She masked it by slamming the dough into a cast iron pan ready to cook in the coals when they were hot enough. "No way. This lifestyle is strictly temporary." Was she protesting too much? She didn't really want to spend more than a month living in the Kimberley, did she?

He didn't seem troubled by her certainty. "That's what they all say."

"All your lady friends?" she asked, carrying the pan to him.

He took the pan from her. "How did you learn to make bush bread?"

He hadn't answered her question, she noticed. "I looked the recipe up when I was doing my research." At his look of surprise she added, "I told you I do my homework. I also know how to make tea in a billycan by covering the tea leaves in boiling water and swinging it around my head to help it brew."

He laughed. "The first time I tried that, I nearly scalded myself."

He hadn't been bred to outback life any more than she had, she remembered. "Did it take you long to settle in?"

He poked among the coals, making a place for the bread pan. "I fought like hell against doing any such thing."

Surprised by his response, she almost cut herself on the old-fashioned can opener she'd been using to open a can of beans and bacon. "You? But you fit in so well."

"When Des Logan brought me to Diamond Downs, I didn't want to fit in anywhere. I did everything I could to make him and Fran throw me out, short of setting fire to the homestead, and I seriously considered that."

She paused in the act of spooning the beans into a sauce-pan. "Didn't you like living in the outback?"

"I liked it far too much."

"Then why…"

He came to stand beside her, the folding table rocking as he planted his palms on it. "I'd been happy with the couple who found me, but then unexpectedly they had a child. I realized later they were afraid I'd be a bad influence on their precious heir. Oh, they didn't mean to shut me out. They tried to keep everything the same, but I knew it wasn't." His gaze grew distant. "She even called the new baby her 'Number One Son.' It was supposed to be a joke. So I started acting up, being what they expected me to be."

"How old were you?" she asked.

"Six or so. When you're branded a troublemaker, it's hard to find another foster family willing to take you on."

She winced. "How can anyone label a six-year-old a troublemaker?"

"Easily enough for the next couple of years, I was fostered by a professional caregiver who was in it for the money. She was already looking after three kids from the system, all older and tougher than me."

"So you became even tougher," she surmised. "Hardly surprising."

He lifted the saucepan out of her hands, his fingers brushing hers and eliciting a wave of warmth. "Want this on the fire?"

"In another ten minutes, when the bread's closer to being done." She opened a folding chair and sat down at the table. "How did you get out of the second foster home?"

"By making the woman's life hell until she gave up on me. Then I was moved to a halfway house for problem kids. It was run on tough love principles supposedly designed to keep us from graduating to jail. Some of the kids had already been arrested. The rest were well on the way. I acted as mean as they were. Better than letting them know how scared I was."

Her heart bled for the frightened child caught in that hell. She tried to justify her response as professional. His experience would make a riveting human-interest story. But the deep-down tug of emotion felt dangerously personal. "You didn't want to be farmed out to another foster home, was that the problem?"

He poked at the fire, not looking at her. "The opposite, in fact. By the time Des and Fran came to the house wanting to foster a son, I'd have done anything to get out of the halfway house, so I put on an angelic act and they bought it."

She got up and moved closer to the fire. Closer to him. "Really?"

Her disbelieving tone earned a raised-eyebrow look. "Not for a second. Des told me later he picked me because he wanted to see how long I could keep up the angelic act."

"What he didn't know was that the toughness was the act," she concluded.

Blake nodded. "Coffee?"

"Thought you'd never ask."

He poured some into two enamel mugs and handed one to her. She cupped her hands around it, thinking of how far he'd come from his early life to his present one. He looked so at ease as he carried the saucepan of beans to the fire that it was hard to imagine he hadn't been born in the outback. "What made you think life with Des and Fran would be an improvement?" she asked.

When the beans began to bubble around the edges, he stirred them with a wooden spoon. "Anything would have been an improvement. I'd heard enough of the other kids' experiences to know I had no future where I was. Then when I got to Diamond Downs, everything was so perfect, I was afraid it was too good to last."

She fetched enamel plates and cutlery and the folding chairs and set them down beside the campfire. "So you decided to hurt yourself before they could do it."

"Des couldn't seem to get the message. No matter what I did, he wouldn't send me away. He added Ryan, then Tom and Cade to the family and I found myself so busy being a big brother that I didn't have time to act up anymore."

He reached for a cloth and pulled the bread pan out of the fire, rapping the top of the loaf with his knuckles. From the hollow sound, she knew the bread was cooked. He tipped it out onto a plate and set it on a rock beside the fire to keep warm.

Recalling Blake's experience at his first foster home, Jo dragged in a deep breath. "But you still felt insecure," she guessed.

He tore two chunks off the bread and put them on plates, then added beans and bacon, and handed one of the plates to her. "I couldn't stand waiting for something to go wrong. So I ran away and persuaded Tom to come with me."

She pulled up a chair and sat down. Balancing the plate on her knee, she leaned forward. "Obviously, Des found you and brought you back."

Blake sat down on the other chair and swirled his bread around in the beans although he didn't eat, caught up in the memory. "Instead of tanning my hide for running away as I'd expected, he made me Judy's godfather. Can you imagine? Me, a flaming godfather."

She could imagine it more easily than she wanted to. For all his tough-guy image and his crocodile-hunting ways, she suspected Blake had a tender heart. He may have had it all but broken on the way to adulthood, but thanks to Des Logan and Blake's inner strength, he'd preserved a core of decency that touched her more than she was willing to let him see.

A cough stopped her voice from cracking too obviously. "Giving you a role to play in his daughter's life would have convinced you, more than anything he could have said, that there was room for all of you in the family."

Blake nodded. "Now you know why I won't let Max Horvath get his hands on this land."

Because he owed Des his life, or at least the worthwhile one he now led. She shuddered inwardly, imaging how things might have gone if Blake had stayed at the halfway house. Another question occurred to her. "How did you come by the name of Stirton?"

He ate quietly. Was he weighing up how much more to tell her, or regretting what he already had? she wondered. She'd decided he wasn't going to answer when he said, "I chose it myself. I got Blake from a piece of paper pinned to the blanket I was wrapped in when I was found. For the first few years, I went by the surname of my first foster family. But I didn't want a connection with anyone who didn't want me. I saw this rugged outdoors man on television, a handler of big cats who ran a wildlife park outside Perth. His name was Bob Stirton, so I adopted his name as my surname. When I joined Des's family, he offered to make me a Logan but by then, I was used to my name."

"A true self-made man," she mused.

He gave her a sharp look. "Haven't you heard the saying that a self-made man has a fool for a maker?"

Chasing beans around her plate with the bread, she said, "Nobody can accuse you of being a fool. Behaving like an angel around Des was pretty darned smart."

"Even though he didn't fall for it."

"You caught his eye, so it worked. And you've made the most of the chance he gave you."

"Now it's my turn to give something back."

He'd been doing that for a long time, she gathered, although he didn't seem to think it was enough. She was fairly sure Des was content that his oldest foster son had grown up to be a decent, hard-working human being who cared as much for others as for himself. From what she'd seen of the older man, he would consider that ample reward for any sacrifice he'd made.

Blake had other ideas. "I'm going to stop Max Horvath in his tracks if it's the last thing I do."

Light suddenly dawned and with it, a blinding sense of disappointment. She hid it by pouring more coffee into their mugs. "That's why you want to stay here with me, to catch your neighbor up to no good. This has nothing to do with helping me put my story together, has it?"

He took the mug. "You'll get your story."

Wrapping her hands around the mug was more comforting than drinking the murky fluid, although she did both. First he would get what he wanted, she reasoned. She had a job to do and so did Blake. No reason to feel slighted.

Except that she did.

As he had reminded her, this wasn't a vacation. She drank the coffee and washed her plate and the cooking utensils in a bucket using the last of the hot water. Apart from not wanting to pollute the pristine waterways with detergent, there was the little matter of the crocodile. No way was she washing dishes at the riverbank ever again.

When she'd finished, Blake washed his breakfast things. "Ready to start on the shelter?" he asked. He seemed immune to her sudden coolness. Or didn't care.

"First, I want to add to my video diary," she said. Avoiding him wasn't the issue.

He used the dishwashing water to douse the fire, making the rocks surrounding it sizzle and pop. "Video diary?"

"As well as writing notes for the magazine, I decided to record my impressions on tape for myself. There could be a documentary in this experience. I'd like to film your comments, as well."

"No," he said.

"Don't tell me you're camera shy?" Not with his film-star looks and powerhouse personality.

"I already told you no interviews."

"How do you promote the crocodile park?"

"I manage. I don't usually talk about myself."

Given how much he'd done so to her, this came as a surprise. "You don't have to talk about yourself. You can talk about surviving in the outback, what a klutz I am in the bush, anything you like."

His eyebrows lifted. "You want me to go on record saying you're a klutz?"

If it got him in front of her camera she could cope. "Whatever."

"Somehow I doubt you'd appreciate such frankness," he said dryly. "I'll leave the on-camera stuff to you."

"I have plenty of tape if you change your mind."

"I won't."

No, he wouldn't. He was a man of his word, she thought as she went into the tent to get her camera. Single-minded pretty well summed up Blake Stirton. Single-minded and determinedly single.

Now where had that thought come from? She was determinedly single herself. She and Blake were evenly matched in that regard.

The hot, airless atmosphere inside the tent made her catch her breath. The undisturbed camp stretcher reminded her that she was short one night's sleep. Before she gave in to temptation and stretched out on the bed, she pulled her pack onto the stretcher and rummaged inside for the camera.

She pulled her hand back with a cry of alarm. Coiled in the pack was the largest snake she had ever seen.

Backing carefully away, she nearly screamed as she came up against Blake. "What's the matter?"

Her voice had deserted her so she pointed a shaking hand at the writhing pack.

Disturbed, the snake was slowly flowing out of the pack, giving her a good look at its golden-tinged head and shining scales patterned in dark cross-hatching.

"It's a king brown, one of the most deadly of all snakes," he murmured. "Do you have a stand or tripod for your camera?"

Her tone mirrored her disbelief. "You want to take its picture?"

"I want to get it out of here. The stand?"

Hardly daring to move, she gestured toward a spindly aluminum contraption resting against the bed. "Can't you shoot it or something?"

"If you want your worldly goods spattered with snake brains." When she shuddered he added, "I don't believe in killing for the sake of it. You can also get bitten by a dead snake."

If he wasn't kidding, she didn't want to know. By now, the snake had flowed over her pack and onto the bed, revealing a body eight feet long and as thick as her wrist. The snake's forked tongue flicked in and out as if tasting the air. She almost forgot to be frightened until Blake moved her to one side.

If she had any sense she would get out of the tent now, in case whatever he had in mind didn't work. Instead, she found herself watching in fascination, wishing she'd been able to retrieve the camera. Since she hadn't, she let her mind become the camera, storing away as much detail as she could.

With the camera stand held in front of him, Blake approached the snake. She marveled at his calmness and air of confidence.

Keeping the legs of the camera stand bunched together, he got closer. As if sensing danger, the snake lifted its head and partly flattened its neck into a hook shape. Instinctively, she recognized the snake's position as a kind of warning before striking. She almost called a warning to Blake but forced the cry down, afraid of distracting him.

In a lightning move he brought the camera stand down so the tangle of legs gripped the snake behind its head, pinning it to the stretcher without injuring it.

Without looking back, he said, "In the Jeep you'll find a burlap sack. Get it for me."

She flew. The bag was on the back seat and she snatched it up. Everything in her rejected the idea of going back into the tent but she did it anyway. Blake was there. She handed him the bag.

"You might want to wait outside now," he said, his concentration never leaving the pinned snake.

"I'll stay," she said. If he was bitten, he'd need her help. What she could do if the snake got loose she didn't know, but she wasn't moving until she knew Blake was okay.

He didn't argue but transferred the bag and camera stand to his left hand. A cry escaped her lips as he used his right hand to grab the snake behind the head. Between his fingers she could clearly see the gaping mouth and glistening fangs. So beautiful. So deadly.

No longer needed, the stand dropped to the floor. He released the snake into the bag, gave the top a few deft twists and held it clear of his body. "Now will you get out," he said tautly.

This time, she had no compunction about complying. The writhing bag seemed more threatening than the snake when it was slithering on her cot.

She followed Blake into the bush well away from the camp-site, to a cluster of rocks where he tipped his burden out and jumped clear in the same movement. Not quite quickly enough as the reptile reared back and struck out at his hand. He let out a salty oath.

Her heart jackknifed into her mouth. "Did it get you?"

"Stay back, I'm fine."

She couldn't see how the snake had missed. Wanting to go to him, she held her ground until she saw the reptile slither between the rocks and away.

Then he came to her. Still not believing he'd survived the encounter unscathed, she grabbed his hand and turned it over, fully expecting to find puncture marks on his wrist. "I told you I'm fine," he said, but he didn't pull away. Instead, his free hand came up and grazed the side of her face. "I have done this before."

"So I gather," she said, annoyed at sounding so shaken.

"In spite of their fearsome reputation, most snakes don't attack people. They'd much rather escape before you know they've been there," he assured her. "No need to look so alarmed."

She forced sound out of her throat. "I wasn't until I thought you'd been bitten."

His expression softened. "So all this concern is for me?"

She tried to bluff it out. "If I lose my guide now, my project is at an end."

"And that's all you were worried about?"

"Of course."

"Liar," he said softly. With his index finger he skimmed her top lip. "You shouldn't worry about me, I can take care of myself."

She nodded. Her chest felt tight. "After all, you wrestle crocodiles for a living."

His gaze never left hers. "I try not to put myself in the position of having to wrestle them."

"Whatever." He took risks she didn't want to think about. And didn't want to think about why she didn't want to think about them.

"You're not so bad yourself," he said softly, pushing strands of hair out of her eyes, the gesture heart-stoppingly intimate. "A lot of women would have dissolved into hysterics."

"I was too busy being glad you didn't hurt the snake."

"I'd rather not cause harm if I don't have to."

Did he mean to the snake, or her? His hand had moved around to her nape, the caressing action sending shivers down her spine. His mouth was a tantalizing few inches away.

Amazed that she was actually doing this, she lifted herself to meet his mouth.

Dimly, she heard him let the sack fall. His arms came around her.

There was nothing gentle about his kiss, and she had no one to blame but herself, knowing she had invited whatever came. His mouth on hers felt hot. Need poured through her, and she felt answering tremors wrack him. Unlike the snake, they couldn't be caught and held. Nor denied.

How could any man make her feel so needy with only a kiss? As he released her and her shaking subsided, she shook her head as if to clear it. She didn't want this. Already it was becoming far too necessary, like breathing.

She pushed herself away from him, trying to pretend she had only kissed him back out of relief. "I'm glad you're all right," she said to strengthen the impression, trying to convince herself as much as him. "Are you always this resourceful?"

He raked a hand through his hair. "You'd be amazed how resourceful I can be."

Her thoughts ran riot, refusing to be corralled. She was glad when he picked up the bag and led the way back to camp. He collected the fallen camera stand and propped it against the tent. "This makes a pretty good pinning hook."

Not as good as the man operating it, she thought. "I'll keep it handy for next time we get a snake in the tent," she said. Trying to match his matter-of-fact tone, she asked, "How do you think it got in? Apart from when I went in to get the breakfast things, the tent was sealed tight." During orientation, Blake had drummed into her the necessity of keeping the tent secure.

He massaged his chin between thumb and forefinger. "I've been wondering the same thing."

And reached the same conclusion she had. "Eddy Gilgai."

Blake nodded. "He could have planted the snake in your pack while we were watching the sunrise."

"Why?"

"The same reason he's feeding the crocodile."

She brought her chin up. "He'll find I'm not so easily scared away."

Blake tossed the burlap bag into his Jeep. "Perhaps you should be. Being bitten by a King Brown is no picnic. The venom is deadly unless you get the right antidote in time."

Thinking of how close they'd both come, she felt herself turn pale. "Max Horvath must really want to get his hands on Diamond Downs if he's willing to kill for it."

Blake poured two mugs of water from their supply and

handed one to her. She was pleased that her hands shook only a little as she took the drink and sat down at the folding table. It was bad enough that someone wanted to sabotage her assignment; she hadn't bargained on it turning deadly.

Blake swung a chair around and straddled it. "Still want to see this through?"

"What do you think?"

"I think I'd feel better if you packed up and went back to Perth."

"Even though your foster father needs the fee my magazine is paying to have me here?"

"No fee is enough to justify this kind of risk. We'll get by."

She had seen enough of Des Logan and his family not to doubt it. "That isn't the point. I want to find out why Horvath would go to such lengths to drive me out of here."

"Only one reason makes any sense. He has a lead on Great-grandpa Logan's lost diamond mine and is afraid we're going to find it before he does."

She thought for a moment. "Could we?"

"Possible, but not likely. Others have looked for the mine over the years. As kids, we searched a lot of this country without success."

"You didn't find the Uru rock art and it was right under your noses, off a cave you were using as a hideout," she pointed out.

"True, although at that age we didn't have much interest in art. Finding lost treasure was more our idea of adventure."

A spirit he still possessed. "Maybe we can both get what we want, and get Horvath off your back at the same time."

His gaze narrowed. "You mean look for the mine? If I'm right about Horvath being behind these incidents, he won't sit still while we search. I can't let you take the chance."

"You can't stop me," she said. "We agreed I'm the boss."

"Unless you're about to put yourself at risk."

"Life is a risk. You have a choice—either back me up or go home to your crocodiles."

He looked infuriatingly amused. "You're firing me?"

She could try. "You bet."

"That's rich, considering you didn't hire me in the first place. I only stayed to keep an eye on you."

She stood up, thinking that his eye on her was way too distracting for her own good. "I'll be fine from here on."

"What if there's another snake?"

"I have my camera stand and I'm not afraid to use it."

"You really would stay out here alone, wouldn't you?"

In many ways, she would find it easier than dealing with the disturbing way he made her feel. But the thought of him leaving wasn't comfortable, either. Make up your mind what you want, she told herself.

"If we get anywhere near the mine, Horvath will turn up the heat," Blake warned her.

A feeling of triumph flooded through her out of proportion to the victory she sensed she'd won. Blake was not only staying, he was going to help her find the lost mine. She'd have the story of her career.

She would also have to deal with the attraction simmering between herself and Blake. Anything Horvath threw at her was likely to seem tame by comparison.

"I can handle it," she said, wishing she could be sure which challenge she was referring to.

Chapter 6

Jo swore as her careful arrangement of bush materials collapsed in a heap. Again.

She hated to think Nigel had been right when he said she'd never turn this mess into a viable shelter, despite following the directions in her survival handbook. The tent that was only supposed to be a temporary home, was looking cozier by the minute.

Blake glanced up from the hunting knife he was sharpening. "Having trouble?"

She fired a what-do-you-think look at him and returned to her puzzle. After a few minutes, he put the knife down and came to crouch beside her. "Want some help?"

Unable to look away, she let her gaze slide to his wide, mobile mouth. Passion lodged there. And desire. And satisfaction. On the verge of swaying toward him, she caught herself and took refuge in irritation. "So you can keep the city girl humble?"

His smoky look negated her defensiveness. "So I can earn her undying gratitude and she'll let me kiss her again."

His idea of a joke, she told herself. No harm in playing along. "Show me how to make something useful out of this, and you've got yourself a deal."

She didn't want him to kiss her. She only wanted something other than failure to write about when she filed her first article from the Kimberley at the end of the week. Jo believed that when Karen Prentiss heard about the snake encounter, the editor wasn't likely to pull Jo off the story because she feared her reporter couldn't cope. If anything, Karen would think the adventure made the story. Jo was the one who wanted to accomplish more. She was hoping the isolation and focus on simple survival would help her get to the bottom of the fears that plagued her whenever she stated getting too close to someone.

Blake reached for a tall forked stick but Jo stayed his hand, pulling back when she was tempted to let her fingers linger on his wrist a fraction too long. "You can show me, but I want to do the work myself."

"A good survival strategy requires that the leader assess what skills are available to the group and put them to the best use," he said.

His abilities were all too obvious, and not only in matters of survival, she suspected. She cleared her throat. "And my skills would be?"

He gathered together a bundle of sticks. "I'll let you know after I collect my reward."

A shiver of anticipation took her, hastily quashed. "I didn't say when I'd make the payment. After the shelter, there's a whole list of survival tasks to be done."

"Helping you work through your list has got to be worth more than a kiss."

Her imagination ran riot picturing what his price might be. "Don't you think I can survive without you?"

A look as soft as velvet, as rich as a promise, greeted the

question. "I'm sure you can, but from my point of view leaving you on your own would be a terrible waste."

While he worked on the shelter she ducked into the tent, letting the flap obscure her view of him. Golden light filtered through the canvas walls and she was assailed by breath-robbing heat. A plastic window with a rolled-up awning gave her a blurred view of Blake at work, his assured movements in startling contrast to her fumbling efforts. Many more of his backhanded compliments and she'd start believing he was really attracted to her, she thought.

Why was it easier to think of herself as a thorn in his side than a woman in his arms? Because the first didn't require anything of her, she knew. The second involved feelings and responses she resisted instinctively without really knowing why. She only knew they were too deep, too dangerous to explore.

She grasped the tent frame to steady herself. Was that the reason she'd felt so comfortable with Nigel? He'd also floated contentedly along on the emotional surface of life, never taking her anywhere she didn't want to go.

Unlike Blake.

From their first meeting, she'd sensed that his energy sprang from a deep inner wellspring. Nothing about him was ordinary, from his start in life to his choice of profession. And Jo guessed he wouldn't be an ordinary lover, either.

Not that she intended to find out, she assured herself, gulping the torrid air. She might—just might—let him kiss her again in fun, to keep her end of their bargain. But that's as far as she would let things go.

Feeling better for having reaffirmed the decision, she reached for her pack, pulling her hand back as she remembered what had been in there the last time she opened it. This time a cautious prod yielded no movement, so she opened the pack and took out her compact video camera.

Absorbed in his task, Blake didn't look up when she approached and the camera was almost silent so she was able to film him working for some minutes before he noticed what she was doing.

He stopped immediately, his gaze darkening. "I thought we agreed…"

"We agreed I wouldn't interview you," she cut in. "This isn't an interview. It's for my private…record."

She'd nearly said enjoyment.

"I prefer that you don't."

She snapped the camera off. "Then I won't. Don't you want to be known as the Indiana Jones of the Kimberley?"

He shook his head. "I'll settle for a kiss, thanks."

"Isn't everybody supposed to want fame?"

"As an abandoned kid, I made enough headlines to last me a lifetime. One of my foster families had all the newspaper clippings. After seeing them, I decided fame is overrated. Now are we going to talk or build?"

Watching him work and helping where she could, she was awed by how easy he made the job seem. One minute there was a bundle of forked sticks and twigs on the ground; the next, there was a rough framework roomy enough to shelter two adults. There was no covering as yet, only thin crosspieces of wood that he said would support a thatch roof.

While she held the last batten, he tied it into position and stood back. "All it needs now is some thatching to keep out the weather, and it's done. Before we do that, does your camera have a remote trigger?"

"Yes." She passed the camera to him. "I thought you didn't approve of making a taped record."

"For this I do."

Curious, she followed him down to the bank of the creek, keeping a wary eye on the water. If the giant crocodile lurked in the green depths, she couldn't see any sign of it. The carpet of water lilies looked tranquil and innocent. All the more reason to be cautious, she reminded herself.

Blake seemed unworried as he set the camera on its stand

on the bank, pulling bushes around the location as a screen. "Are you hoping to photograph the crocodile?" she asked.

"We might catch a predator in action."

Understanding grew. "You're after Eddy." Why hadn't she thought of that herself?

"A court may not accept the recording as evidence of any wrongdoing, but Eddy's clan elders certainly would, and he'd have to account to them for his actions." Blake fiddled with the settings and then trailed the remote control to the landing, covering the cord with leaf litter. Anyone stepping onto the rocks would trigger the camera. "I hope you brought a supply of spare batteries."

She nodded. "Do you plan to hide and wait for him?"

"It could be hours before he shows up or not at all. You have a roof to thatch."

She stepped over the concealed cord to his side. "I've never thatched a roof in my life."

He checked his handiwork one more time. "Think of it as knitting with grass."

"Do I look like a woman who knits?"

"You look like a woman who does anything she sets her mind to."

About to accuse him of chauvinism, she blew out a breath instead. "I hope you realize, if I do the work our agreement is off."

His smile slanted wickedly. "Then I'd better collect while I still can."

"That wasn't what I…"

Whatever else she might have said was swept away as he took her in his arms and found her mouth with unerring precision.

She should kiss him back lightly, playfully, in the spirit of their deal. Not splay her fingers across his back and meet the pressure of his mouth with shameful eagerness. But choice seemed to have fled with his touch.

Heat skipped across her skin. Her heart pumped. This

wasn't a game. It was seduction, pure and simple. Against everything she believed she wanted. "The shelter…" she said shakily, striving to ground herself in ordinary matters.

He chose to misunderstand. "Good idea."

Too overwhelmed to think straight, she let herself be held against his side and steered back to the campsite, where the unfinished shelter beckoned. She longed to enter it with him and give in to the desire pouring through her. The primitive setting demanded primitive responses. But accompanying the desire was a terrible feeling of foreboding that worsened as they neared the shelter.

Moving toward the structure, her steps faltered as she tried to figure out her confused feelings. Wanting Blake wasn't a crime. They were both free and consenting adults. Was she worried about what would happen when this adventure ended? She already knew she would return to her city life and he to his crocodile park, and they'd probably never meet again. Cause for regret but surely not for the fear gripping her.

"Our deal was for one kiss," she said, pitching her voice low to hide the tremor.

"Any deal can be renegotiated."

He sounded as edgy as she felt. But a lot more sure of what he wanted to do about it. "We should finish the shelter."

"Testing it would be more rewarding."

She resisted the temptation to agree. "But not very practical."

"You're really going to stick to business, aren't you?"

"For now." Not what she had intended to say at all.

He nodded as if he'd heard the thought. "Very well, we'll stick to business for now. But what's between us isn't going away."

"I'm not ready," she said.

Blake frowned. "Ready for what?"

She spread her hands. "Your family history may make you see relationships differently than I do."

"My history may not have sold me on happy ever afters, but what's wrong with happy for the moment?"

"I *am* happy for the moment," she insisted less than honestly, then threw his own words back at him. "Are we going to talk or build?"

He could also twist words. "Build. For now."

While he went looking for suitable roofing material, she made a sketch of the shelter in her notebook. She couldn't help admiring the ingenious way Blake had planted sticks in the ground to make an A-frame, tying each pair of sticks at the top with lengths of vine. Thin pieces of wood were tied at intervals to the long sides of the shelter. It looked strong enough to stand for some time.

Striving to be practical, Jo couldn't help thinking what a beautiful, primitive bower the shelter would make for a tryst. The floor could be carpeted with leaves, making a soft, fragrant bed for two as moonlight filtered through the thatched roof.

She tore the page out of her notebook and crumpled it. The shelter was designed for survival, not lovemaking. She had Blake to thank for making her think in those terms. And in any case, though she might be prepared to kiss him, her idea of a romantic hideaway came with five stars and room service, not crocodiles and snakes.

She was here to do a job, not fall in love. What was it about Blake that made her forget why she was here? What was it about him that made her turn a deaf ear to her common sense and listen to her heart instead?

Ruggedly handsome he might be, but he had a complicated history, and his interests were a world away from hers. She couldn't imagine him in a crowded nightclub where you could hardly hear yourself think. He needed wide open spaces and being close to nature.

The Kimberley suited him, she thought, remembering how often she'd longed to get away from the noise and strobe lights when she'd been out with Nigel. She'd have to be careful not to confuse her enjoyment of the outback solitude with her feelings for Blake.

Blake returned with an armful of long, pliable tufts of grass. Demonstrating, he said, "You take a handful, bend it over the side battens and secure it by twisting a strand around the sheath just under the batten."

His hand closed over hers, directing her inexperienced movements. "Then you slide the sheaves along the batten so they overlap and form a weatherproof barrier, like this."

With an effort, she focused her mind on the task, although it was difficult when every movement brought her into contact with him. Somehow they got the thatching completed.

"If this was a true survival exercise, we'd make a bed out of forest debris," he said.

Remembering her vision of sharing a leafy bower with him, she said, "There's a limit to how authentic I'm prepared to be for the magazine."

"Survival with a few frills," he reminded her. Disappearing into the tent, he soon came back carrying one of the cots, with a sleeping bag draped over his shoulder.

"What inspired your editor to assign you to this story?" he asked as he set up the stretcher.

Jo came back with the second stretcher and sleeping bag, trying not to notice how close together they would be in the narrow shelter. "I've been asking myself the same question ever since Karen dreamed up the idea. The Prentisses are hardly outdoor types, but she was determined to have this story."

"Ron Prentiss is a property developer, isn't he?"

"Big-time. He's the main reason I agreed to do this."

She'd snagged Blake's interest, she saw. "Is he involved with the magazine?"

She shook out the sleeping bag and handed it to him. "He owns it, but leaves running it entirely to Karen. He calls it her little hobby."

"Expensive hobby," Blake observed.

"Not in their circle. She told me he bought the magazine so she'd stay out of his projects. One of which could leave a friend of mine homeless."

"How so?"

She stopped rummaging through the food stores. "Lauren Gale and I have been friends since my school set up a kind of mentoring relationship with her school when I was fifteen. She's a great kid, full of laughter and energy, just a few years behind her age group developmentally.

"Ron Prentiss wants to put up an apartment block that would mean tearing down the group home where she and her friends live. I hate to think how she'll manage if that happens. She's happy and well-adjusted where she is, but she doesn't cope well with change."

"So by writing your boss's pet story, you're hoping she'll use her influence with her husband," Blake surmised. "Sounds like a long shot. What will you do if it doesn't work out?"

"Then I'll think of something else," she said. She dived back into the food box. "You have a choice of soup or soup with the leftover bread. I'm too tired to cook tonight."

"I could do it."

She yawned hugely. "Thanks, but I'm too tired to eat, as well. Staying up all last night is taking its toll. I might settle for a hunk of the bread and some fruit, and call it a night."

"At least you won't lie awake out in the open, wondering what's out there," he pointed out.

She nodded, sure that his nearness would be more disturbing than anything in the bush. Luckily, her tiredness wasn't an act. What with snakes, crocodiles, Nigel's departure and Blake's effect on her, she was genuinely worn out.

All the same, after they ate and cleaned up, she lay awake for some time listening to the sounds of him moving around the camp. He had elected to stay up, claiming he never went to bed early even after being up all night.

She turned her head to look at his bed, less than a hand's span away from hers. They might as well be sharing a double bed. They would have been if she had been willing. The thought sent alarm rushing through her, and she turned abruptly away to gaze at the thatching through which moonlight filtered.

In the distance, she heard a dingo call and relaxed, enjoying the primitive night sounds and imagining Nigel's astonishment that she could actually like sleeping in a rustic shelter under the stars.

In this state of mind, she drifted into a dreamless sleep.

Blake cradled his coffee mug and stared into the embers of the campfire. Behind him he heard the small sounds of Jo settling to sleep. Everything in him urged him to join her and finish what they'd started earlier in the day.

She'd said she wasn't ready but in his arms, she had felt more than ready. Eager. It wouldn't have taken much persuasion on his part for them to have made love. The thought made his groin tighten. But he didn't want to persuade her. Didn't want her having second thoughts later. When they made love—and he had no doubt it was when, not if—he wanted her as hungry for him as he was for her.

She thought she had unfinished business with Nigel, but she was wrong. In Blake's experience, no man walked away from a woman he cared about unless he was sacrificing himself for her benefit. And Nigel didn't strike Blake as the self-sacrificing type.

He had a feeling Jo knew it and was using Nigel as a shield against whatever was between her and Blake. The thought made a smile of satisfaction play around his mouth. He could live with that until she was ready to accept reality. Then it wouldn't matter whether he came to her in a luxury hotel room or a leafy shelter under the stars. The result would be spectacular.

Cold shower time, Stirton, he told himself. Or the next best thing the outback had to offer. He kicked soil over the embers, making sure no sparks remained, then went to wash his cup and himself in a bucket of water. Some time later, chores completed, he was stretched out on the cot beside Jo, the pleasure of watching her sleep threatening to undo the benefits of the cold sponge bath.

Wearing a knee-length T-shirt with a Kisses From The Kimberley logo rising and falling with every breath, she sprawled half-out of the sleeping bag as if she was hot. One arm was crooked over her head, and her smile suggested a pleasant dream. He yearned to share whatever was provoking that Mona Lisa smile. He yearned for a lot more, and had to remind himself of his vow to wait until she was ready. The wait would make their joining all the sweeter.

If he'd learned one thing on his crocodile hunts, it was the virtue of patience.

Unable to stop himself, he leaned across the narrow space between their beds and brushed his lips over hers. Only a taste to hold him until she was ready, he told himself.

Instantly liquid fire tore along his veins and he bit back a groan. He should have known a taste would only sharpen his need. He lowered himself onto his own cot, taking deep breaths and willing the tremors to pass. He'd desired other women and satisfied himself and them without feeling this all-consuming hunger. It scared him. He'd built his life around not needing anyone. He might choose their company, as he'd done with Des Logan and his family, but Blake had grown up determined not to need anyone. Not to leave himself open to being abandoned ever again.

He had reckoned without Jo Francis.

"What are you so cheerful about?" he groused, hearing her hum as she prepared muesli and toast for their breakfast. He'd already made coffee and was on his second cup, needing the caffeine fix after a night of fitful sleep.

"It's a beautiful morning. I slept well. Didn't you?" she asked innocently as they ate.

He debated telling her that she'd kept him awake long into the night, wondering how she fit into his self-contained life and finally deciding she didn't. He kept quiet because the logical conclusion hadn't swayed the part of him she touched so effortlessly. He shouldn't want her, but he did.

"I slept well enough," he said. "What's on this morning's agenda?"

"I need to work on my article for Karen."

"While you're doing that, I'll replenish our water supply and check on the video camera."

"Watch out for the…" she started to say, then intercepted his pitying look and remembered who she was talking to. "Just because you're a crocodile man, you can still get eaten."

"I won't," he assured her. He had no intention of taking risks when he still hoped to catch Eddy Gilgai. Hoping to make love to Jo gave Blake another incentive to take care.

Jo pushed the breakfast things aside and opened her laptop computer on the folding table. She couldn't remember when she had felt so energized. Was it the outback setting, or sharing it with Blake? She banished the possibility as ideas and fragments of sentences began to take shape in her mind. Soon the words were pouring through her fingers almost faster than she could type.

She hardly looked up when Blake returned, until he set the water container down and came to her at the table, the video camera in his hand.

Then she noticed his set expression. "Did we get anything useful?"

He pulled a chair up beside her. "Lots of footage of animals coming to the landing to drink early this morning. Then this."

He showed her the tiny preview screen. She could make out a figure stepping up to the landing and dropping down to examine the rocks, unaware of the camera recording the activity. She frowned. "It isn't Eddy, so who?"

"Take a closer look."

She took the camera from him, went back to where the figure arrived on the scene, and studied the sequence that followed. Something about the person was familiar. Then it came to her and she looked at Blake in confusion. "Your sister,

Judy? Why would she be hanging around the creek at sunrise?"

His mouth tightened into a grim line. "I don't know but I intend to find out."

Chapter 7

"Where is everybody?" Jo asked as they neared the Logan homestead. The sprawling house that sat on a ridge of grassland between river and rain forest looked deserted.

"Des had to let a lot of the staff go when he couldn't meet the payroll," Blake said. "The few who remain are taking care of the cattle. Andy and his people told Des he can pay them when he's able. Without Andy and his friends, Diamond Downs wouldn't survive."

"Karma," she murmured.

"What?"

"For years, he's given so much to others. Now it's coming back to him in the form of love and loyalty."

He parked the car under the shade of a sprawling gum tree and they got out. "You really believe in karma?"

"I believe what goes around comes around." Her tone dared him to disagree.

Instead he said, "Then Max Horvath is due some mighty big shi…stick any day now."

Cade was in the office, studying figures on a computer screen. He looked up when Jo and Blake walked in. "Judy around?" Blake asked in the direct way of outback men.

Cade tilted his chair back. "Out at the airstrip, working on her plane. Des is at the muster camp with Andy. I'll be going there myself after I finish here."

Jo chewed her lip. "Should Des be doing that?"

Cade stacked files into an untidy heap. "Try and stop him. Don't worry, Andy won't let him overtax himself."

Blake stabbed a finger at the screen. "Are those figures getting any better?"

"Not since I was last home. I paid some of the bills and I see you and Tom have been doing the same, but it's like trying to turn off the wet season. If one of us doesn't win the lottery soon, or find Great-grandpa Logan's diamond mine…" He left the rest of the prediction unspoken.

"So much for your karma," Blake said as they walked back to the Jeep after refusing Cade's offer of coffee or a cold beer. She had thought longingly of a shower, but such luxuries weren't in the spirit of the survival exercise, so she had settled for leaving an assortment of batteries with Cade to recharge. She knew that Blake was anxious to get out to the airstrip.

His frustration wasn't with her, Jo sensed. As a man of action, Blake had a low tolerance for situations he couldn't change or control. Not so different from Jo herself. She was also curious to hear Judy's explanation for her secret dawn visit to Dingo Creek.

Homesteads on many of the properties in the Kimberley had been established before aircraft came into regular use, Jo was aware. Only in later years did the owners have to consider where to put an airfield, preferably one that would remain dry and accessible during the monsoon season, when it might become their only link with the outside world.

The site for the airstrip on Diamond Downs had been selected with The Wet in mind, Blake explained as they drove. The surface was so well compacted and the runoff so efficient that even several inches of drenching rain overnight wouldn't close it to aircraft. Even so, the site looked primitive to Jo, used to sleek black surfaces and modern buildings.

The airstrip was no more than a gash of red earth, bulldozed flat and with every stick and stone scoured away. The perimeter was marked by white-painted oil drums. A wind sock hung limply from a small building made from corrugated iron.

The cloud of dust thrown up by the Jeep announced their arrival long before they reached the plane that was Judy's livelihood. It was Jo's first close-up look at the single-engine Cessna, and she was impressed by the plane's well-maintained appearance.

Judy emerged from the engine cowling, wiping her hands on a grease-stained rag. "To what do I owe the pleasure? Not that I'm not pleased to see my big brother anytime," she added, her smile including Jo. Then she frowned. "Oh no, don't tell me something's happened to Dad?"

"Des is fine. He's with Andy out at the muster camp," Blake hastened to assure her. He looked over her shoulder at the Cessna. "Problems?"

"A leak in the exhaust port. Nothing a five-dollar gasket and an hour of my time won't fix. If I leave it until the next oil change, I might have to replace the exhaust riser and that means sending out important bits to have them machined, costing me thousands of dollars and days of unscheduled downtime."

Jo let her surprise show. "All because of a leaking gasket."

Judy dropped the rag onto an oil drum. "It's usually the way with planes. Leaks, cracks and chafes in the engine compartment always get worse, and costly, very fast. Left unattended, that gasket could end up in an in-flight fire. So I hope you don't need to be anywhere important for at least a couple of hours."

"We didn't come looking for a ride," Blake said. He gestured toward the small building. "Let's go inside out of the sun."

Judy looked alarmed. "It's hotter in there than out here. I don't think you…"

"Everything okay, Judy?" came another male voice.

Blake spun around, an oath dropping from his lips and dragging Jo's attention to the building. Framed in the entrance was a man of about Blake's height and build but with a fleshier look to his features, as if he'd once been as ruggedly fit as Blake but had let himself go.

Another foster brother she hadn't heard about? Jo wondered, but Blake's angry body language contradicted the idea, even before he said, "What the devil are you doing here, Horvath?"

So this was Max Horvath, the neighbor who held the mortgage over Diamond Downs and wanted ownership of the land more than he wanted repayment. His gaze roved over Jo's body, making her feel distinctly uncomfortable. She knew why, having met his type before in the city, usually on the wrong end of a story about something like organized crime. What on earth was he doing at the Logan airstrip with Judy?

The other woman stepped into Blake's line of sight. "I invited him, Blake. No need to get agro about it."

"No need at all, Stirton," Horvath said, moving closer to Judy.

Jo saw Blake's hands ball into fists. "Get away from her."

Instead, Horvath dropped an arm possessively around Judy's shoulders. "Is that any way to talk to your future brother-in-law?"

Blake looked as if he might explode. Pointedly ignoring the other man, he asked, "What's going on, Jude?"

Judy shifted from foot to foot, plainly less comfortable than Horvath. "I haven't agreed to anything yet, only to give Max the chance to convince me. I was going to tell you, Blake, but I haven't had the opportunity."

Her foster brother folded his arms across his broad chest. "You have it now." His tone said she'd better make it good.

"Max came to see me to discuss Dad's mortgage. We started talking about the old days."

"We had no old days with him."

"That's not true, at least on my account. We did date for a time," Judy reminded him. "And when you and the other boys were younger, we did a lot of things together—swimming, fishing, endurance rides, lessons with School of the Air together."

Blake's face didn't change. "All that was a long time ago, because our fathers were such good friends."

"Before you moved to Perth?" Jo asked.

Horvath switched his attention to her. "You're the journalist Judy told me about."

She nodded. "Jo Francis, *Australian Scene Weekly*."

He didn't offer his hand or move from Judy's side. "G'day. To answer your question, when my folks split up I drew the short straw and went to live with my mother in the city."

"Hardly the short straw," Blake argued. "You never made any secret of disliking outback life."

"I came back for visits whenever I could."

"When the court ordered you to spend time with your father, you mean."

Judy's expression darkened. "Stop it, both of you. Anyone would think you were both still thirteen instead of thirty."

"Some things don't change, like leopards and their spots."

Horvath tightened his hold on Judy. "You're right, some things don't change. I've always cared about this little lady."

For a fraction of a second, Jo saw something flare in Judy's gaze, then it was gone. She wasn't as relaxed about this as she wanted Blake to think. What was going on here?

Blake was too furious to notice the discrepancy. "You can't be serious about taking up with him again? You know he's only after Des's land."

Judy's head inclined in agreement, surprising Jo, as well as Blake. "I should probably be insulted by that, but you're right. Max has been honest about wanting to find the old diamond mine. But if he does, think what a difference it will make to Dad."

"You really think he plans to share the spoils? As soon as Horvath takes possession of Diamond Downs, Des will be out of here faster than a crocodile grabbing a calf drinking at his water hole. And the consequences will be just as deadly for your father."

"Max has promised to take care of Dad and me."

"And you believe him?"

"Of course she does if we're to become engaged," Horvath said. "Judy's an adult. She doesn't need your approval."

"What she needs is her head read," Blake snapped. "I don't see a ring on her finger."

Judy glanced at her left hand. "It's much too early for that."

"Do me one favor," Blake asked. "Hold off making this official until you've had time to think things over."

"She's had years since I first popped the question," Horvath insisted.

Blake ignored him. "Jude?"

"I won't be rushing to a jewelry store, if that's what's worrying you. In any case, I can't go anywhere until I finish up here. While I have the cowl doors pulled, I may as well do a complete engine compartment inspection. I also need to take a look at the overvoltage annunciator. The alternator is tripping off-line and I suspect the relay may be bad."

"You didn't mention other problems with the plane apart from the oil leak before," Horvath complained.

She shrugged and moved away from his side. "As I told Jo, there's always something to worry about with a plane. So you see, Blake, I won't be going anywhere at least until tomorrow."

"I have to accept that," Blake said grudgingly.

"You have to accept that you can't come between us," Horvath insisted. "Your sister has finally realized how much I love her and want to be with her."

"How much you love Diamond Downs is more likely."

Horvath looked uneasy. "We haven't decided which property we'll live on after we're married. Probably this one, as it needs the most work to bring it back up to scratch."

"And promises you the most benefit." To Judy, he said, "What does Des think about your decision?"

She glanced away. "We haven't told him yet. I want to talk to his doctor first and make sure we choose the right time. I'm sure Dad will be glad to see an end to this pointless feud."

"If it doesn't kill him first."

Judy's sudden pallor made Blake's cold expression soften: "I shouldn't have said that. I know you always have your dad's best interests at heart."

Judy touched her brother's arm. "This has nothing to do with you, Blake."

He really looked at her then, and Jo saw a frown furrow his brow as if he'd finally realized that all was not as it seemed. She watched him master his anger with an obvious effort. "Then I'll have to trust you, won't I?"

Rather than finding the exchange reassuring, Horvath looked irritated. "This is very touching, but I don't think she needs your trust or your good wishes, Stirton. This is between Judy and me."

Blake gave his sister a thoughtful look. "I hope you know what you're doing."

"You trusted me to share the secret of your hideout cave when we were kids," Judy said. "That worked out okay, didn't it?"

An odd expression came over Blake's face. "Yes, it did. You think the situations are comparable now?"

"I sure do, so there's no need to pull the big-brother act," she said, looking relieved. Then she frowned a little. "What did you come to talk to me about?"

Jo waited to see if Blake would mention the videotape of Judy taken at the creek that morning, but he shook his head. "I'd rather discuss it later."

Out of earshot of Max Horvath, Jo surmised and wondered if Judy would get the message. Evidently she did. "I'll be home this evening if you want to drop by the homestead. Why don't the two of you come to dinner?"

"I can't make it tonight. My bank manager's coming over," Horvath said as if he'd been invited.

"We're seeing each other, not joined at the hip," Judy said, sounding tired. "I'm sure I can entertain Blake and Jo without you."

Not exactly a doting girlfriend, Jo thought. "Maybe I should stay at the camp."

"We both should, to keep faith with the terms of your assignment," Blake told her. "Why don't you come to the camp and have dinner with us?"

Judy thought for a minute. "Why not? Dad's spending the night at the muster camp with the men, and Cade's driving out there this afternoon to make sure everything's all right."

"Then we'll see you tonight at camp."

Horvath looked from brother to sister. "Should I put the bank manager off?"

Judy's smile didn't reach her eyes. "Sweet thought, Max, but only if you really want to. I'm sure the dinner won't be anything special and it's probably best that you go ahead with your plans."

In light of Judy's discouraging response, Horvath mumbled something under his breath. Jo didn't catch what was said but evidently Blake did.

"Care to repeat that?" he challenged.

Judy gestured with the spanner. "Max, did you find the multimeter for me?"

Looking almost relieved, Horvath nodded. "I'll get it."

Judy shrugged. "Duty calls. See you both later."

Blake was deep in thought as they walked silently back to the Jeep. "You don't think she's really in love with Horvath, do you?" Jo asked when they were safely away from the other two.

He pushed his hat back on his head. "At first, I didn't know what to think. Horvath's always had a thing for Judy, but she wouldn't give him the time of day until now. Of course, women are a strange mob."

"Thanks a lot." Jo let him open the car door for her, wincing at the blast of heat that greeted her. Leaning on the door, she said, "What do you think she's up to?"

"She mentioned the hideout cave. When we were kids, Tom and I found it first, and planned to make it our secret headquarters. The last person we wanted in there was a girl, so for ages we wouldn't tell her how to find the concealed entrance."

"She didn't give up?"

"Not our Jude. She got Tom and me alone and pretended that the other one had shown her the way. Each of us showed her the way in. When we realized we'd been duped we were ready to black each other's eyes, but we thought there was no longer any reason to be secretive, so we grudgingly welcomed her."

Jo laughed. "So Judy learned what she needed to know." She sobered abruptly. "Do you think that's what she's trying to do now?"

"If she is, she's playing a dangerous game. Horvath's mention of his bank manager means he's getting increasingly desperate for funds."

Jo eased herself into the car, avoiding the heated metal parts as she fastened the seat belt. "What makes you so sure?"

Blake slid behind the wheel and gunned the motor. "Before Shara became engaged to Tom, she was promised to a man called Jamal, a powerful but unscrupulous member of her father's government in Q'aresh. Des gave her refuge on Diamond Downs while Jamal and his retinue stayed with Horvath."

Jo put two and two together. "Entertaining a man like Jamal wouldn't come cheap."

"Right. Horvath was never good with money, and his father put most of his income back into the property."

"So Max is asset rich and cash poor?"

"Probably a good deal poorer after Jamal's extended stay. Word around the district is that the prince ordered the best of everything and charged it all to Horvath's account. When Jamal was jailed in Q'aresh for plotting to overthrow the King, Horvath got stuck with the bills."

"Finding a lost diamond mine would solve a lot of his problems."

Blake swung the Jeep around and headed back in the direction of their camp. "It's the only thing that will."

"Do you think he's getting close?"

"Judy evidently thinks so. With Eddy Gilgai's help, it's possible. Gilgai's people were always said to know where the mine is, but they won't reveal anything because they believe Jack Logan's spirit guards the site."

"He died there, didn't he?"

"So the legend goes. His body was never found."

He lapsed into thoughtful silence and Jo watched the bush jolt by, lost in her own thoughts. She couldn't help remembering the lecherous way Max Horvath had looked at her, hardly appropriate for a man who was supposedly committed to Judy. His readiness to take up with Jamal against Shara suggested he had few scruples. She really hoped Judy would watch her back.

By the time they reached camp, heat was shimmering off the landscape in waves. Jo looked longingly at the creek, wishing she could safely swim there.

Blake saw the look. "Don't even think about it."

"There must be a water hole around here that isn't owned by a crocodile."

"I can think of one or two."

She was sorely tempted. "No, as Judy said, duty calls. My video diary needs updating and I'm on a deadline for my article. I'm surprised Karen hasn't called to ask why she hasn't received it yet."

"Your editor sounds like a tough lady."

Jo thought for a moment. "She's good at what she does."

He spread his arms. "You can be honest. There's no one to overhear."

Loyalty forbade it, even so. "Let's say she's fine to work for as long as you do your job."

"And if you don't?"

She let a smile show. "There's hell to pay."

"Then I'd better let you get on with your work."

"What will you do in the meantime?" she asked.

"Go catch our dinner, unless you actually prefer freeze-dried rations?"

She shook her head. He also wanted to see if Eddy or Max had left any more clues, she assumed. "You get to have all the fun."

He gave her a knowing look. "I believe you would rather explore along a muddy, croc-infested creek than sit behind your laptop."

She hadn't thought of it in those terms, but he was right; the adventure had far more appeal. Or was it the adventurer? "Too bad I can't."

He came up to her. "You know, Jo Francis, you're an amazing woman."

"For a city woman?"

"For any woman."

Her pulse jumped in instant response to his nearness. But she didn't move back. Didn't push him away when he invaded the last of her personal space. Worryingly, she even lifted her face so he could kiss her more easily. How could you want something and not want it at the same time?

He threaded his fingers through her hair and the wanting intensified. "This is getting to be a habit," he growled.

"A bad habit," she said without much conviction. "Didn't somebody once say the only way to deal with a habit is to give in to it?"

"Is that what you want?"

Her gaze locked with his. "I shouldn't."

"Because?"

Words were hard to summon. Hard to argue against a need so powerful. "My career. Your outback life."

"I'll grant you one out of the two."

And he was right. Their lifestyles weren't incompatible. But the one impediment she hadn't mentioned was fear. She valued her independence and hated feeling so needy. Whenever anyone became overly protective, she instinctively pushed them away. She felt the urge to be wanted and needed by Blake so strongly she could almost taste it, and it scared the devil out of her.

Could he possibly know? And why was her independence so important to her that anything threatening it filled her with mind-numbing fear? Being with Nigel or any of her former boyfriends had never triggered such intense feelings. But then none of them had never affected her as strongly as Blake did. Something nagged deep down inside her, but when she reached for it, it scurried out of the light, out of her conscious reach.

"There's something else, isn't there? Something you're not telling me."

She shifted uncomfortably. When had he become so in tune with her? "What makes you think so?"

He tilted her chin up. "It's in your eyes. I've been around wild creatures a long time and I've seen that look before. You want to trust me but for some reason, you can't let yourself. Someone hurt you pretty badly once. Was it a man?"

Tension gripped her as the nebulous thought in her subconscious scuttled deeper into shadow. She moved her head away from his hand. "I don't stick around long enough to get hurt." Now what had possessed her to say that?

He nodded as if he'd heard more than she'd said. "And you don't plan to this time, even though you can feel the power of what's between us."

"What's between us is pure, unbridled lust," she said on a brittle note. "Maybe we should just make love and get it out of our systems."

His head whipped around in instant negation. "I can't deny the idea has plenty of appeal. Nor that it will happen. But when we make love, it's going to be for all the right reasons."

She tried to keep her tone light. Failed miserably. "What do you call the right reasons?"

"The certainty that what you're doing is so right you can't hold back a moment longer. The hope that it will lead to an unbreakable bond between the two of you."

"And if it doesn't?" she was practically whispering now.

"Sometimes it doesn't, but you keep trying. Keep hoping."

She had to move, to busy her hands. If she didn't, they would be wrapped around him and her mouth would be reaching for his. Setting up her laptop was the safe antidote, the familiar activity, and she took refuge in it. "How have you stayed so positive after all you've been through in your life?" she asked without looking at him.

He watched her for a moment. "I only had two options, sink or swim. A long time ago, I made up my mind to swim. Everyone has the same choice."

Not everyone had his strength. She dragged a folding chair up to the table and opened a file on her computer. The article she'd begun that morning leaped onto the screen, the letters fading in the strong sunlight. Then she realized her view was blurred. She blinked hard. What was it about Blake that pierced straight to the heart of everything she was?

He was still watching her, she noticed out of the corner of her eye, but kept her attention fixed on the screen. "I made more progress than I realized," she said. "All I have to do is write some snappy closing paragraphs, polish up the rest, and it will be ready to send to Karen."

"Real life doesn't always lend itself to snappy closing paragraphs," he observed. "Most of the time, we have to muddle through with what we've got."

She was tired of feeling so open and exposed to him. She'd had experts trawling through her mind to try to get at the source of her fear of being dependent on anyone. He wasn't going to do better in a few days. He wasn't a thera-pist. Maybe there wasn't anything to find. "Don't you have a crocodile to wrestle or something?" she demanded. "I have work to do."

"You got that right," he said softly, his tone making it clear that he didn't mean the article. "I'll help you."

"So you can get me into bed?"

"Low blow," he said. "We both know I could get you into bed in the next thirty seconds if I wanted to."

She couldn't deny what he'd felt for himself when he'd held her in his arms. Her resistance to his appeal was zero. She half turned and opened her arms in a theatrical gesture. "Then what are you waiting for? Take me, I'm yours." Heat flooded through her, the invitation not entirely in jest.

He heard it, too. "If I believed that, I'd sweep you into the shelter so fast your head would spin. But it isn't true, not yet anyway. When we make love, I want you with me in spirit as well as body."

Going to the Jeep he pulled out a sturdy-looking rod and reel, slung a pack over his shoulder and strode off into the bush, leaving his words hanging in the air behind him.

When. Not if. He'd said it as if it was only a matter of time. "I have to write," she mumbled, feeling her fear return. How she hated this. Why couldn't they have a fun fling and be done with it?

Because of his blasted code of the outback, she thought, raising her head from the screen. How did it go? You don't back down, you don't give up and you stand by your mates.

Even when they didn't want you to?

So it would seem. Releasing a breath composed of equal parts longing and exasperation, Jo got to work.

Chapter 8

Karen must have picked up the phone as soon as she received her e-mail, Jo decided when her cell phone rang moments later. In the middle of recording a video diary entry, she stopped the camera and opened her phone. "Jo Francis."

"Great work, Jo. The article really sizzles. The digital photos are excellent, too."

Recognizing her editor's voice, Jo let her eyebrows lift. "You didn't waste any time reading it."

"I'm as fascinated by your experience as our readers are going to be."

Jo pulled a face at the phone. "So my deathless prose isn't the reason you rushed to call me?"

"You don't need me to tell you you're a good writer," Karen said briskly. "But the best writer in the world can't make a silk purse out of a sow's ear."

They didn't talk in clichés either, Jo thought good-humoredly. "Then you're not concerned about me finding the snake in my bag?"

"Why? It's exactly the sort of adventure you're supposed to be having. You are all right, aren't you? The snake didn't bite you?"

Contrarily, Jo was irritated at Karen's evident complacency. Jo didn't want Karen pulling back on the story, because she considered it too dangerous. But she might show some concern for her reporter's well-being. *Make up your mind*, she thought. "If it had, I wouldn't be here talking about it," she told Karen. "Blake knew exactly how to deal with the snake."

"He's quite an asset, isn't he?"

In more ways than one, came the swift thought. "He's at home in the outback. And surprisingly tolerant of my inexperience."

"And?"

And he pushes every one of my buttons, and there's every chance we'll go to bed together before this assignment is over, Jo thought. She wasn't about to share such an admission with her editor. Other than at the office party, when Karen had talked about not having children, they'd never indulged in much girl talk and Jo wasn't comfortable starting now. It wasn't like Karen to take much interest in the private life of a staff member. Maybe Karen also found Blake attractive.

The swift, sharp stab of jealousy caught Jo unawares. "And he'll make sure I don't kill myself before this is over. Although you have to agree, it would make a heck of a closing article for the series."

"Don't even joke about it," Karen snapped. "I'm well aware that what you're doing has its dangers and I trust you to be sensible."

Now she sounded like the headmistress from Jo's old high school. "Yes ma'am," she murmured dutifully, deciding that the image didn't suit the older woman. "Have you spoken to your husband about saving Lauren's house?" she asked to change the subject.

There was a long pause. "Ron has been very busy lately."

In other words, no. "You will talk to him before he goes any further with his development plans, won't you?"

"I've said I would."

Subject closed, Jo heard. Had she made a mistake leaving Perth before the question was resolved? She'd taken the assignment to please Karen, on condition that the editor would use her influence with her husband to let Lauren and her friends remain in their home. If Karen didn't keep her end of the bargain, this had all been for nothing.

Not quite for nothing, Jo thought with a glance at the track Blake had taken into the bush. She would still have her memories of him and his primeval world. The thought of leaving the Kimberley behind—leaving him behind?—was surprisingly disconcerting. "I'm sure you'll do everything you can," she told Karen.

She heard computer keys tapping as the editor multi-tasked. "I'm not as heartless as you seem to think. I'm well aware of how much you care about your friend, and how important it is for someone like her to have a settled home and familiar surroundings."

Jo didn't like hearing Lauren described as "someone like her" but she was careful not to risk offending Karen further. She was still Lauren's best hope. Ron Prentiss was on record as saying he'd do anything for the wife he adored. Jo remembered seeing an interview with the millionaire property developer in which he crowed about how impressed he'd been at Karen's virginal state when they'd met, and how he always wanted to be first with her in everything. He'd added that if another man so much as looked at her, he didn't know what he'd do.

Jealous? Jo asked herself. While she wouldn't want the world knowing the details, she knew she'd give a lot to have a man feel that way about her.

Who was she kidding? The moment a man took such an intense interest in her, she'd run a as fast as she could to get away from him. She valued her independence too much to want what Karen and Ron Prentiss had.

Didn't she?

"I have to go," she said. "My phone battery's running low." Unless she collected the spare batteries she'd left with Cade to recharge, she would soon be off the air completely.

"I will talk to Ron," Karen promised. "In the meantime, see if you can persuade Blake to give you an interview about himself. Use your feminine charms."

They might work for Karen on Ron, but Jo couldn't see them having much effect on Blake. "He's publicity shy," she said, wondering again why the editor was so interested in the crocodile man. Given her husband's possessiveness, she would seem to be playing with fire.

"And send me more photos," Karen said as if Jo hadn't spoken. "One of Blake handling a snake or a crocodile would be sensational."

What am I, invisible? Jo thought. Anyone would think Blake was the focus of this story. Karen seemed far more interested in him than in Jo's activities. She *was* jealous, she decided, of her editor playing favorites. Jo couldn't possibly feel territorial about Blake, or could she? She should be glad she had something she could use to persuade Karen to keep her end of their bargain.

"I'll see what I can do. Let me know when you've spoken to Ron," she said. She started to say goodbye, but Karen had already hung up.

Blake had meant what he'd said to Jo. They wouldn't make love until she wanted him as much as he wanted her. Something was keeping her from giving herself to him. Perhaps had stopped her from giving herself completely to any man.

If she didn't resolve whatever was getting in her way, taking her to bed might make things worse. The better their lovemaking—and Blake fully intended to make it spectacular— the greater the likelihood that her unnamed fear would send

her running afterward. And Blake didn't want her running anywhere but into his arms.

Reaching the rock landing overhanging the creek, he hun-
kered down, looking for signs of human intrusion but finding
no fresh evidence. Had failing to scare Jo away by luring the
crocodile in close to the camp and by planting the snake in
her bag, or knowing she was now under Blake's protection,
forced Max to change his tactics?

At the thought of the man pawing his foster sister, Blake
stood up, his fingers white around the fishing rod. He didn't
think there was a chance of Judy being seriously interested in
the man, but the idea of Max as a prospective brother-in-law
turned Blake's stomach.

Since there was nothing he could do about the situation
now except trust both the women in his life, he set about
catching a barramundi for their dinner. The barra was the leg-
endary eating fish of the tropical north, gracing the menus of
the finest restaurants. Right now was the prime time for catching the fish around the inland creeks and lagoons.

From his pack, he retrieved a minnow-shaped plastic lure
designed to swim about three feet below the surface. Tying it
to a sixteen-pound line at the end of a heavier leader and
sinker, he cast the rig out over a cluster of fallen trees where
the water tended to be warmer and the fish food plentiful. Then
he twitched the rod tip to make the lure jump around in the
water in imitation of the insects that were the barra's favorite
meal.

He didn't have too long to wait. After a series of fruitless casts,
working the lure all the way back to his feet and then casting it
out again, he felt something strike the lure hard and his rod bent
almost ninety degrees. He began to wind the line in as fast as he
could, concentrating on keeping the line taut while the aggres-
sive fish indulged in a series of rod-bending lunges that made
Blake's arms feel as if they would be torn from their sockets.

Several times, he thought the fish had snagged his line
under fallen trees or rock bars but he kept up the pressure,

gradually playing the fish closer and closer to the rocks until he could slip a net under it and bring it to shore.

All the time, he kept a wary eye on the water at his feet, alert in case the big crocodile that frequented the creek decided to take an interest in his catch. It wouldn't be the first time he'd left fish lying half in and half out of the water to keep them cool, and returned to find only the heads remaining. But the crocodile must have fed recently because Blake saw no sign of it.

The barramundi was a good fifteen pounds in weight, he assessed as he cleaned and prepared the fish well away from the water's edge. No sense in tempting fate more than necessary. When he'd finished the job he threw the fish head and trimmings into the creek, knowing they wouldn't go to waste.

By the time he returned to camp, Jo had put away her laptop and had dragged the folding table into the center of the clearing. She was setting it with enamel plates and mugs for three. She looked so attractive that his breath caught and he stopped at the edge of the clearing, and enjoyed the view.

She'd bunched her hair up on top of her head for coolness, and a few tendrils curled onto her neck. Her skin was turning golden from the sun, despite the sunscreen she applied conscientiously. The top three buttons of her checked western-style shirt were undone, revealing a generous expanse of creamy flesh. She looked so enticing that he almost forgot his vow not to make love to her until he could be sure not to frighten her away.

He instantly suppressed the low groan that collected in his throat. The urge to take her into his arms was almost overwhelming. He wasn't a psychologist. Maybe he was wrong. She might not be spooked. She might even thank him for showing her that her fears were groundless.

And he might wake up one morning to find her gone without explanation.

The prospect made his blood turn to ice. He knew once he had possessed her he would never want to let her go. For a moment, he shared her fear. Until Des and Fran came into his life, he hadn't experienced much in the way of happy families, starting with the most elemental relationship—his mother. What made him think he had what it took to create something lasting with Jo?

Was she also afraid that love didn't last? Unlike his there was nothing in Jo's family history to support the fear. She had loving parents who were still happily married and brothers whose main crime, according to Jo, was overprotectiveness. Until he knew what was making her so afraid to trust him, he would have to take extra care with her.

Jo hummed to herself as she prepared the table. She was probably being overly fussy. This was a bush camp, after all. Placing wildflowers in a glass in the center of the table was hardly essential to their survival. But they looked pretty and added to her sense of occasion. For a foolish moment, she wished she and Blake were dining alone under the stars.

This was a business arrangement. He wouldn't be here at all if he wasn't being paid by the magazine to assist her, she reminded herself. He had hardly fallen over himself to make love to her when given the chance. Telling herself he'd pulled back for her sake didn't help. She hadn't wanted him to. She'd wanted...in truth, she didn't know what she'd wanted. Maybe he was right. It was better to wait until she was free of doubts.

Would she know when that time came? As a young teenager, she'd asked her mother how you knew when you were in love. Frustratingly, her mother's answer had been, "You'll know." Jo guessed the same applied now. If Blake was right and some deep-seated explanation for her fear needed to be dislodged before they made love, then she'd better start working on the cause of the fear.

The instinctive way she felt her stomach clench suggested he *was* right. Yet she'd never felt fearful when she was with Nigel. Perhaps because he'd meant less to her than she suspected could be the case with Blake. With him, there would be no half measures. No easy friendship-and-see-where-it-leads, such as she'd known with other men. He would give her the world, but he would want everything she had to give in return. Now all she had to do was figure out why the notion scared her witless.

She'd scooped up a handful of knives and forks when a prickling sensation on the back of her neck warned her she was being watched. She turned slowly, a cry forming on her lips. She stifled it, seeing Blake standing at the edge of the clearing.

Her heart slammed against her ribs. Not in fear this time. More like excitement. She covered it with a light tone. "I hope you've caught dinner because the alternative is freeze-dried Irish stew."

He held up the glistening fish. "Will this do?"

She whistled softly. "Nice fish. Barramundi, isn't it?"

He carried it closer. "One of the best eating fish in the Kimberley. Or anywhere."

She was glad of the mundane conversation giving her time to recover her emotional balance. Finding him watching her when he'd haunted her thoughts only moments before had shaken her more than she wanted him to see. "I've eaten it in restaurants."

"Not the way I intend to cook it," he assured her.

"I thought that's my job."

He stripped a palm leaf from a bush and placed it on the table, setting the fish down on top. "This is a job for an expert."

She felt laughter dance in her eyes. "That sounds suspiciously like, 'Me Tarzan, you Jo.' I'm not sure I like it."

"Then it's time you learned your place, woman. Step aside and let the hunter-gatherer…ah…hunt and gather."

She laughed, relegating the fear to a far corner of her mind. Tonight, she was going to enjoy Blake's company without complications. "I think you already did that." She lifted her hands, palms up. "But if you want to slave over a hot campfire, be my guest."

His gaze narrowed. "Why do I get the feeling I've been outmaneuvered?"

"No such thing. You volunteered to cook. I'll do the cleaning up afterward. Isn't teamwork important to survival in the bush?"

"It's important to everything," he agreed. He lifted a hand

and brushed a few strands of hair away from her face. Her heart quickened pace. But he let the hand drop and stepped away. "I'll start dinner."

By the time Judy arrived, the sun was low in the sky. Blake had banked up a roaring fire and then allowed the flames to die down before making a pit in the center of the glowing embers. He'd seasoned the fish with butter, black pepper and some bush herbs he'd collected on the way back. Now their meal was wrapped in layers of aluminum foil and nestled on a bed of hot coals with more coals piled on top. At the appetizing aromas, her mouth had already begun to water.

"Hope I haven't held you up," Judy said when she joined them. "The problem with the alternator relay was more stubborn than I anticipated, but it's all fixed now. I brought cold beer."

Blake straightened from supervising the fire. "You're a candidate for sainthood."

Judy rolled her eyes. "You're only saying that because Jo's here. He had other names for me when we were kids," she told Jo.

"I have two brothers. I can imagine," she replied. "Mine used to baby me, too. It was okay for them to jump off the garage roof and pretend they were superheroes, but I was only allowed to be the wide-eyed girl sidekick."

"I used to wait until the boys weren't around before I jumped off the stockyard shed," Judy confided.

Blake looked up. "So that's how you twisted your ankle. You told us you'd jumped away from a snake."

"Well, there could have been a snake waiting below when I jumped off the shed," his foster sister defended herself.

To Jo, the exchange sounded so much like those she'd had with her own brothers when they were growing up that she felt a flash of homesickness. "When we get together for holidays, we still carry on much the same," she said.

Judy popped the tops off three cans of beer and handed one each to Blake and Jo. "And we probably always will. Just as long as we agree that everything is their fault."

"Now wait a minute," Blake protested.

But Jo nodded full agreement. "Exactly what I tell my brothers. I've tried to teach their wives the same rule."

"Wives are different. They have built-in rose-colored glasses where their menfolk are concerned."

Blake gestured with his can of beer. "If you two have finished amusing yourself at my expense, the fish is almost cooked."

Judy changed tracks seamlessly. "Good. I brought a bowl of coleslaw. And the batteries you left with Cade," she added.

Jo nodded her thanks. "I'm not sure how honestly this can be called a survival exercise when we have modems and cell phones, but they're a comfort all the same."

"No sense taking greater risks than you have to," Blake agreed.

He opened the blackened, foil-wrapped parcel and lifted portions of the fish onto a plate to bring to the table, while Judy retrieved a covered container and a basket of fresh bread rolls from her car.

Blake gallantly pulled a log up to the small table, leaving the folding chairs for Jo and Judy. With the evening chorus of bush sounds around them, Jo couldn't imagine a finer restaurant anywhere. In the way of the outback, day had tumbled into velvet night with no perceptible twilight in between. Now the stars blazed overhead, their numbers dizzying. Blake had hung a lantern from a tree, and a citronella-scented candle flickered on the table.

Jo lifted her can of beer in a toast. "To the Logan family."

Blake touched cans with her and Judy. "I'll drink to that."

"And to a future for Diamond Downs," Judy added.

Jo saw Blake's features tighten but he let them enjoy their meal in peace. Then he said quietly, "Diamond Downs will have a future. You don't have to sacrifice yourself."

Judy licked traces of fish off her fingers before answering. "I'm not sacrificing myself. I don't actually intend to marry Max."

"What about the wedding night?"

Judy looked angry. "In the first place, that's none of your business. In the second, Max is the last man I'd sleep with."

"Does he know that?"

"Of course not. The whole point of the exercise is to let him think he has a chance with me so he'll reveal how much he knows about the whereabouts of Great-grandpa Logan's diamond hoard."

Jo began to stack the plates and cutlery. "Do you think he knows where the mine is?"

Judy passed her plate along. "Thanks to Eddy Gilgai, he knows more than we do."

"But if Max finds the mine on Logan land, it still belongs to you, doesn't it?" Jo asked.

Judy inclined her head in agreement. "Unless he forecloses on Dad's mortgage." She shot her foster brother a look of appeal. "You must see why I can't let that happen."

Blake's glance included Jo. "We're doing everything we can to prevent Max taking ownership of this place. I've been looking into refinancing the crocodile farm."

Judy covered his hand with hers. "Oh, Blake, you were so close to having it paid off. This is the shed roof all over again, isn't it?"

"What?"

"You'd rather hock your home and business than let me play my part."

"Getting involved with Max Horvath isn't the answer."

"Because I thought of it," Judy said with an exasperated look at Jo. "I don't plan on marrying the man, only of gaining his confidence and finding out what he knows."

"Is he likely to turn violent?" Jo asked.

Blake frowned. "That worries me, too. If he finds out what you're up to, you could be in real danger."

"I can handle Max," Judy said with what Jo thought might be a touch of overconfidence.

"That's what Tom and Shara thought, and she almost got

herself kidnapped back to Q'aresh and forced into an arranged marriage," Blake pointed out.

"I'm not taking this lightly," Judy insisted. "I know Max is desperate for money, and he hasn't always acted above the law, but I'll take care, I promise."

"Like you took care wandering around the creek yesterday morning?" Blake demanded.

Jo saw Judy's eyebrows go up. "What do you mean?"

"We set up my video camera to film movement around the creek, hoping to catch Eddy or Max up to their tricks with the crocodile."

Judy traced a pattern on the tabletop with her finger. "Oh."

"And you can guess who we caught on camera, can't you?"

Judy lifted her head. "I was hoping to find more information. I should probably have told you what I was doing."

"Probably?" Blake sounded as if he was about to explode. "If the croc had been hungry, you could have been dragged into the water."

"But I wasn't."

Feeling the need to defuse the situation, Jo stood up with her hands full of dishes. "Can we agree that you won't sneak around the camp again without letting us know?" she said to Judy.

"The next time I sneak around, you'll be the first to know," the other woman promised with a wry smile.

"I'd rather you agreed to keep out of this," Blake groused at his foster sister.

Judy began to help clear the table. "How can I when my home and family are at stake?"

Blake's eyes blazed. "Are you suggesting they're not my home and family, too?"

Judy's hands stilled. "Oh, Blake, of course I'm not. I didn't think you had any doubts left."

A fist clenched around Jo's heart as she watched the interaction between the siblings. Did Blake want to solve Des Logan's problems all by himself to prove himself worthy of his position in the Logan family? Did such deep-seated doubts ever fully go away? He'd accused Jo of having hidden fears. It sounded as if he had a few of his own to resolve. Maybe everybody did.

"Judy's a grown woman. She has to make her own decisions," she said, speaking from the experience of having brothers of her own.

"This one doesn't feel right," he snapped. "I don't trust Max Horvath any more than I'd trust the crocodile in that creek."

Judy snapped the lid back on the salad container. "Neither do I. But I don't have to trust him, just use him."

"As long as you're not the one who ends up being used," he said.

Judy shot Jo a look of triumph. Jo wasn't sure that Judy had actually won any victories, but her tactic had gained his acceptance if not his approval. In leading Max Horvath on, Jo wasn't convinced that Judy was taking a safe route, but she understood the frustration driving the other woman to act. Sometimes any action was better than inaction.

"Has Max told you anything useful yet?" she asked.

Judy shook her head. "He showed me a few tiny diamonds he took out of the creek near the hideout cave. Where the Uru artwork is located," she added for Jo's benefit.

"We're going to hike to the cave tomorrow," Jo informed her. "Should I keep my eye open for diamonds lying around?"

"You have to know what to look for and where. But if Max found the diamonds where he said he did, there's a good chance the mine itself is somewhere in that region."

"He first showed the stones to Shara at the foot of the escarpment near the hideout cave," Blake said. To Jo, he explained, "He and Jamal thought they had Shara cornered so they probably felt they had nothing to lose by letting her see the diamonds."

Judy smiled at the reminder. "Then the cavalry arrived and we snatched her off Jamal's plane as it was taking off. It was like a scene out of a movie."

"Except that this isn't a movie," Blake growled. "Max showing you the diamonds as well doesn't exactly reassure me."

"He thinks his secret is safe because we're going to be lovers," Judy said. When Blake frowned, she touched his cheek. "It's all right, big brother, I'll be careful. You never know, you and Jo might find the mine yourselves and give me the satisfaction of telling Max what he can do with his proposal of marriage."

"Do you think we stand any chance of locating the mine?" Jo asked Blake a short time later as Judy's car headlights were swallowed up by the darkness.

His face was too deep in shadow for her to see his expression, but his tone left her in no doubt. "I think we have as much chance as Max Horvath has of marrying my foster sister."

Chapter 9

Awakened from a pleasant dream of being waited on hand and foot in a five-star hotel, Jo groaned as she opened her eyes to predawn grayness. She could just make out Blake standing at the entrance of the shelter. "What time is it?" she asked groggily.

"It's almost sunrise," Blake informed her cheerfully. He was dressed in khaki shirt and pants. Outside the shelter, the crackle and pop of flames told her he already had the campfire going.

She levered herself up on her elbows. "This isn't civilized."

He shrugged. "It was your idea to hike to the Uru cave."

"Not mine. My editor's. Wouldn't it help to be able to see something when we get there?"

"It will be full daylight in half an hour. The best time to walk through the bush is before the heat of the day builds up."

She could hardly disagree, and she hadn't argued when Karen had suggested they walk to the cave when they were planning this assignment. Of course, Jo had been safe in the magazine's offices in Perth, imagining an easy walk through lush tropical greenery, with an occasional stop at a water hole to cool off.

Arising before dawn to walk through some of the most inhospitable terrain on Earth, with no chance of a swim that didn't involve the risk of being eaten alive, painted a far less attractive picture.

Still, she had gotten herself into this. And she appreciated having Blake as her guide. She hated to think how she and Nigel would have coped on their own.

She sniffed the air. "Do I smell coffee?"

"Coffee, rolls and the rest of last night's barramundi," he informed her.

Since the camp had no refrigeration, Judy had taken most of the big fish home with her and still there had been enough left for breakfast, Jo recalled. She remembered her dream. "No chance of room service?"

"Then I'd never get you out of bed," he said.

Sometime during the night, she had pushed aside the sleeping bag. Suddenly, she became aware of how much of her long, bare legs her skimpy T-shirt nightgown exposed to his view. Defiantly, she tossed her head. "Some men would consider that a good thing."

His face was in shadow, but there was no mistaking the appreciation in his voice when he said, "They'd be crazy if they didn't."

Desire as hot and fierce as an out-of-control bushfire leapt inside her. She tamped it down by remembering that they'd been in this situation before, and he hadn't taken advantage of it. Of her. The fear of commitment he'd recognized might stop her from planning anything long term, but it didn't have to get in the way of healthy, mutually satisfying sex.

At the same time, she knew it wouldn't work. Blake wasn't the type to settle for a one- or even several-night stand, however incredible. And she had a gnawing certainty that it wouldn't be enough for her, either. In fact, the more incredible the experience, the more she would want it to go on and on. Better not start something she wasn't up to finishing yet.

Damn him for being right, she thought again, and swung her legs over the side of the camp bed. "Give me ten minutes to wash and dress."

She was ready in less and Blake had a mug of steaming coffee waiting for her. She took it and sniffed appreciatively, savoring the rich aroma. "Why does food smell and taste so much better in the outdoors?"

"Fewer distractions for the senses. And you're usually more physically active, so your appetite is sharper."

She took a drink. "My parents used to take my brothers and me camping and fishing when we were kids. Food always tasted wonderful then, too."

He nodded as if she'd confirmed a theory. "I guessed this wasn't your first experience camping out."

She gestured with the mug. "A campground at the beach or in the hills hardly compares with building your own shelter and navigating through unmarked country without getting lost. I gather you had lots of practice at camping after you joined the Logan family. But what about before you came to the Kimberley?"

"Once, although it was more like a forced march with full pack than a camping trip. The caregiver I had at the time was in the army reserve and thought the experience would toughen me up."

She cursed herself for bringing up what was obviously an unhappy memory. "I'm sorry, I…"

"It's all right. As the saying goes, what doesn't kill you makes you stronger."

"You make it sound as if he was right to treat you like that."

His shoulders lifted. "Who's to say? They all did the best they could. I wasn't the easiest kid to manage."

"With good reason. No child should be passed around from one home to another."

From the hot coals he removed two foil-wrapped packages.

From one, he took a roll heaped with succulent barbecued fish and handed it to her. "The world is full of injustice. All we can do is work on our corner of it and hope others do the same thing in theirs. Like you're doing with Lauren."

Another wave of indignation surged through her. "Lauren isn't a good cause. She's my friend."

He unwrapped a second roll and bit into it before answering. "The best kind of good cause is the one you choose because it benefits you as much as the person you're helping."

The warm fish melted on her tongue along with most of her indignation. "It's true. I get far more out of the time I spend with Lauren than she gets from me. She's so full of life, sweet and trusting. Everybody's her friend until proven otherwise. Sometimes I wish I could be more like her."

"Unlike Lauren, you have the wisdom to know it isn't safe to trust too readily," he pointed out. "I'll bet her sweet nature sometimes gets her into difficulties."

She felt her eyes shadow. "When she was a teenager, a man tried to entice her to go to his house to see his puppies. Luckily, she was waiting for me and I arrived as she was about to go with the man, in time to put a stop to it. I reported the incident, but he wasn't caught. Lauren was furious with me. I had to take her to see some puppies at a local pet shop before she'd speak to me again."

Blake finished his roll and dusted crumbs off his hands. "Still, she was luckier than you."

Unease nagged at her. "In what way?"

"She had you. Who was there for you when you were kidnapped?"

"Lauren will always have me," she said, not wanting to admit that her anger over the incident might be related to her own abduction.

He didn't push. "You're a kind person, Jo."

"Anyone would have done the same."

"And you don't take well to hearing compliments about yourself."

"Maybe I recognize a line when I hear one."

"Telling you you're kind is hardly a line." His hand came up and touched the side of her face. "If I tell you how beautiful you look first thing in the morning, with your hair all mussed and your eyes clouded from sleep, would that be a line?"

Striving to ignore the wisps of sensation curling through her, she darted her tongue out to moisten her lips. "I don't know. Would it?"

His palm cupped her cheek. "It would be the truth."

"Oh."

Blake liked the note of surprise he heard in her voice. She really had no idea how beautiful she was, he thought. Sometime, somewhere, her confidence in herself had been undermined, and he'd like to get his hands on the culprit. So many times in his life people had tried to do that to him and never succeeded because he had made up his mind not to let them touch the essence of who he was. He hated the thought that someone might have violated her in any way.

"Even so," he went on, "my opinion doesn't matter a darn."

She looked startled, a little wounded, but he pressed on. "The only opinion you need to take into account about you is yours."

Her smile blossomed, making him hunger to taste her again. Patience, he schooled himself. Until she came to him, heart completely open and body willing, he couldn't possess her and keep peace with himself. All the same, it took a mighty effort to lift his hand away.

He couldn't resist letting his fingers trail down her face. She tilted her head a little and nuzzled his hand, making his stomach muscles tighten. Inwardly, he cursed himself for being so blasted noble, but he knew with her he had no choice. She affected him in ways he couldn't begin to count, and he didn't want to do anything to drive her away from him.

With seeming reluctance, she moved away. "You're very hard to get mad at."

He pretended to be offended. "Why would you want to?"

"Because one minute you're listing my shortcomings, and the next you're making me feel like the most beautiful woman in the world."

"Have you considered both might be the truth?"

Her breath gushed out. "I certainly know I have shortcomings."

"Very few, and mostly the result of misguided good intentions," he said. "I get the feeling you have a bigger problem dealing with the other part."

She tossed the dregs of her coffee into the fire. "Now that *is* a line."

Over the hiss and spatter of the moisture on the hot coals, he said, "Only if you take it as one. It isn't meant to be. You are beautiful."

How was she supposed to respond to a man who confused her as completely as Blake did? Sparks of reaction danced through Jo although she tried to ignore them. "You could try keeping your opinions to yourself," she suggested.

"Ah, but that would take all the fun out of this adventure."

"Speak for yourself."

"I was."

The simple statement cut right to the core of her fear. He wasn't playing with her when he called her beautiful, and it wasn't a line. He truly believed what he was saying. But she wasn't beautiful or kind, or any of the other noble things he attributed to her. She felt uncomfortable imagining herself having to live up to his expectations.

"Isn't it time we started for the cave?" she asked.

"If you've had enough to eat."

On safer ground, she nodded. "More than enough. I think barramundi has become my favorite fish. Not that I'll ever taste it like this again."

He piled dirt over the coals to suffocate them and prevent any chance of escaping sparks causing a bushfire. "Unless you come back to the Kimberley, then I'll catch and cook a barramundi for you anytime you want."

She stood up and stretched. "This assignment is a one-off. I don't see myself making a career of being Jo Francis, outback reporter."

"Or you could stay."

Her breath shallowed. Looking down at his broad shoulders and tousled hair as he worked on the fire, she felt a longing so strong it was like a hunger. No place she had ever visited had worked such magic on her. And no man. All the more reason to put as much distance between them as she could. "I don't think so," she said.

If he heard the note of finality in her voice, he didn't react. "The fire's safe to leave. We can go now."

Since she wasn't an experienced bush walker, he had proposed taking the Jeep part of the way and then hiking the last few miles through Cotton Tree Gorge to where the Uru cave was located. The day was already hot with the promise of becoming hotter and steamier, so she accepted without demur. Before they left camp, he had telephoned Andy Wandarra and arranged to have the Jeep moved to the road below the Uru cave so it would be waiting for them at the end of the hike.

All through the jolting drive over rugged cattle tracks, his words echoed through her mind. *You could stay.* It was impossible, of course. She had her career, her friendship with Lauren, her whole life in Perth. Yet as they approached the canyon where storm-fed torrents had gouged out crevices and undermined giant cliffs, the magic of the Kimberley did its level best to seduce her.

She couldn't deny that the man at her side was part of the plot. He infuriated and attracted her in about equal parts. She disliked the way he delved into her psyche and disliked even more that he seemed able to see into her soul. But the attraction was strong, too. Stronger than the dislike? She hoped not, or she was in real trouble.

Nothing to be done about it now, she told herself, and made an effort to focus on the changing landscape around her. Blake pointed out one of the world's most primitive plants, a member of the cycad family he told her, adding that it had grown in this location since the time of the dinosaurs.

She should be taking notes for her next article, but found herself content to feast her eyes on the craggy outcrops clothed in paperbarks and bloodwood, bottlebrush and she-oaks. A gently diffused light hung over the countryside and their passage was noted with disinterest by kangaroos, wallabies, eagles, a dingo, and even a few wild donkeys and a buffalo that Blake said would have wandered west from the Northern Territory. Clouds of parakeets, budgerigars, finches and larger, graceful brolgas and jabirus clustered around the watercourses.

Whoever called this land barren was out of his mind, she thought. She had never before seen a place so teeming with natural life.

When Blake steered the Jeep into the shelter of a tree and cut the motor, the sudden silence seemed deafening. "This is where we get off."

Ahead lay a wide, picturesque valley. "Cotton Tree Gorge?"

He nodded, reaching for the day packs they'd prepared before going to sleep the night before. Each pack contained sufficient water and food to see them through the hike. Looking at the creek cascading through the gorge, she couldn't imagine them running short of water. Unless crocodiles were a problem here, too.

"Only in the lower reaches of the gorge. Higher up, they're the Johnstone River variety, more commonly known as freshwater crocodiles, and generally harmless to humans," he explained when she voiced the comment. "You can recognize them by their long, narrow snouts."

She swung her pack onto her back. "I'm still dealing with the 'generally harmless' part."

He adjusted his own pack. "Freshwater crocs are fine as long as you give them plenty of room. I've swum with dozens of them and never come to any harm."

"So the Johnstone River crocodiles live in freshwater, and

the salties, the ones that eat you, live in salt water, right?" That should simplify matters, she thought.

He shook his head. "Sorry, no. The term saltie is a misnomer. Both types can live in fresh, brackish or salt water, so it's wise to be cautious until you know a body of water is safe to swim in."

"I'll stick to dry land to be certain," she decided. "I suppose that means the beach is out of the question?"

"They're a saltie's favorite hangout. Dozens are removed from the harbors around the northern Australian coastline every year by people like me."

"Why am I not surprised? Tell me again why you love this place?"

His smile widened. "Look around you."

She did and felt the peace of the valley enveloping her. There might be dangers, but not if you were careful. And the rewards in beauty were beyond price. How was she to do justice to the Kimberley in her writing when she could barely wrap her mind around its wonders? Millions of years had gone into shaping the spectacular landscape. How could mere words ever capture such grandeur?

"Cotton Tree Gorge is also a misnomer," Blake explained as they set off. "It's actually a main gorge with a series of side gorges branching off it. Easy to get lost. You need to watch your step."

"I believe you." They had only started the climb and already the footing was tricky. The track snaked upwards between ever-narrowing stone walls. In places they had to clamber over giant boulders to penetrate the upper reaches.

When they had gone about three miles by her estimation, Blake led them into yet another branching chasm. "Careful of the fallen logs," he warned, holding out his hand to help her over an obstacle.

His grip felt warm and sure. She welcomed the assistance, but wished he didn't have the power to unbalance her with every touch. Needing to focus her thoughts on something other than her inner turmoil, she asked, "Can you drive into the gorge?"

"There's a rough access road from the other end that goes as far as the Uru cave. It's where I asked Andy to have the Jeep waiting for us."

"So we're doing this the hard way?"

"It's also the most spectacular way."

She couldn't disagree. And she had wanted the experience of hiking through the bush to write about. Did she also want the experience of seeing it with Blake? Her knees went weak and it was just as well he had hold of her hand, or she might have slipped between the boulders. She was so confused. Part of her wanted to be anywhere but where he was, while the more insistent part was blissfully happy. She didn't have any idea how she would handle leaving him when the time came.

"We've come far enough. Time for a lunch break," he said.

"I'm fine to go on."

"You slipped and almost fell."

"The heat is getting to me a little." No sense telling him he had contributed to her near miss.

He led her to a rock overhang, festooned with thickets of vine, and slid the pack off her shoulders, letting it drop to the ground. When his hands lingered for a few seconds on her upper arms, she had to struggle to keep her breathing even. Was he going to kiss her again? Did she want him to? The answer must have been transparent in her gaze because he bent his head and brushed her lips with his own.

She held still, afraid to respond in case she couldn't stop. She saw something similar reflected in his gaze, because he gathered in a deep breath and stepped back. *I won't always back away,* she read in his expression, and knew that the time was very near when he wouldn't. When she wouldn't want him to.

He was leaving the choice and the timing up to her.

Blake shouldered out of his own pack and rummaged in it. "We're all out of lobster and caviar. Will cheese, crackers and fruit bars do?"

"I'm hungry enough to try anything," she said, only aware of how he might take her words after they'd left her mouth.

She saw his eyebrows lift but he said nothing as he passed a package to her. She willed herself not to react to the momentary contact and covered her awkwardness by reaching for a bottle of water. The droplets spilled down her chin as she drank. "This bush walking is thirsty work."

Her composure was almost shattered anew when he skimmed her lower lip with a finger, wiping away the moisture. "You're in good shape for a desk jockey," he commented.

She settled herself on a convenient rock ledge, resting her back against the sun-warmed stone wall. "The magazine has a private gym, and I belong to a walking group. Nothing as challenging as this though. What about you?"

"Wrangling crocodiles keeps me fit enough."

Thinking of the monster that had leaped out of the creek and grabbed Nigel's canteen, she asked, "Don't you ever get scared?"

"Only a fool isn't scared of such a dangerous reptile."

And he was no fool. "What got you started working with crocodiles?"

He stopped eating. "What is this, an interview by stealth?"

"If I'd wanted our conversation on the record, I'd say so." Her tone reminded him he wasn't the only one who lived by a code of ethics.

He got the message. "Bad habit of mine, sorry. Nothing good ever came of delving too much into my past."

Forgiveness came quickly. Perhaps too quickly. "You've never wondered about your family?"

"Sure I have. I wonder whose genes I carry, what I might pass on if I have children. But it's pointless losing sleep over something I can't change. The police would have found anything there was to find thirty years ago."

How would it feel to have a total blank where your personal history should be? Jo's grandparents were among her favorite people in the world. Her grandfather on her mother's side was a retired doctor, still active in his local community. On her father's side, they were farmers who swore they'd leave their land feet first. Jo was sure they meant it. Visiting them and hearing their stories made her feel connected to her past. She couldn't imagine not having that sense of personal history.

"Right after I decided that animals were smarter than people," Blake said, recapturing her attention.

"Excuse me?"

"You asked what got me interested in crocodiles. Seeing how fascinated I was with animals, Des encouraged me to study zoology. It turned out that my namesake, Bob Stirton, had captured a rogue crocodile on Diamond Downs some years ago, while he was still establishing his wildlife reserve. Des introduced me to him, and I was able to work with Bob's big cats while I completed my degree."

Memory came rushing back. "Tiger Mountain, I know it. A few months ago, I did a story on their conservation program for the magazine. What did Stirton think of you borrowing his name?"

"I don't know if he was flattered that I'd modeled myself on him, or hoped that the tigers would get this upstart out of his way. Either way, he let me work alongside him. He was still involved with crocodiles and took me along on some of his expeditions to relocate problem reptiles. After the first trip, I was hooked. When a run-down animal park came up for sale near Halls Creek, I bought it in partnership with Tom and we set up Sawtooth Park. He's a silent partner these days."

"I'm sure Shara's glad he is," she said.

Blake nodded. "It takes a unique woman to tolerate a man disappearing into the wild every so often, knowing he might not come back in one piece."

A shudder gripped her. "Is that why you've never married?"

"That and the lack of a suitable candidate," he said. "You must have heard that eligible women are in short supply in the Kimberley?"

She had a feeling his single state had more to do with his first reason than the second. He was right. Jo knew it wouldn't be easy living with the risks he took every day, trusting his experience and skill to bring him safely back to her.

Now where had that thought come from? She wasn't planning on waiting at home for him or any man. She had crocodiles of her own to hunt, not the reptile kind, but goals that were every bit as challenging. "Maybe you should let me interview you," she suggested, not sure how lightly. "You'd have eligible women beating your door down."

"One woman would be quite enough," he said, his gaze warm on her.

Oh, no, he'd better not start seeing her in the role, she told herself. And if he did, it was no concern of hers.

She snapped a cracker in half and sandwiched a piece of cheese, biting into it while she thought. She might be seriously considering making love with him. Her insides jittered at the very notion. She did hope to have a family one day, but her plans didn't include settling down for a long time.

Finishing her meal, she gathered up the debris and replaced it in her pack, then climbed to her feet. When he started to join her, she gestured for him to stay where he was. "I'm going to take some pictures. I'd like you in the shots. Don't worry, your face won't be visible. I need a human figure to give an idea of the immensity of this place."

"Don't wander out of sight. And watch out for snakes."

She grimaced. "Did you have to mention snakes?"

"They won't bother you if you tread heavily. They're more afraid of you than you are of them."

"Has anyone told the snakes?"

Leaving him chuckling, she stamped away, adjusting her camera as she went.

Blake watched her go, fighting the urge to call to her when she disappeared behind some rocks. She was right, she didn't need a minder, but he was sure tempted. The desire to protect her was palpable. Watching the outback seduce her had been like seeing it anew through her eyes. He knew he was close to falling in love and, for the first time, didn't feel a need to resist. If anything, he wanted to fall harder, faster, taking her with him on the ride of their lives.

He was so caught up in looking for her and thinking about the future he wanted them to have that he didn't hear the noise behind him until it was too late. He spun around, catching a glimpse of a figure emerging from the shadows, arm upraised. Blake barely had time to lift his own arm as a shield before pain exploded through him.

Crouched among the rocks, Jo fiddled with the camera but it was no use. The delicately tinted bush orchids blooming in a crevice were too petite for her to get a good shot of them. Did they even have a name? She had heard that new wildflowers were being discovered all the time in the Kimberley. Perhaps she'd stumbled on a new species. She took some shots anyway, then stood up. Karen wasn't likely to thank her for pretty pictures of wildflowers.

She had to clamber between more rocks before she could frame the overhang in her lens. Blake had stretched out full length on the rock taking a nap, she assumed. If she had any sense she should do the same. The heat was oppressive.

The hand she swiped over her face came away damp. The sun beat through her hat and long-sleeved cotton shirt. But she felt too restless to follow Blake's example. Too aware that his interest in her went deeper than she wanted. Frustration gnawed at her. Weren't men supposed to be the ones wanting sex without commitment? Trust her to attract the one exception.

She climbed along a series of ledges to photograph a collection of rock paintings above her head. They looked fresh so must have been retouched by the modern-day custodians of the work. She had been warned that some galleries were off-limits to women, but Blake had assured her that these galleries weren't among them. She snapped away to her heart's content.

The faint sound of pebbles rattling away into the gorge brought her head around. Blake couldn't have reached her so quickly. So who—she felt her color drain. A man was climbing toward her ledge. A man she thought she recognized, and he was carrying a traditional club.

Her knees almost buckled but she made herself back slowly into the shadows. The man hadn't seen her yet, although from his purposeful progress he must know she was up here. A new terror swamped her as she pictured Blake asleep in the overhang. Her blood ran cold. Not asleep—unconscious. The man must have reached him first.

Suddenly, she felt the ground give way beneath her. Then she was slipping and sliding between the steep, moss-covered walls of a hidden crevice. Too shocked and winded to scream, she scrabbled desperately for a handhold. The slippery walls offered none and she hurtled down into blackness.

Chapter 10

Winded but conscious, Jo revived to the sound of water trickling into a pool. At first, she thought her sight had been damaged because she could barely make out ferns and mosses clinging to the rock overhang above her. Gradually, her vision adjusted and she saw she was in a gloomy underworld, resting on a living carpet of green that had broken her fall.

Cautiously, she sat up. Nothing seemed to be broken, but the cavern lurched around her. She held still until the dizziness passed before getting shakily to her feet. An assortment of aches told her she was going to have an interesting collection of bruises soon.

The sheer rock walls towered above her from a fern-shrouded pool. She had fallen into a long, sinuous cavern that was almost completely screened from the sunlight, allowing a garden of mosses to thrive.

Another fact became abundantly clear. There was no way she could climb out the way she had fallen in. If she could manage the climb, Blake's assailant could be waiting for her. It was agony not knowing how badly Blake was hurt. She needed to get to him, and the only way was to walk out.

Shivering slightly in the damp air, although she had been sweating before she fell, she tested the narrow rock ledge surrounding the pool. While slimy, it felt solid underfoot. With exaggerated care she put one foot in front of the other, her heart trip-hammering as she nearly slid into the pool at one point. With no way of knowing how deep it was or what lurked in the water, she wasn't anxious to take a dip.

At the far end of the pool, her way was blocked by a fallen log, also slick with mossy growth. She inched across it, catching her breath as it shifted under her weight before settling. The log formed a bridge to a wider, fern-filled amphitheater. If she wanted to go any farther, negotiating it was her only option.

Stepping off the log was a relief and she gave herself a few seconds to take stock of her surroundings. What looked like a tide mark ran the full length of the cavern at about head height. Above the mark, Aboriginal paintings adorned the walls. A reassuring sign, she decided. Someone had found their way down here at some point, and since there were no sign of human remains, they must have found their way out again.

So could she.

At her feet, a thin stream of water trickled out of the rock, meandered along the cavern floor and disappeared somewhere in the distance. Maybe she could follow the watercourse to the open gorge. Feeling her spirits lift slightly she set off, only stopping when something glittered where she was about to put her foot.

She crouched and picked up four sparkling stones the size of pinheads, sluicing them in the water before turning them over in her palm. Could they be diamonds? Hadn't someone said that Max Horvath had found some of the gems in a creek somewhere near the Uru cave? Perhaps the creek traversed a good part of the gorge's length.

Her heart sank. If most of the creek traveled underground, it might not be any help in guiding her to safety.

An unwelcome thought came to her: Blake's grandfather had died in a cavern like this. His body was never found. The stones she buttoned securely into her shirt pocket might have come from his mine. Was she, too, destined to disappear into Kimberley folklore?

Don't wimp out now, she told herself firmly, pushing away the panic fringing her mind. Blake needed her. She had eaten recently. She had access to water. Sooner or later, she would make her way to the open gorge. All she had to do was remain calm.

Easier said than done, she discovered after exploring her surroundings without finding any sign of a way into the main gorge. To her eye, all the rock walls looked the same, angling upward to meet overhead like the rim of a volcano, the opening thatched by heavy greenery screening out most of the sunlight.

She turned her gaze to the aboriginal paintings. Someone had created them and presumably knew the way out. It could be right in front of her, perhaps camouflaged in a fold of rock.

The silence, broken by the sound of trickling water, felt eerie, as if the place was haunted. She shook herself. Better not start thinking of that now. Later, when they were together again, she and Blake would laugh about her fears. She was staking a lot on him being all right, she realized. He would be. He had to be.

Lifting her wrist to check her watch, she saw it had stopped. Now she had no way to tell how long she'd been here or when she could expect someone to be looking for her. She could only keep going. And hope.

Blake shook off his grogginess and gained his feet in almost the same breath. The ledge shifted under him and he stilled, breathing deeply until his legs no longer felt like buckling. He blinked to clear his vision. He had to get to Jo before the attacker did. He had a good idea who had hit him, but there was no sign of the man now, and the gorge slumbered undisturbed in the afternoon heat.

Worry gnawed at Blake. He should never have allowed her to go off alone. Now she could be in real danger.

Where the devil was she?

Gaining strength from action, he made his way cautiously down the slope to a cluster of boulders and looked around. This was where he'd lost sight of her. Tiny bush orchids bloomed among the rocks and he smiled grimly, imagining her stooping to photograph them. Blake didn't have Andy Wandarra's skill, but he was a pretty fair tracker when he needed to be. Besides, it didn't take much ability to spot Jo's footsteps leading back to their lunch spot. Or the second set following hers. At the sight of them, ice shivered through his veins.

Halfway there, both sets of tracks headed to the right and continued climbing until Blake lost them on the baking rock. They petered out in the direction of another vine-clad overhang, this one decorated with aboriginal paintings that had been recently touched up by Andy's people. Blake would bet Jo had gone into the cleft to photograph the paintings.

Sure enough, he found more footprints under the overhang, and something a lot more worrying. Her camera lay on the ground where she'd evidently dropped it. And beyond that, a tangle of torn greenery told its own story, though there was no sign of their attacker.

Heart slamming against his chest, Blake inched toward the broken bushes, parting them so he could see what lay beyond. His worst fears were realized when he saw the slick stain of green plunging down between steep walls into blackness.

Dropping to his full length, he peered over the edge. "Jo, are you there?"

No answer.

"Jo, speak to me if you can." Oh, God, don't let her be lying at the bottom, broken and unable to respond, he prayed.

Cupping his hands to his mouth he gave the traditional outback call, "Coo-ee," stretching out the last syllable so it had the best chance of carrying over a long distance.

Still no response.

Everything in him wanted to hurl himself over the edge and into the abyss, to reach her the quickest way he could. What if she was injured? He wouldn't let himself consider that she could be dead. He would have felt something. He had to hold to that certainty.

Think, he ordered himself. This isn't Jo lying at the bottom of the crevice. She's a woman you've been hired to guide around the Kimberley. How would you deal with this if she meant nothing to you? His heart tried to reject the order outright as blatantly untrue, but he willed himself to focus.

He was about to start back down the rocks when he heard the faint sound.

"Blake, can you hear me?"

He dropped again and leaned over the fissure. "I hear you. Are you all right?"

"What?"

"Are—you—all—right?"

"I'm uninjured but there's no way to climb back. What about you?"

He cupped his hands to his mouth. "I'll live. Stay put while I try to get to you."

"Blake?"

Hearing the alarm in her voice at the prospect of him leaving, he felt torn. But he wouldn't help her if he stayed. "Hold tight. I'll be as fast as I can," he promised and tore himself away before he could reconsider.

Back at the overhang, his pack was gone, along with his cell phone, but their assailant had evidently overlooked Jo's pack in the shadows. He pushed her camera into it and hoisted the bag over one shoulder. He debated trying for the Jeep, but Andy could well have moved it by now. No sense wasting time.

Back at the crevice, he used his knife to hack free a length of the vine thicket growing down from the escarpment above. A few minutes later he was snaking down the improvised rope into a cold, damp cave with a low ceiling. A dozen feet from the bottom, the vine snapped and he had no choice but to jump. His landing was cushioned by a bed of ferns and mosses that had evidently also broken Jo's fall. Although she'd said she was uninjured, he drew his first whole breath in an hour when he didn't find her crumpled at the bottom.

There was no sign of her anywhere. Damn it, he'd told her to stay put. She must have tried to walk out in the only direction available. He adjusted her pack on his back and headed after her.

Although Jo had been straining to hear Blake's footsteps, her heart lurched when she heard a sound behind her. She had to force herself to turn and her knees weakened as she recognized his tall, commanding figure.

She retraced her steps to his side. "Blake, are you okay?"

He shrugged off the concern. "I told you to wait."

"You told me to hold tight. I was looking for an easier way out."

He began to run his hands over her body, across her shoulders and then down her arms to her sides. When he reached her legs, she batted at his hands. "What are you doing?"

"Making sure nothing's broken."

She endured the examination with outward calm, but inwardly she trembled at the intimacy of his touch. "Don't you think I'd know?"

"Desperate people have been known to walk for miles on broken legs."

"And stubborn men have been known to walk around with a possible concussion."

He massaged the back of his neck. "I wasn't knocked out completely, only dazed for a few minutes. I'd half turned, so he only managed a glancing blow," Blake said, with more than a hint of male bravado.

"Did you see who hit you?"

Shaking his head produced a grimace. "I was hoping you had."

"I must have just missed seeing him. It looked like you were taking a nap."

He grinned without humor. "A long one, if my friend with the nulla nulla had gotten his way."

"The what?"

"It's a traditional weapon used for killing. Usually thrown, but sometimes wielded as a club."

"By Eddy Gilgai?"

"I thought you said you didn't see him?"

"I recognized him when he came after me. I was backing away when I slipped into the crevice."

"And he took off and left you there?"

"Left both of us," she reminded him.

"Back at the homestead, when I called to ask Andy to move the Jeep, Horvath must have been with Judy, and sent Gilgai after us," Blake said. "Horvath must be getting desperate, thinking we're closing in on the location of the diamond mine."

She fumbled in her shirt pocket. "Maybe we are. I found these beside the creek not far from the crevice."

He examined the specks in her palm. "It's too dark in here to tell if they're real. They could be quartz crystals or zirconias."

"But you don't think so?"

He shook his head. "Horvath claimed he'd found diamond traces near the entrance to the Uru cave. If your creek is the same one that surfaces there, the mine could be somewhere in between. We would need a properly equipped expedition to find out for sure. First, we have to get out of here."

"We wouldn't have the problem if I hadn't stupidly fallen in."

His gaze was warm on her. "Not stupid at all. You probably saved yourself from much worse at Eddy Gilgai's hands. And you were ready to walk out on your own, if that's what it took."

"Until I heard your voice, I couldn't see much alternative."

He lifted a hand to her cheek, pressing the back against her heated skin. "A lot of women would have gone into hysterics right where they fell."

She didn't care to be lumped in with other women, and let her flashing gaze tell him so. "I'm a city girl, remember? Bred to be self-reliant."

Without warning, his mouth fastened on hers. She reeled, her reaction making nonsense of her claim to self-reliance as he devoured her as if to reassure himself that she was truly in his arms.

For the first time since she'd tumbled down the Kimberley's equivalent of Alice's rabbit hole, she felt safe, felt as if they had a chance of getting out of here. The crazy thing was, her sense of urgency had receded. There was something remarkable about being kissed by the man of her dreams in a lost world where they were the only human inhabitants.

The mystical twilight filtering through the fern ceiling gave everything a surreal quality. Even the feel of being in Blake's arms was like a dream. She lifted her hands and clung to him, testing his flesh to assure herself she wasn't dreaming. He was really here.

She needed him so much, but didn't like needing him. She leaned on him anyway, comforted by his support.

After a time, he held her at arm's length. "Have you any idea how I felt when I discovered you'd fallen down that fissure?"

About as despairing as she'd felt thinking Eddy might have killed him. "Blake, don't."

His fingers dug into her flesh. "Don't what? Don't care about you? Tell me how to stop and I will."

She tried to move away. "This isn't supposed to be happening."

"Do you think I want this any more than you do? My life was supposed to be clear-cut, and it didn't include falling in love."

"No!" The protest was out before she could stop it.

"You think it's that simple? I don't fit into your plans any more than you fit into mine. But denying what we both feel won't change reality."

She pulled in a strangled breath. "I can't deal with this right now, and you're hurting me."

Becoming aware of the strength of his grip on her arms, he freed her as if he were scalded. The relief wasn't as great as it should have been.

"I'd never intentionally hurt you," he vowed.

She met his gaze out of her own pain. "It's the unintentional that worries me." He had already hurt her. Not by his grip on her arms or the bruising she'd sustained in her fall. Those she could handle. The deeper pain in her heart troubled her far more.

"I have plans for my future," she said, wondering who she was trying to convince. "Editor at thirty-five. Maybe publisher at forty."

"I suppose Lauren's the closest you're going to come to having a child," he rasped.

"Lauren isn't," she protested, then her voice stalled. Could he possibly be right? Was she using Lauren as a substitute for having a family of her own? "She's none of your affair."

"Everything about you is my affair. From the moment you walked into my crocodile park. You were so sure of yourself, or so you pretended. At heart you were scared stiff of what you'd bitten off."

"I was not."

"When I gave you that baby crocodile to hold, you almost freaked out. Oh, you kept your cool on the outside. I admired that. But when I took the croc from you, I felt you trembling."

She stalked to the rock face and pressed her palms against it. She was trembling now. Could he guess?

"If you must know, I was imagining confronting its big brother in the wild," she said, keeping her voice low so he wouldn't hear the tremor in it.

"Yet you went ahead with the assignment anyway. I've never met a woman like you, Jo. Outwardly all tough ambition. Inwardly—"

She held up a hand to cut him off. "Stop it, before my halo strangles me."

"I'm not saying you're perfect."

Cold fear swept though her. How she hated that word. "I'm not," she agreed.

"Just perfect for me," he went on as if she hadn't spoken.

* * *

There, he'd said it. The words he'd never expected to say to any woman. But he recognized the truth of them the moment they left his mouth.

Jo *was* perfect. Not in any saintly sense, but in her combination of healthy self-preservation and willingness to meet life head-on.

In his opinion, courage was doing what you were afraid to do—exactly what she did. He couldn't ask for more.

She was beautiful. Even battered and dirty, she was the most gorgeous thing he'd seen in a long time. He doubted whether the best hairdressers and fashion designers could make her any more lovely to his eyes than she was right now.

Her beauty was real.

"Shouldn't we focus on getting out of here?" she asked when the silence lengthened.

He cursed himself for being self-indulgent. Yet he couldn't give her what she most craved at that moment. "I'm afraid it won't be tonight."

"What?"

He schooled himself not to take her into his arms again or he wouldn't answer for the consequences. "The vine I used to climb down broke before I reached the bottom of the fissure. I had to jump the rest." He might manage to climb up the sheer rock face but he doubted she'd have the strength.

He saw her accept the inevitable. "Then we walk out."

"My guess is this valley runs parallel to the main gorge, ending somewhere near the Uru cave. If there was another way in, I'm sure one of my foster brothers or Judy would have stumbled on it years ago. Trying to find our way in the dark would be foolhardy. We're better off staying put until dawn, then making the attempt when we're fresh."

"You're the expert."

He admired her confidence in him but thought it was misplaced. "In this, I'm no expert. This is way out of my league.

I have some basic rescue skills, the ability to read the land, find food and navigate around, but not much more."

"It's more than I have going for me," she said, sounding shakier.

"You have a lot going for you. You discovered this valley. Who knows, Des might name it after you."

He was gratified to see her spirits lift visibly even as she waved away the suggestion. "I'm hardly the first to discover it." Her gesture indicated the rock paintings high above them.

He followed her gaze. "I'd say they haven't been retouched in over a century."

She studied the paintings curiously, the fading light making them seem more vivid when logic suggested they should be harder to see. "Why are they so high up?"

He frowned, wishing she hadn't asked. "They're painted above the level the water rises to during the wet season."

She glanced at the creek. "You can't mean this trickle of water gets as high as those tide marks?"

His smile was rueful. "It's true. Once the monsoon rains start, creeks like this fill up and spill across the land in sheets as far as the eye can see."

Her brow furrowed. "The wet season is due to start soon, isn't it?"

"Not for another few weeks. Your project will be finished before it happens."

"But sometimes the rains come early."

He couldn't lie to her. "Sometimes."

"And if we're trapped in here when they start?"

This time he did take her into his arms. "It's a long shot. We have more immediate worries, like getting through the night."

"It's going to get cold, isn't it?" She could feel the air chilling as the last rays of the sun left the valley.

"Luckily, Gilgai overlooked one of the packs. Yours has a space blanket and emergency rations in it," he said. "We'll have to share the blanket and pool our body heat."

She rested her forehead against his shoulder and then lifted her head, striving for humor. "This must be a dream come true for you."

He stroked her hair, his heart turning over as he realized she was trying to make light of the situation. "You're on to me. I arranged for you to fall down that fissure for the sole purpose of getting you under my space blanket."

She touched his cheek with her hand. "Wouldn't it have been easier just to ask?"

The light banter had given her time to regroup, to master her fears and deal with the reality of spending the night with Blake in a hidden valley, cut off from the outside world.

There was no difference between what they were about to do and sharing the rough shelter at Dingo Creek. If anything, the valley gave them more space than the narrow shelter.

Until nightfall.

For the moment, it was business as usual.

From her pack, Blake produced a nutritious if unexciting meal of half a high-energy fruit bar each and the remains of the cheese and crackers from lunch, washed down with water from the creek.

The atmosphere was too damp to start a fire, even if the smoke wasn't likely to choke them. The temperature was still mild, so the cold food and drink didn't bother her. More worrying was the thought of huddling under a space blanket with him during the long hours of darkness.

He made the process as painless as he could. In an attempt to lessen her nervousness, he joked about letting her use the bathroom first, while he made a bed of ferns for them in the shelter of a rock wall. She noticed he chose a ledge a few feet up from the valley floor. A precaution against an unseasonal flash flood?

She recoiled at the thought of being caught in the valley when a mountain of water came crashing down on top of them and then told herself she was worrying needlessly. Blake had assured her the possibility was remote and even if it wasn't, obsessing over it wouldn't make any difference in the long run, except to guarantee her a sleepless night.

Not that she expected to get much sleep anyway under the circumstances.

Blake shook out a thin, crackly sheet of what looked like cooking foil. "How will that keep us warm?" she asked, a delaying tactic if ever she'd heard one.

"The thermal material is designed to reflect our body heat back to us, instead of dissipating in the air," he explained. "Some cave explorers carry one folded up inside their helmets, both to keep them warm while caving, and in case of emergency."

"And it's called a space blanket because you huddle together in a small space," she hazarded, her pulse racing at the prospect.

He shook his head. "You might think so, but in reality the material was designed for the space program."

Houston, we have a problem, she thought, looking at the bed of ferns and the silvery sheet he held open for her. His large body took up a daunting amount of the available room. She joined him on the fern cushion, trying not to tense when he tucked the blanket around the two of them, pulling it over their heads like a tent. Within seconds, she could feel the heat radiating from him.

He put an arm around her shoulder. "Try to relax and get some sleep."

He might as well have suggested she fly around the valley under her own power. The problem wasn't the strangeness of the night closing in around them, or the knowledge that there were no other people for miles, but the tiny amount of distance she was maintaining between herself and Blake. If she did fall asleep she might slump against him, and what would happen then?

So what? she asked herself angrily. Strangers slept on each other's shoulders in planes. It didn't have to mean anything.

And if the contact aroused them to the point where they made love, again so what? She was an adult with a contraceptive implant in her arm that still had a few weeks of life left in it. Everything she knew about him suggested that Blake was

as healthy as she was. Neither of them was committed to anyone else. And they'd already agreed they cared for each other.

There was the problem.

It would be easier if he didn't care for her. His insistence
on placing her on some kind of pedestal of female perfection
scared the devil out of her. She didn't want anyone thinking
her as perfect. The burden felt too heavy.

Several times in her life, she'd tried to pinpoint why being
the object of other people's high expectations made her feel
so ill at ease. As usual, she got nowhere. It wasn't as if her
family had created the problem. On the contrary, her parents
had made her feel as if every achievement was wonderful, provided she'd done her best. Yet somehow the fear persisted.

"You're thinking," he said into the gathering darkness.

"Everybody thinks."

"Not as loudly as you're doing."

She laughed without humor. "I'll try to think more quietly."

He shifted slightly and began to massage her nape. "Better if you stop thinking and go to sleep."

He couldn't know it but his touch had just about guaranteed wakefulness. At the contact, hot, eager arousal flooded
her and it was all she could do not to turn her face and seek
his mouth with her own. That way lay madness.

She took deep breaths, willing her body to relax. Gradually, the kneading at the back of her neck did its job and she
felt herself sinking. She was barely aware of his hand sliding
away from her nape, to drape around her shoulders. Snuggling
into the crook of his arm, she let herself drift at last.

And woke up countless hours later, screaming.

Chapter 11

Someone was holding her down. She couldn't get away. She fought and struggled wildly but iron hands held her firm. "Jo, you're dreaming. You're all right."

Still, she thrashed around, trying to escape. "Let me go."

"Not until I know you're fully awake."

Awake? She'd been asleep. Dreaming. Was she still dreaming? Blearily, she looked around, seeing the shadowy outline of rocks silvered by moonlight. Feeling the hardness of a ledge beneath her, and hearing the labored breathing of the man holding her as if he'd never let her go.

"I'm awake," she said, aware of her pounding heart and clammy hands. Aware of being cradled against the solid wall of Blake's chest, his arms tight around her.

"You must have had some dream."

"An old one." She tried to sound dismissive but could hardly muster her thoughts. They kept wanting to slide back into the nightmare. "It hasn't bothered me for years."

He rubbed her back with a circular motion. "Probably the result of the fall and the strange surroundings."

Shivering, she pressed her palms against her eyes. "Oh, God, I've never known it as bad as that." Although she was awake now and remembered falling into the cave and settling down for the night with Blake, the dream seemed more real. The fear that went with it so vivid that she shook with it.

He smoothed her hair back. "It's all right, I'm here. Lean on me."

She was too distraught to do anything else and burrowed into his embrace with childlike eagerness. He felt so strong, so good. So solid. Not soft and cushiony like…no, she wouldn't think of the person in the dream. She wouldn't.

Without letting go of her he rummaged in the pack one-handed and came up with a bottle of water. Popping the top, he offered it to her. "I wish we had some light," she said when the dryness in her throat was gone.

"We have moonlight. It's a lot more romantic."

But less reassuring than the bright glare of lights she craved. "Do we have a torch?"

"Sure." He delved into the pack again and came up with a small flashlight. When he clicked it on, the cave receded and a circle of yellow light enveloped them.

Her ragged breathing started to ease. "Thanks."

"We can leave it on as long as you want."

She nodded, too unsettled to speak.

"Want to talk about it?"

She shook her head. Even if she could drag the remnants of the dream together enough to make sense, she couldn't share it. The very thought speared her with dread.

"I'm sorry I disturbed your sleep," she said, striving for normalcy.

He offered her the water bottle again and she cupped her hand around it, guiding it to her mouth, ashamed when she spilled as much as she swallowed.

He wiped away the water with the back of his hand. "You

screamed something about an old woman. You were telling her not to touch you."

"Was I?"

"Who is she, Jo?"

She lifted her shoulders. "A figure in a dream. Who knows?"

"I have the feeling you do."

"Then you know my mind better than me, because I haven't a clue. She's probably a witch in a story I read as a child, the sort of person who looks kindly and sweet but hides an evil core."

"A pretty specific description of someone you claim not to recognize."

His persistence began to ruffle her. "Whose dream was this?"

"Judging by the effect on you, it was more than a bad dream."

She needed to move, to pace, to dissipate the energy charging through her, but didn't want to leave the shelter of his arms. Logic told her there was nothing to harm her beyond the circle of torchlight, but she still recoiled from the darkness. She drew her knees up and hooked her arms around them, wincing when stray bruises from the fall made themselves felt. "This particular dream started when I was a little girl. I thought I'd outgrown it."

"Do you think something down here triggered it?"

"Probably. I'm okay now. We can go back to sleep."

"Do you think you will?"

"No."

Blake heard the tremulous note in her voice and his heart turned over. Jolted awake by her screams, he'd felt helpless, wanting to do something to ease her fear, but unable to reach her through the nightmare. He could feel tremors sweeping through her like the aftershocks of an earthquake, and tucked the thermal blanket closer around her. "It's almost dawn. If neither of us is going to get any more sleep, we may as well talk until it's light enough to move."

"As long as it isn't about the dream," she insisted.

"Have you ever spoken of it to anyone?"

"Not for a long time."

He stroked her hair, felt her tension. "Don't you think it might be time?"

"I'll find a therapist as soon as I get back to Perth," she lied.

"What's wrong with right now? We don't have anything else to do." She tried to squirm away, but he held her tightly. "Does this have something to do with you being abducted when you were a child?"

He felt her stiffen in his arms. "What makes you ask?"

"You said you were taken by a demented old woman who thought you were her child, although her daughter was middle-aged by then." It was a long shot but he had to ask. "Could that woman be the one you were screaming at to leave you alone?"

"It happened a long time ago. I barely remember anything about her."

"Consciously. Unconsciously, you probably remember every detail," he said.

"So what?"

"So the buried memories could be causing the nightmares."

She frowned. "And you want me to dig them out now, for your entertainment?"

"No," he said, refusing to be goaded. "For your peace of mind."

She buried her face against his shoulder. "Oh, God, it's so hard to talk about. I haven't for years."

"But you did at the time?"

Keeping her face against his shoulder, she shook her head. "Not really. Twenty years ago, nobody thought counseling or debriefing mattered, especially to a six-year-old. A doctor checked me over to make sure I hadn't been harmed sexually—*interfered with* was the term he used then. I hadn't. And the police asked me to identify the woman. That was about it."

He smoothed her hair with his fingers. Her forehead was damp. "What about your parents?"

"They took me away for a vacation. They thought spending time at amusement parks and the beach would be the best way to help me forget."

"Or help them get over it," he observed.

She stirred in negation. "My parents did the best they could at the time. I won't have them demonized for not knowing any better."

"I'm not fixing blame, only trying to understand why you might be haunted by the experience and still wake up screaming more than twenty years later."

"Assuming I am," she said overbrightly.

"Do you doubt it?"

Her sigh whispered between them. "No, damn you."

"Then talk. Tell me what you remember."

Accepting that he wasn't going to be diverted, she took a deep, shuddering breath. "What can I say? According to my mother, we were at a children's concert in a park. I remember being in a crowd with lots of other families. Some of the kids, including my brothers, went up to the front where other children were dancing. I went with them. An old lady approached me and said my mother wanted me. I went with her but she took me away from the park."

"Nobody saw you go with her?"

"Everybody was watching the concert."

"Something your abductor counted on. Maybe she wasn't as demented as she let the police think."

"The same thought occurred to me many years later, although nobody thought about it at the time."

"What happened after you went with her?"

Jo came more upright and felt the press of the rock wall at her back. Instead of comforting her, the rock felt alien, dangerous somehow. Instinctively, she wanted to shrink away from it. Another breath steadied her enough to continue. "We went to her home across the road from the park. She told me I'd have a better view of the concert from there. She kept calling me Lisa, although I told her my name was Joanne. Later, I found out her daughter's name was Lisa."

In the torchlight, she saw his smile flicker. "So Jo is short for Joanne."

"Privileged information. Use it and you're a dead man," she warned, feeling less shaky by the second as she felt herself drawing strength from him.

He skimmed her hairline with his lips, eliciting a sharply indrawn breath. "I prefer to live, so I'll stick to Jo."

"Smart man," she said, feeling shaky for an entirely different reason. The temptation to seek solace in his arms rather than keep talking was almost overwhelming.

He wasn't letting her off so lightly. "What happened after the woman took you to her home?"

"We watched television, ate ice cream. She seemed happy just to have me there."

"What about the cave?" he asked out of the blue.

Jo crammed her fingers against her mouth. "How do you know about the cave?"

"I don't, I was guessing," he said. "Being down here triggered your nightmare, so I figured there's some connection between this place and your childhood experience."

"It wasn't really a cave," she said, hearing her voice coming as if from a great distance. "It was a shallow grotto in her garden. If I had to describe it now, I'd say it was one of those kitschy concrete structures made to look like stone. In the middle was a religious statue decorated with plastic flowers. I'd almost forgotten about it."

"Consciously, anyway."

She took his point. "She took me outside to show me the grotto. I don't remember much else until the police came and took me home."

"Did the old woman give you the idea it isn't safe to be perfect?"

She stared at him in the torchlight, feeling chilled. "That's crazy."

His hold tightened. "Somehow you got the idea that being perfect is dangerous."

She could hardly speak for the lump clogging her throat. She couldn't breathe. Everything in her urged her to get up and run, but there was nowhere to go. She clung to Blake, biting her lip to keep from whimpering.

Suddenly, like a door opening in her mind, fragments of recollection tumbled back. "In the grotto, she started to act strangely. She called me her darling child, her perfect angel. She said she'd make sure nothing bad ever happened to me."

He put both arms around her and held her close. "It's all right. You don't have to go there if you don't want to."

"I want to. I have to. It's been so long. She— Oh, God, I can't, but I must." She lifted her chin. "She said angels were too perfect to live on Earth with ordinary people. She told me—oh, this is so hard—she told me I would go to sleep in the grotto and wake up with the other angels where I belonged."

"Did she try to drug you?"

She nodded with an effort, her neck muscles stiff as if with disuse. "I think so. I don't know with what. I was too young. But young as I was, I knew I shouldn't drink whatever she tried to give me. Although she could have put something in the ice cream I'd already eaten."

"She probably wanted to gain your confidence first."

"I guess."

"She sounds fiendishly clever. If I ever get my hands on her—"

It was Jo's turn to soothe. "She died not long after, before anything could come to trial."

"So that's why nothing ever came out. My poor, poor Jo. To have gone through such an ordeal and kept the details inside all these years."

"I didn't know what was there," she whispered. "The dreams about a motherly woman trying to give me something to drink make sense now. I used to wake up sweating and pushing her away, with no idea who she was."

"And tonight I made you sleep in the grotto again." His tone was filled with remorse.

She put a finger to his lips. "Don't blame yourself. If I hadn't landed here, I might never have made sense of the dream."

"Or your resistance to being overprotected and called perfect."

Even now, knowing what she knew, she bristled with rejection. "I'll never like hearing it."

"Then I won't say it," he assured her. "I'll show you in ways you're guaranteed to like. Not now," he said when she stirred. "It isn't the right time. You need to rest, to process what you've uncovered. When you go back to the city—" strange how hard he found it to say the words "—you can get professional advice to help you deal with this."

"Repressed memory syndrome," she said. "Karen Prentiss wrote a series of articles about it. Never in my wildest dreams did I think it ever would apply to me."

"I used to doubt there was any such thing. Not anymore."

She grazed his cheek with the back of her hand. "Thank you."

He took her hand and kissed the tips of her fingers. "For what?"

"Believing me. Not treating this as a joke."

"Why wouldn't I believe you? What you went through was hardly a joke."

She shrugged. "I was six and already well-known for flights of imagination."

"Do you think it's why you buried the angel thing in the recesses of your mind?"

"Probably. My parents used to give me grief about making things up. I was already afraid of getting into trouble for going with a stranger, when I'd been told countless times never to go with anyone. I probably didn't want to make things worse for myself."

"I'm sure blaming you would have been the last thing on your parents' mind. All they would have cared about was having you back safely."

She freed her hands from the space blanket to link them around his neck. "You don't think like that at six years old. You think everything's your fault."

He unlinked her hands and kissed each palm in turn, sending shivers coursing through her, but of desire this time. Then he gave a slight smile. "I remember the feeling."

She inclined her head in understanding. "You blamed yourself for being abandoned as a baby?"

"Not after I was old enough to work things out, but for a long time."

She managed an unsteady laugh. "What inflated opinions we have of ourselves as children, thinking the world revolves around us."

"Until reality comes along and knocks it out of us."

"Just as well or we'd become egomaniacs."

He touched her chin, lifting her face. "Des and Fran taught me that, in the middle, there's healthy self-esteem."

She was aware of sounding slightly out of breath. "Sometimes I think I've found the middle, then along comes a night like tonight."

"Things will be better after this."

She didn't ask how he knew. She felt it, too. "Yes."

"Is it okay if I turn the torch off now?"

She nodded. "I'll be fine."

There would be no more bad dreams tonight.

A pale stream of morning sunlight threading through the ferns into her eyes awoke her. Blake was gone and the space blanket had been neatly tucked around her and the pack placed under her head as a pillow. Determined not to feel cheated of his arms, she sat up and looked around. He must have gone exploring.

Shrugging the space blanket off her shoulders, she folded it into a compact bundle and pushed it into the pack. Then she saw his note wrapped around a high-energy food bar. "Looking for the exit, Sleeping Beauty. Room service left breakfast. Back soon. B."

Self-reproach rolled through her. After her performance last night, he probably hadn't known how to face her. How could she have thrown all that angel stuff at him and expect him to want to be beside her when she awoke?

His words about healthy self-esteem came back to her. He'd claimed to understand, she remembered. Okay, he might not hold last night against her, but her outpouring wasn't likely to improve their relationship.

She had enough balance to know she couldn't be blamed for the repressed memories. Burying them had been a child's act of self-preservation. Dragging them into the open meant they had far less power to hurt her any longer.

As for Blake, she could only hope he would take his cue from her and leave well enough alone. Letting her guard down with him so completely had rocked her. What was she supposed to do with real closeness? Just because she understood why she'd gravitated toward shallow relationships where she'd felt safe—like her relationship with Nigel—didn't mean she was ready to deal with anything deeper.

Thinking she might be the focus of a man's hopes and dreams still made her uneasy. Didn't scare the hell out of her, true. So she was making progress. But she had a way to go yet to feel comfortable with real intimacy.

Lost in thought, she unwrapped the food bar and took a bite. It was like eating dry cereal but, according to the wrapper, it was full of essential nutrients. Alternating bites with swallows of water she managed to get it down, then used what passed for the bathroom. The trickling stream provided washing facilities but no change of clothes, unfortunately.

One way or another, she felt as desirable as yesterday's pizza.

By the time Blake returned, she had convinced herself that not only was she not falling in love with him, after last night she was the last woman he'd be interested in.

So why was he looking at her as if she was the eighth wonder of the world?

* * *

After her revelation last night, Blake hadn't wanted to leave Jo alone, but she was sleeping so peacefully he'd decided to risk it, hoping to have some encouraging news for her when she woke up.

Instead, he'd have to tell her that his first conclusion was the right one. It seemed the only way out was to traverse the full length of the hidden valley until it merged with the main gorge.

Too bad her cell phone didn't work in the valley or they could have contacted Judy and asked her to drop a longer rope down to them from the overhang. As it was, his foster sister wouldn't raise the alarm until a few more hours had passed without him reporting in. Before then, he hoped to be back in cell phone range and able to assure her all was well.

He could imagine the ribbing he'd get from Judy and the family once they knew he'd been stuck down here. He could blame Jo and come out looking like a hero, but that wasn't his way, either. Last night, she had bared her soul to him and he had no intention of taking advantage. Not because he hadn't wanted to. Making love to her last night would have been the easiest thing in the world. But seeing how vulnerable she was, he couldn't have lived with himself.

She was washing her face in the creek when he got back, and his heart felt as if a giant hand had grabbed it and was squeezing tight. Tousled from sleep she looked young and fragile, and his protective instincts went on full alert.

Thinking of what had been done to her, he wanted to kill. Since that wasn't possible, he settled for the next best thing— wishing a long stay in purgatory on her tormentor.

So Jo wouldn't see how angry he felt on her behalf, he pinned a smile on his face. "Good morning, Ms. Francis. I trust the room was to your liking?"

She matched his jocular tone. "Room service leaves a lot to be desired."

"I'll speak to the management."

"While you're at it, tell them there's no hot water in my bathroom."

He sketched a bow. "Immediately, madam. Anything else?"

She became serious. "How are you feeling?"

He dropped onto a rock beside her, resisting temptation by staying out of touching distance. Where he'd been knocked out cold, the back of his neck was sending messages of pain all the way to the top of his skull, but he kept the details to himself. "I've lived through a lot worse."

Her look said she understood what he wasn't saying, but she played along. "What about a way out?"

"It looks as if there's nothing before the main gorge."

Her shoulders drooped and he saw the shadows in her eyes. She was bracing for his reaction to her revelation last night, he realized. Didn't she know that nothing could change the way he felt about her? Should he say something or nothing? Which would make her happy?

He decided to say nothing. Coward's way out perhaps, but he trusted his instinct. She would talk to him if and when she was ready. "Ready to take a hike?" he asked.

Bingo, he thought as he saw her eyes brighten. So much for the theory that women always wanted to talk about their feelings. Silence could be golden for them, too.

"I wish I had my camera. I took some shots of you lying under the overhang, resting I thought. I might have caught Eddy at the scene," she said after they'd walked in silence for a while.

"You do have your camera. It looked okay when I found it, so I shoved it into the pack. We can check when we get back. How are your bruises this morning?"

She rotated one arm, then the other, sharing about as much of her discomfort as he'd done with her. "Not pretty, but I'll survive."

He hooked his thumbs into the straps of the pack. "I admire your resilience."

He saw her shoot him a sidelong glance, probably wondering if he'd meant anything by his remark. He had, but he'd leave it to her to draw whatever conclusions she liked.

"Thanks," she said softly. "For everything."

Wrapped up in three words, he heard her acknowledgment of his support and appreciation for not rubbing in the necessity. "You're welcome," he said in the same code. "You always will be."

This time, she looked startled, as if he'd given her more than she'd expected. If she only knew it was taking a lot not to sweep her into his arms. In fact, the more he considered the matter, the more inevitable it seemed.

They were in a scenic part of the hidden valley. Dappled light sifted through from above, highlighting a thick carpet of mosses and ferns that gave with every footfall. No one would be worried about them before afternoon, and they would reach the main gorge long before then, even taking time out for themselves.

He imagined letting the pack fall.

He saw them tumbling together onto the mossy carpet. She would shriek, but wouldn't fight him. The slightest resistance and he would back off at once. But there would be none. Instead, she would link her arms around his neck and pull his face down, kissing him as if he were the room service she'd missed out on earlier.

Instantly, his gut tightened and his hormones went into orbit. Walking became distinctly uncomfortable. He lifted his head and smiled at her, but determinedly kept moving.

She looked at him, frowning a little. "What?"

"I was just thinking."

She knew, he saw, when her color heightened. Had she been imagining a similar scenario? Was she waiting for him to make the first move? Hoping he would? He felt like a bush tracker who had lost the ability to read signs. Adrift, directionless.

This love business was tougher than it looked, he thought. For with a blinding flash, he knew he *was* in love with her.

Not just wanting to make love to her, but the full deal. The white dress, walking-down-the-aisle, kids and a dog, till-death package. The kind of package Des and Fran Logan had shared.

A tremulous sensation tore through him. How could he be picturing any of that with Jo when he had no idea if it was what she wanted?

She had to, he decided. For the simple reason that he didn't intend to live without her.

Chapter 12

The discovery kept his thoughts busy for the hour it took them to complete the walk.

"Do I see sunlight up ahead?" Jo asked, perking up visibly through her tiredness.

For the past thirty minutes, he had been aware of walking slightly uphill. "We're almost at the junction with the main gorge."

He pushed his way through a curtain of greenery like a waterfall cascading over sheer rock. The greenery completely curtained the entrance to the valley. Unless, like Jo, you literally fell into the side gorge, you could walk right past and never know it was there. "No wonder we never stumbled on Francis Valley before," he said.

"Francis Valley," she tried the name on for size. "I like it, although I'm not sorry to be out of it for now."

"Amen to that."

Blissfully she lifted her face to the sunlight as they walked on. Another thirty minutes and she was staring in undisguised joy at the Jeep parked ahead of them in the shade of a eucalyptus tree. "If that Jeep were a horse, I'd say you whistled and it came like they do in old cowboy movies, but I guess we have Andy to thank for leaving it here."

"We could also have my call to thank for spending the night in the side gorge."

"You think Max was with Judy when you contacted Andy?"

"How else did he know where to send Eddy to find us?"

"I hope you're not blaming yourself? I was the idiot who fell down the fissure."

"You weren't an idiot. The crevice was so well camouflaged that anyone could have made the same mistake."

"Then we're even," she said.

It was his turn to say, "Thanks for not holding last night against me."

She summoned a smile. "Is a thank-you all I get?"

"We could shake hands."

But even as he said it, she was moving toward him, her expression intent. As in his fantasy, he dropped the pack to the ground and welcomed her into his arms.

Her kiss was chaste enough to start with, but he'd settle for what she was offering, and the wonderful feel of her pressing against him. For now, anyway.

When she wrapped her hands around his neck, his temperature soared. Her lips moving against his felt like more of the fantasy. When she pulled away, he let her go with only the slightest exhalation of regret. He didn't think she heard. Being noble was playing havoc with his hormones.

"Look, there's a cooler in the Jeep," she said, going to the vehicle and yanking open the passenger door. Was it wishful thinking or did she sound as shaky as he felt?

"I promised you room service."

She lifted the lid and gave a slight moan. "Cold drinks. Real food."

Above them loomed the escarpment where the Uru cave they'd set out to visit was located. He looked over her shoulder. "How much do you want to see the rock art?"

She replaced the cooler lid and turned to him. "The truth? I've had about all the caverns I can handle for the time being."

"You won't have a problem with your editor if we save the visit for another time?"

Jo shook her head. "By the time I write about how we discovered the hidden valley, Karen will have more than enough headlines to keep her happy."

"Then how about a swim instead? If your photos do provide evidence against Eddy Gilgai, they'll keep for a while longer."

This time, her moan was less restrained. "I'm starting to like this hotel."

He hoped she'd have a little time for the management, as well.

She surveyed the sparkling expanse of water he drove them to. Water poured in from upstream, forming a series of pools down the hillside, linked by miniature waterfalls and rapids, that eventually spilled into the main part of the Bowen River below. "Are you sure there aren't any crocodiles in this pool?" she asked.

"Only a few of the freshwater variety. As I told you before, if you don't corner them they won't bother you."

She gave him a trusting look. "You're the crocodile man. I don't know whether I want to swim or eat first. After the night we spent, both seem sinfully tempting."

"I can think of other activities with the same potential," he said.

Not so long ago, his comment would have made her apprehensive, knowing how attracted she was to him. Now she was amazed to feel an answering torrent of desire race through her. At the same time, she recognized there was more going on here than simple sexual need. She wanted him, yes, but there was more. She felt open to whatever developed between them in a way she'd never done before.

For the first time in her life, she wasn't afraid of the close-ness. Or where it might take them.

The exhilaration of it made her want to sing and shout. Or make love.

Her stomach betrayed her by rumbling loudly.

"Sounds like we'd better eat first," she said ruefully.

"I like the part about first," he agreed. He didn't ask what might come second.

Judy had thoughtfully included half a bottle of Pinot Noir with the feast of smoked salmon, potato salad, green grapes and crusty bread.

Blake spread a blanket in the shade and sprayed the perim-eter with something mint-smelling he carried in the car to deter marauding insects. The clear blue sky, red-and-ocher rock cliffs, vine thickets and glinting water made a backdrop so picturesque it seemed unreal.

Lolling on the blanket, her taste buds singing with the rich-ness of the picnic, Jo felt as if she'd died and gone to heaven. "Oh, my, this beats energy bars by a long shot."

Picking grapes off a stem, he said, "Probably not as nutri-tious."

"But more sensual," she said, wondering why her thoughts kept returning to that.

He topped off his glass of water and her tumbler of wine. "You're really happy, aren't you? Even after being attacked, hiking for miles and sleeping rough."

She sipped wine. "I could have done without the first part. For the rest, the company makes a difference." Knowing how at home he was in the outback, she had felt safe with him. Un-settled definitely, especially after delving into her subcon-scious. But she had never doubted they would survive.

He lifted his glass in a toast. "I'm glad you think so."

"I know so." She gathered in a breath and made herself say the words she'd been avoiding for hours. "Not many men would have held my hand the way you did last night, without a word of recrimination."

"You couldn't help what happened to you."

"It helps to have that understood."

"My own experience puts me in a unique position."

She braced herself on one elbow. "You put yourself in a unique position. You don't only know how it feels to have your life controlled by others. You've found a way to rise above your history and make your life your own."

"You've done the same," he pointed out. "I had the advantage of knowing what was driving me. You've only just found out."

She toyed with her glass. "Yeah, I'm still trying to take that in."

"It won't happen in an instant. You need to give yourself time."

"I'm trying to do that, too."

He started to stow the remains of their lunch in the cooler. "Ready for that swim now?"

She finished the wine and handed him the glass. "Don't we have to wait for an hour or something before going in the water?"

"Old wives' tale," he said. "As kids, we never waited five minutes."

"Me, neither. We lived within walking distance of the beach and spent hours in the surf. I don't remember ever letting food settle before plunging in. And we didn't die of cramps, or whatever's supposed to happen to you."

He slanted a grin at her. "It's a plot by grown-ups to give them a break. If you're dutifully resting on a blanket, they get to rest, too."

She scrambled up. "What is it about the outback that makes me want to defy every social convention?"

"It's the air of freedom. Want to defy another one?"

Wondering what he had in mind, she cocked her head. "What?"

"Ever been skinny-dipping?"

She felt herself turn hot. "You mean as in nude? Without any clothes?"

He seemed to enjoy her confusion. "That's generally what's meant by skinny-dipping."

"I don't…I mean I've never…"

"Then it's time you tried. Isn't this supposed to be a voyage of discovery for you?"

"I'm also supposed to write up everything I do."

"Everything?"

"Well, it doesn't have to be blow-by-blow."

Just as well, he thought. The way this day was shaping up, he wouldn't want to read the details later, and he was fairly sure she wouldn't, either. Some things were not meant for public consumption.

He returned the cooler to the Jeep and came back. "I'll avert my eyes while you get into the water, then I'll join you."

She was glad to get out of the clothes she'd worn since yesterday. The balmy air felt wonderful on her bare skin. "You're sure about the crocodiles?" she asked as she approached the pool.

As promised, he had his back to her. "Want me to come and double-check?"

Conscious of the bruises blossoming on her skin from the fall, she wanted to be up to her neck in water before he turned around. "I'll take your word for it."

Pushing undergrowth aside, she stepped across the green silk of the river flat and into water which felt refreshing as it lapped around her legs. It was also crystal clear, reassuring her that nothing lurked in the vicinity. Emboldened, she sank up to her neck and struck out across the pool. Rushing water was the only sound.

By the time she turned to swim back, Blake had discarded his clothes and was wading in. She almost forgot to tread water in the shock of seeing him naked, a god of the outback in his tanned magnificence.

The lack of tan lines around his hips suggested he made a habit of swimming nude. Her mouth went dry. Did he bring other women here? Was she mistaking a practiced ploy for something more personal?

He swam out to her. "You're frowning. Don't I live up to your expectations?"

He far exceeded them. "I was wondering if you do this with all your dates?"

"And if I say yes?"

She splashed water at him. "Don't make jokes, I'm serious."

He turned over on his back, letting the water support him. "You are, aren't you? That means you care."

"You already know I do."

"I know, and it matters to me. For the record, you're the first woman besides my foster sister I've swum with in this pool."

Her eyebrows lifted. "You swam naked with your sister?"

"It's normal in the outback. When you live this close to nature, modesty seems like a waste of time."

"And a waste of a sensational feeling," she said, relieved that she was not one of a long line of women he'd brought to this magical place. She didn't want to think of this as a setup for seduction. She didn't have a problem with the seduction part, only the setup.

"Look," he said, pointing behind her. "There's a crocodile."

Heart leaping into her mouth, she flailed around in the water. "Where?" All she could see were dark specks at the water line a dozen feet away. They must be small, she guessed from the distance between eyes and nostrils, but her heart rate continued to escalate. Where there were small crocs, could man-eaters be far behind?

She began to swim toward Blake. "Shouldn't we get out of here?"

"No need, they're the freshwater variety, *Crocodylus johnstonii*."

"I'm swimming with a crocodile and you're spouting Latin at me?"

"They're the freshwater Johnstone River crocodiles I told

you about, harmless to humans unless you bother them. They only grow to about eight feet long. Watch."

Linking his hands, he sent a wave shivering in the direction of the dark spots showing above the water. In a blur of speed, a five-foot crocodile swirled its tail around and vanished into the depths. Moments later ripples in the water showed where its companions had similarly made themselves scarce.

Then he pointed out what she had taken to be a piece of driftwood farther up the opposite sand bank. It, too, hurtled into the water with astonishing speed and sank without a trace.

Treading water, she leveled a suspicious look at him. "Did you know they were here when I got in?"

His expression was all innocence. "I offered to check for you."

"Next time, you come first."

He grinned. "Best offer I've had in a long time."

"Oh, really?" As her racing heart gradually slowed, she pondered whether to kill him or kiss him. Since she might need him again later to defend her against crocodiles, there was only one option. She swam up and kissed him.

Startled, he began to sink, swallowed water and came up spluttering. "You might warn me before you do that."

"Like you warned me about the crocodiles?" Pleased with her revenge on him, she let her hands play over his muscular flanks. "What about when I do this?"

"Lady, you're playing with fire."

Legs pumping in the water, he pulled her into his arms and towed them both into the shallows where he trailed kisses over her upturned face.

She closed her eyes and then opened them, wanting to see him. She was lying in his arms, the water taking her weight. She stroked his chest, feeling the powerful beat of his heart under her fingers. Exertion or desire? A test was in order. She kissed him again.

This time he didn't go under, except perhaps figuratively.

Instead, he kissed her back, his mouth moving over hers as he took all she was offering.

When her lips parted, he deepened the kiss. For the first time in her adult life, no ghosts lay in wait to sabotage her pleasure. There was only a wanting so acute she ached with it.

For the first time, she was ready to give herself without reservation, she knew. Without having to guard herself against her partner's expectations. She could be open, taking and giving without fighting herself.

She had never felt so exhilarated. Or so needy.

"Please, Blake," she pleaded.

Chest heaving, he pretended ignorance. "Please what?"

"Do I have to beg?"

"It could get interesting."

She pummeled his chest. "If you keep pushing my buttons, I may have to harm you later. But not now. Now you have to follow through or I'm going to explode."

A grin of pure pleasure split his features. "When you put it like that—" Leaving the sentence unfinished, he swept her into his arms and stood up. Water streamed off him in ribbons, outlining the sleek contours of his body.

She had never been carried in a man's arms before and the sensation was unexpectedly pleasurable. Being crushed against him, his hardness to her softness, heightened her anticipation in ways she could hardly believe.

When he settled her on the blanket in the shade and leaned across her, she saw his gaze darken with pure, potent desire. For her. No clothes came between them. No barriers of any kind. In his gaze, she saw them all stripped away, down to the basic need of a man for his woman.

He fussed for a moment over her bruises, kissing them better one by one until she writhed beneath him. After covering her face with kisses, he moved down her body, spending agonizing minutes on each breast until she arched her back and cried out from the heat searing to the center of her being.

"Blake, this is too much."

"It's no more than you threatened to do to me," he said between caresses.

She arched again. "I didn't mean...not literally. Not like this."

"Then how about like this?"

At the intimacy of his touch, a volcano of needs erupted inside her. She was all heat, all wanting. She couldn't think straight. Her breath came in strangled gasps and her heart felt as if it would beat right out of her chest.

Desperately she clung to him, wanting to give as much as take. But he would have none of it yet. He was in command and this was his show. And she was in no position to protest, even had she possessed the strength. Or the will.

He stroked her and feasted on her alternatively. "Your turn will come," he promised. "For now, this is my gift to you."

And what a gift. How could a rugged man of the outback have the hands of a surgeon or a violinist, playing on her nerves with the skill of a virtuoso, until she vibrated in time to his pleasure?

He got to his feet. Guessing what he needed, she caught his hand and pulled him back down. "It's all right, we don't have to worry." She pressed his fingertips to the bump in her forearm. "A contraceptive implant, see?"

"And you accused me of making a habit of this."

"I had the implant put in because I travel and work odd hours," she said hotly, then caught his slanting grin. "You bastard."

Her fists drummed against his chest, but he spun her onto her back, claiming her mouth and making her pay with her sanity for taking him seriously.

Somewhere between his exploration of her breasts and the core of her womanhood, she lost control. Lost it as completely as if she'd never owned such a thing in her life.

She screamed, startling the native birds from the trees. Their cries mingled with her own as every muscle in her body trembled with the waves of sensation rolling through her.

Hearing her cry of release, Blake felt his own pleasure start to peak but fought it. Not yet. Not until he was buried in her would he allow himself to crest that wave. This was for her, his demonstration that everything he'd learned about her last night had only increased his love for her.

He sensed that she was ashamed of the outburst. Ashamed of revealing so much of herself to him. He wanted to show her that it had been as much a gift to him as he wanted to give her in return. True love had no shame. No barriers. He would allow none between them.

Seeing her tumble over the edge, he knew it was time. Levering himself up, he gave in to the needs battering at him and buried himself in her.

Her throaty cry of pleasure was all he needed to drive deeper, faster, harder, finally giving full rein to his own needs. With each thrust, he heard her drag in breath after breath and felt her fingers clawing at his back.

He had meant to go slower, to take her to the climax together. Her frantic movements beneath him destroyed not only his lofty intentions but any ability to think at all. He could only plunge and take, aware at some level that she had matched his rhythm and was with him every inch of the way. Her eyes were open and she met his gaze boldly, as if daring him to leave her behind.

This he had no intention of doing. He held on, held on, almost destroyed himself with waiting until he sensed she was ready, before he abandoned himself to a last frenetic thrust of utter release, his hoarse cry twinning with hers.

Gulping in air, he rolled her onto her side with him while the tremors slowed and finally ebbed. "Skinny-dipping with the other kids was never like this."

She frowned. "I hope not."

"Nothing was ever like this," he added. He lacked the energy to move for the time being, although conscience drove him to ask, "I hope I didn't aggravate your bruises?"

Her eyes sparkled. "What bruises?"

He kissed the one he could reach on her shoulder. "My mistake, beauty spots."

"The others will get jealous," she murmured.

"They'll have to wait while I recover my strength." She seemed content to wait. Since he was still inside her, he didn't mind, either.

"I never guessed that guilt could feel this delicious," she said.

He appraised her curiously. "Guilt about what?"

"I should get back to camp and check the photos in my camera. If Eddy Gilgai shows up in any of them…"

Blake touched a finger to her lips. "If he does, we'll know soon enough. It's not exactly flattering to hear you're thinking about another man while making love with me."

"Hardly comparable," she insisted. "He's the bad guy."

"Women sometimes prefer the bad guy."

"Fishing?" she asked. Before he could answer, she said, "No need. Right now, you're the only man on my mind, I promise."

"Then I'd better make sure it stays that way."

As he leaned over and kissed her, she shifted beside him. He felt himself start to harden again, her movement enough to send him spinning toward the edge again. Then she sat up and the only diamonds were the ones in her eyes as he lifted himself to meet her.

Chapter 13

Later that day, they were back at camp when Jo pointed to the screen on her laptop. "Look there. See that blurry figure among the bushes above the overhang? How could I have missed seeing him? When I lined up this shot of you, I must have been looking right at him."

Blake rested a hand on her shoulder. "You weren't expecting anyone else to be there. I didn't spot him or any sign of a vehicle until it was nearly too late, and I'm supposed to be the bushman."

She covered his hand with hers. "We were both distracted."

His lips grazed the junction of her neck and shoulder. "Hardly an excuse for almost getting us killed."

She shuddered, thinking of his own painful reminder of the encounter with Eddy's nulla nulla. "You didn't exactly get away unscathed yourself."

Closing his eyes, he rolled his head in a circle, then opened them and looked at her. "Paying him back will be a pleasure, but this photo won't do it."

It was the only shot showing any sign of Eddy. "Why not?"

Blake's finger stabbed at the screen. "You and I both know who it is, but the figure is too small and fuzzy for positive identification."

"Unless the figure can be enhanced to show more detail."

A pause, then, "Cade," they said at the same moment.

Des, Judy and Cade were enjoying a beer on the homestead veranda when Blake and Jo drove up. "Told you Blake can smell a cold beer a dozen miles away. I'll get two more glasses," Judy said as they climbed the steps to the veranda. Then Judy stopped in her tracks. "What happened to you two?"

"Long story," Blake said from behind Jo.

"You had a fight and Jo won," Cade suggested unhelpfully.

His foster father shot him a chilly glare. "The day any of my boys puts marks like those on a woman, I kick his butt to hell and back. I'm not so far gone I can't do it, either."

Wishing she'd worn a long-sleeved shirt to cover her bruises, Jo felt herself flush. "We had a run-in with Eddy Gilgai at Cotton Tree Gorge."

Judy let out her breath. "Don't say another word till I get those beers. I want to hear this."

When Blake and Jo were seated on canvas chairs with foaming glasses in front of them, Des leaned forward. "Now tell us what happened?"

Jo let Blake tell the story. When he reached the part about being clubbed by Eddy, he didn't spare himself, although it must have embarrassed him to admit to being caught off guard. As if sensing this, even Cade kept his mouth shut.

He also skipped over what happened after they'd walked out of the hidden valley, she noted. She didn't really expect Blake to share the details with his family, but she wondered if they could read anything from the heat she felt suffusing her face at what he wasn't telling them.

Once or twice, she caught Judy regarding her speculatively, but nothing was said.

When Blake finished, Des nodded in satisfaction. "We've got the bugger. This time, he's gone too far."

"The difficulty will be in proving anything." Judy looked at the photo Jo had put up on her laptop screen to show them. "Without your say-so, I wouldn't have recognized Eddy."

"Our conclusion, as well," Blake agreed. "Cade, you're the photographer. Can you do something to make the figure clearer?"

The others looked expectantly at Cade. "These days, you can make a photograph show almost anything you like."

"That's not what we meant," Jo put in. "We both know Eddy was the one who attacked Blake and then came after me. All we want is for the photo to back us up."

"This is my fault, isn't it," Judy said. "If I hadn't tried to outsmart Max, he wouldn't have been hanging about when Andy agreed to move the Jeep for you, and he wouldn't have sent Eddy after you."

Des's head came up. "What's this about you and Max?"

"I meant to tell you, Dad. While you were at the muster camp, Max came around asking me for a date. I thought it would be a good idea to humor him so I can see what he's up to."

"We know what he's up to. He wants this land," Des growled. "If this mess is anyone's fault, it's mine for borrowing money from his father in the first place."

"You couldn't have known Clive would have an accident and Max would inherit your mortgage along with his place," Blake insisted. "Maybe Judy is doing the right thing, keeping an eye on him."

His sister looked surprised, then pleased. "I thought you were against me having anything to do with him."

"Don't get me wrong, I hate the thought of that snake being anywhere near you. But yesterday, he showed he'll stop at nothing to get what he wants."

Des shook his head. "Shouldn't this be a matter for the police?"

Blake nodded. "I intend to give them a full report of what happened at the gorge, but they can't do much without proof. I didn't get a good look at who hit me, so it's Jo's word against Eddy's."

Cade traced a pattern in the condensation on his glass. "You can bet he'll have half a dozen witnesses swearing he was nowhere near Diamond Downs yesterday."

"Max must need those diamonds really bad," Des said.

"He does," Judy agreed. "After Jo and Blake left us at the airstrip, he stuck around while I was servicing the Cessna. I think he expected more of a payoff, but he was out of luck. I made sure I was too greasy and dirty for him to think of getting up close and personal."

"He mentioned a meeting with his banker," Blake remembered.

Judy sipped her beer. "At the airstrip, I got the impression he's in a lot of money trouble. Jamal left him a string of debts from when he was stalking Shara, but there's more. It seems Max invested heavily in some dodgy dot-com companies using his inheritance as security."

Blake whistled. "So unless he gets more capital from somewhere, he could lose the lot. Serve the bastard right."

"It isn't that simple. If he goes under with the mortgage over Diamond Downs still outstanding…" she didn't finish.

"There's another solution," Des said into the silence that followed. "I sell up, pay him out and use what's left to start over. I didn't take you boys into the family to rescue me from my problems."

"Too bad," Blake and Cade said at the same time.

"You're being rescued anyway," Judy said in a tone brooking no argument.

Des matched her for annoyance. "How, precisely? If you think I'll let my daughter get involved with Max Horvath to get me off the hook, you've got another think coming."

Judy gave a theatrical shudder. "I've no intention of getting involved, as you put it. I only want to find out how close he is to finding great-grandpa's mine."

Blake rubbed the back of his neck. "I'd say very close. Jo and I have the bruises to prove it."

"And these." Jo took a twist of paper out of her shirt pocket and spilled the contents into her hand. "I found them in the streambed in the hidden valley Blake told you about."

Des touched a forefinger to the pinpoints of crystal. "If they're real, you could be on to something. Andy's people regard Cotton Tree Gorge as a sacred place. According to them it's haunted."

"Could they mean by the spirit of Great-grandpa Logan?" Cade speculated. "Wouldn't that be something?"

Judy got up and refilled the beer glasses. Blake covered his glass with his hand. "Got to drive back to camp tonight."

His foster sister frowned. "After what you've been through, I thought a soft bed and a hot shower would have more appeal."

"I can't deny it appeals. But a deal's a deal."

"My deal," Jo amended. "You've already done more than I had a right to expect."

His level gaze swept over her. The meaning might escape the others, but she felt his eyes on her as if they were his hands, caressing and arousing, evoking the same heated sensations as if he were making love to her all over again. How was she to think of anything else when he could make her whole body vibrate with a look?

"I'm coming back to camp with you," he said. "I don't like to leave anything half finished."

Judy looked from Blake to Jo, her eyes alight with interest. "Is there something else you two want to tell us?"

Blake assumed a look of innocence. "Not a thing, why?"

Judy held her hands up. "Just curious."

"I hope you'll take care," Des warned. He seemed oblivious to the undercurrents between Blake and Judy. "Now Max and Eddy have resorted to violence, you might not be safe at that camp."

"He won't get by me a second time," Blake vowed. "If either of them tries anything, I'll be ready."

"And I'll do what I can to find out what Max's plans are.

Maybe we can put two and two together and get four before he does," Judy said.

Blake finished his beer and stood up. "You're the one who should take care. If Horvath finds out what you're up to, we might not be around to help."

"You're not around every time I put the Cessna down on a rough-and-ready airstrip in the middle of nowhere," she reminded him. "I can look after myself."

Blake gave her a rueful look. "That's what I thought right before Eddy king-hit me."

All business suddenly, Judy got to her feet. "Better let me take a look."

He ducked away from her hands. "Don't fuss. The swelling's already going down."

But she persisted and pulled in a disapproving breath at what she saw when she turned back his collar. "You're lucky you're not seeing stars."

"I was at the time, but I didn't lose consciousness. At least, not entirely."

His sister swung on Jo. "Did he?"

"I was too far away. All I saw was Blake lying on the ground," she said with scrupulous frankness, then met the searing look he gave her with one of her own.

"That does it. You're spending tonight here," Judy said.

Blake gave Jo a now-see-what-you've-done look, but she couldn't bring herself to object. She'd also seen the livid mark when Judy pulled back his collar, and she was horrified that she'd let him make love to her in such a state. How could she have been so selfish? That the feeling had been very, very mutual hardly excused her lack of consideration.

"This time, I have to agree with Judy," she said, not much liking the idea of sleeping in the open tonight with Eddy Gilgai on the rampage.

"I'd also feel a lot happier if you stayed the night," Des said. "Not because you need mollycoddling. I've never done that with any of you. But I'm a sick old man. You should humor me."

"So now you're sick and old, are you? That didn't occur to you yesterday when you went to the muster camp with the stockmen," Blake said, sounding aggrieved, as well he might be with his whole family ganging up on him. His expression accused Jo of taking their side against him.

"Yes, well that was yesterday. The experience took a lot out of me."

Blake huffed out a breath. "All right, already. We'll stay here tonight."

Des got up and clapped him on the shoulder. "Sensible man. I'm going to lie down for a while before dinner. See you all later." And he stomped off into the house.

"For a sick old man, he has a knack of getting his own way," Blake said as he sat back down. "Since I'm not driving, I may as well have that second beer."

"You didn't say anything to Judy about us, did you?" Blake asked as he showed her to the bedroom wing of the house after dinner.

Jo hadn't been aware there was an *us*, except physically, but the word sent an unexpected frisson of pleasure through her. "No, why?"

"Just a hunch." He threw open a door and she found herself in a spacious, high-ceilinged bedroom with a double bed at the center. A door stood open onto an adjoining bedroom. "The other room is mine. Judy gave you this one."

Looking from one room to the other, Jo felt herself flush. "Oh."

He stroked her hair. "That doesn't sound like an objection."

How could she object, when every minute having dinner and making small talk with his family had been agony? She had wanted to touch him and had to settle for trading glances when no one else was watching. "I didn't object when we shared a cave and a riverbank. This is a lot more civilized," she said.

He closed the door into the corridor behind them and then took her into his arms. "Not everything here is civilized."

She shivered but with anticipation. "Now I know why you didn't protest too much about staying the night."

His lips skimmed over her brow. "There are compensations."

She already had a good idea of what they were, but allowed him to show her, slowly and with consummate skill.

"Do you think Judy will be surprised when she finds that one of the rooms and none of the night clothes she put out for us has been used?" Jo asked much later as she lay in Blake's arms.

He kissed her deeply, his fingers splaying over her stomach in a gesture both familiar and so arousing she could hardly stand it. "I think anything else would have disappointed her."

"You have a remarkable family."

He nuzzled her ear with his tongue. "When they're your family by choice, it makes a huge difference."

She squirmed, on fire again more quickly than she would have believed possible. Blake had that effect on her. And she had the same effect on him, she saw, as he leaned over her, his mouth and hands telegraphing how he wanted to deal with the situation.

The part of her mind still functioning marveled at the effortless way he carried her along on a tidal wave of sensation. No not carried, she thought—she was an eager voyager. With her fear of closeness quickly becoming a memory, she felt like a starving person given access to all the food she desired.

They feasted on each other.

As soon as he awoke next morning, Blake sensed that he was alone in the bed. Hearing the tapping of Jo's computer keyboard, he relaxed. She'd gone into the other bedroom to work, leaving the connecting door open between them. He saw her fingers still and her gaze wander to the window. Then she bent her head and typed furiously, her delicious mouth curving in satisfaction.

He went to her and gathered her hair into his hand so he could kiss the back of her neck. "Do the words flow better when you're naked?"

She arched her back and took in his state of undress. "Uniform of the day. Besides, no clothes means fewer distractions."

"Speak for yourself." He skimmed a finger down her spine. "It's past eight. Judy must have decided we needed to sleep in. Do you have to work?"

"I wanted to get the hidden gorge story written while it's fresh."

"And then?"

"I'll send it to Karen. She's always in the office early. Then I'm all yours."

She already was, only she hadn't fully accepted it yet, he thought. He let her hair slide through his fingers, then padded to the unused bed. Stretching out on top, he linked his hands behind his head, enjoying watching her as she dispatched her work into cyberspace. His old student's desk had never been occupied so entrancingly, he decided. Her back was half turned to him, straight and lean, her flank taut, her skin creamy but for the blemishes from her fall. He'd kissed them better last night, but from the look of them, a repeat therapy wouldn't go astray.

Waiting for the nanoseconds to tick by until then was murder.

"Done." She closed the computer and sat back, improving his view with every lithe move. He swung his legs off the bed and then cursed as her cell phone rang. He'd have ignored it, but she was more conscientious than he was. With a regretful smile, she palmed the phone.

"Karen," she mouthed, turning her lips down in a grimace.

A man only had so much patience. He encircled Jo with his arms and pushed the phone aside so he could kiss her ear. She choked back a laugh. "I couldn't hear you, Karen. Something got into my ear."

Sure did—his tongue, he thought. If he kept it up, she'd have to end the call. If she didn't, he wouldn't be able to keep it up.

Instead, she switched the phone to her other ear, although goose bumps rose nicely on her skin as he drew patterns on her stomach with his fingertips. Frantically, she arched her eyebrows at him. "Yes, he's around somewhere. And no, he still doesn't want to be interviewed." She squirmed away from his exploring hands. "Oh, Lord. No, nothing's the matter. He told me where his surname came from, but we were talking off the record." There was a pause while Karen said something he couldn't hear. "I guess he didn't like being a Baracchi. From all accounts, they weren't any great bargain as foster parents," Jo replied.

As if it had never existed, Blake's passion vanished, replaced by white-hot anger so explosive he could hardly contain it. Moving as stiffly as a robot, he withdrew his hands and clamped them around the chair back. He held back from snatching the phone and demanding to know what the devil Karen Prentiss was playing at, but it took a supreme effort of will.

There had to be an explanation for what he'd just heard.

He could think of only one.

"Blake, what is it?"

Blinded and deafened by anger, he hadn't heard Jo end the call. Now he came back to her as if from a vast distance. "I want to know what that was all about."

She looked bewildered, then resolute. "There's no need for you to get angry. I reminded Karen you don't want to be interviewed. I can be every bit as persistent as she can."

Ice frosted his words. "I'll bet you can. You two make a good team, don't you?"

"I wouldn't call us a team, exactly."

He steeled himself to ignore her obvious bewilderment. "But you *are* working together?"

She stood up and groped for the robe Judy had draped over the foot of the bed. It happened to be a man's shaving coat, but Jo pulled it on anyway, seeming to need the thin layer of protection.

Blake felt a momentary twinge of conscience for frightening her, but if his suspicion was true, she should thank her stars he wasn't given to doing more.

"Of course we work together. Karen's my boss," she said as she tugged the robe around herself and belted it. Meant for him, the garment went around her almost twice, and she had to grasp the front to keep it from gaping.

He watched the feminine movements dispassionately, keeping himself as unmoved as if he were made of stone. "And you're depending on her goodwill to save your friend's home."

She nodded warily. "You know I am. Why…"

She gasped as his hand snaked around her wrist and he yanked her against him, the sudden movement almost spilling her out of the robe. He wouldn't let himself be affected by that, either. "Did she promise you your friend would be safe if you sold me out?"

Her eyes went round as saucers, the pupils growing huge as her anger surged. "What's this about, Blake? Nobody's sold you out, least of all me. I don't know what you mean."

Moments before, without even touching him, she'd had the power to set him reeling. Holding her against his nude body with only a skimpy robe between them, he allowed himself to feel nothing but cold fury. "Oh, no? Then how did you hear of the name Baracchi?"

"I didn't until two seconds ago, when Karen said the name."

She sounded so credible and so worried that his determination wavered. For a heartbeat he held Jo in his arms, her fluid body setting his senses ablaze with longing. Her mobile mouth was set in a grim line that he'd put there. All he had to do was kiss her and she'd melt and everything would be as it was. The ache in his loins told him how desperately he wanted that.

He couldn't. Not without answers.

He thrust her away. She stumbled against the desk, putting her hands behind her to steady herself while he stalked to the window and turned his back to her. "You expect me to believe this is all coincidence?" he demanded over his shoulder.

"I expect you to tell me what the hell you're so worked up about."

He had to admire her style. Her tone held just the right mixture of hurt and anger to be convincing. He didn't turn around, not wanting to see if her expression matched the tone. *Afraid you'll weaken and start believing she didn't know what she'd just done?* he asked himself. He laced his voice with sarcasm. "You really have no idea?"

"All I know is one minute you can't keep your hands off me, the next you're looking at me as if I'm something you've picked up on your shoe. I can't believe this is because Karen mentioned the first name you were known by. You may not have fond memories of it, but it's a matter of public record."

"No," he said with steely softness, turning. She looked small and fragile. He refused to let the sight sway him. "That name isn't on public record."

"You're making no sense."

"I'll spell it out for you. I was left on a doorstep in Perth and adopted by the family who found me."

She hugged herself as if cold. "And their name was Baracchi. So?"

"No, it wasn't. A few days before I was left there, the Baracchis had flown to Rome. Their daughter and her husband were living in the house. When my real mother couldn't be located, they took me in. They were the ones the media photographed and wrote about. Their surname was Hutchins."

Confusion colored her features. "Anyone could have researched the original owners of the house."

"The Baracchis had moved to Italy indefinitely. They sold the house to their daughter and son-in-law. By the time I turned up on their doorstep, Lou and Donna Hutchins were the legal owners."

It was her turn to look angry. "So what? A good journalist can uncover such details. Karen probably went digging."

"Why would she? As far as anybody knows, my first name was Hutchins. Then I was placed with Jane Creedy, the woman who made a living out of fostering kids. She didn't care what I called myself as long as the support payments arrived on time. So I chose Stirton. The only time I ever saw the name Baracchi was on the back of letters Donna Hutchins got from her mother. She and her husband never returned to Australia."

"Karen has shown a lot of interest in you, but then your story is unusual," Jo said. "Maybe she knows someone in the Baracchi family and got the name from them."

"Or maybe there's another explanation altogether."

Jo pushed herself away from the desk, taking a faltering step toward him, but was stopped by his implacable expression. "Oh, my God! Do you think Karen knows your natural mother?"

"Or she *is* my natural mother."

Jo was thunderstruck. She studied him intently. "There is a slight resemblance if you look for it."

"And it never occurred to you to look until now?"

"Not for a second, I swear."

He began to pace. "Add it up. Karen leaves me with what she thinks is the Baracchi couple who, I'm told, adored kids but couldn't have more than the one daughter. Unknown to Karen, they're heading overseas and have sold the house to their daughter. They do the noble thing by taking in the dumped baby until he's usurped by the arrival of their own child."

"If it's true, your mother tried to do the right thing by you," Jo said.

"The right thing would have been to go through proper adoption channels, not toss your child out like so much garbage."

"Unless she was too young and panicky to think straight."

"I might expect you to side with her. This whole thing was a setup, wasn't it? Our family got plenty of publicity after the Uru cave was discovered. It was all the excuse Karen needed to send you here as her mole. Were you making the video diary to satisfy her curiosity and save her from having to face me herself?"

Jo drew herself up, seemingly too angry to care about keeping the robe closed. "The diary was my idea. I'm nobody's mole, and if you think I'd do such a thing, it's as well we find out now, before we get in any deeper."

How much deeper could they get? he asked himself. He was in love with Jo. Discovering she'd duped him from start to finish felt like a knife twisting in his gut. He'd always believed what his natural mother did to him was the worst cruelty he could endure. He was fast learning there were worse hurts. Loving someone who'd deceived him on Jo's scale was hell on wheels.

Even so, he still wanted her with every fiber of his being. He ached to lose himself in her and pretend none of this had happened. But it had. Karen Prentiss *was* his natural mother. He'd stake everything he had on it. He would find out for sure, of course. But inside, he already knew the truth.

Jo's eyes sparked with anger as she watched him pace. "You know the worst of this? It isn't that Karen abandoned you as a baby—if it turns out to be true—or that she planted me here under false pretenses, although both are almost beyond forgiving. For me, the worst is having the man I care about think I could be a willing party to any of it."

She tightened the robe and headed for the door. Panic coiled through Blake, far more terrifying than his anger. "Where are you going?"

"Back to Perth to get some answers. Evidently, there's nothing more here for me—if there ever was."

Chapter 14

Jo found Judy at the stockyard where she was rubbing down one of the horses. When she asked about flight times from Halls Creek to Perth, Judy said, "Great Western flies via Newman three times a week. There's a flight today at noon, getting to Perth at five. Why?"

The timber rail felt rough under the palm Jo pressed against it. "Something's come up. I need to get home in a hurry."

Judy's brush stilled, earning a soft whicker of protest from the horse. "Anything I can do to help?"

Short of Judy flying Jo to Perth in her own plane, she couldn't think of anything that would make a difference anymore. "Thanks, but I'll be fine. I have some urgent business with my editor."

That was putting it mildly, she thought as she thanked Judy for the family's hospitality and promised to be in touch soon about finishing the survival story. If she ever came back to finish it, she thought but didn't add.

"Is everything okay between you and Blake?" Judy asked as Jo started to walk away. "I hope I didn't misread your signals and make a mistake with the rooms."

Jo glanced back, unable to keep the bitterness out of her voice. "You didn't. If anyone made a mistake, it was me."

All the time Jo had been showering, dressing and forcing down some coffee and toast, her mind had been rejecting the unfairness of Blake's accusation. Jo wasn't convinced that knowing one obscure name necessarily made Karen his birth mother. The editor probably had a perfectly simple explanation for the slip.

Whatever the reason, it wasn't going to help Jo. How could she forgive Blake for thinking she had conspired with Karen against him? His distrust felt like a weight on her shoulders, bowing her down. The comfort and passion of the previous night were fast becoming a memory.

Not fast enough, she thought as she located the rental car that had remained at the homestead while she'd shared Blake's Jeep. Seeing the Jeep a few feet away, she felt a tug deep inside as she pictured his strong hands on the wheel, steering them over a rugged stretch of road. In the vehicle's shadow, he'd made love to her for the first time after they'd emerged from the hidden valley. Wonderful, heated, exhilarating love.

Would she ever look at that model car again and see only a car?

She was starting to think of Blake as part of her past, she realized. Wasn't he? It was a long way back from the things he'd said to her this morning to where they'd been last night. Trying to imagine bridging that gulf, she lowered her head to her crossed arms on the steering wheel and closed her eyes.

But she didn't cry. She was damned if she would let him reduce her to tears. The minute she got back to Perth, she was going to confront Karen and demand to know what was going on. Then she would find a way to throw the truth back in Blake's face as payment for his lack of faith in her.

What she would do afterward, she had no idea.

If Karen did have a hidden agenda and had been using Jo to further it, she would start by looking for another job. Her resume was excellent and her savings would last until she found something. The state of her personal life was a different matter.

The secrets of her past were no longer hidden from her. She was free to commit or not as she chose. She didn't need to stick to safe relationships. The thought should have been liberating. Instead, she felt hollow inside, as if something had been taken away and nothing new left in its place.

Time heals all wounds, she assured herself, smiling a bit ruefully at the top-gun writer thinking in clichés. On the drive back to camp, she occupied her mind trying to do better, before deciding she was too demoralized to care.

The timing of the flight left her little time for soul-searching. By the time she'd telephoned GWA to reserve a seat, changed clothes and grabbed her bags, she barely had time to drive to Halls Creek.

Returning the rental car took a few more precious minutes. After check-in she had to cross the tarmac at a run and join the end of a line of people climbing the fold-down steps into the twin turboprop aircraft.

The seat beside her was occupied by a mother traveling to Perth to introduce her baby to the child's grandparents for the first time, so there was plenty of distraction on the long flight south. Jo couldn't decide if that was good or bad. The baby's antics kept her from thinking too much about the world she'd left behind in the middle of Diamond Downs.

Blake couldn't be right that the project was just a cover to let Karen learn more about the son she had abandoned. It would mean he was also right about Jo being used to get to Blake.

She focused on the blur of the propellers taking her ever closer to Perth. One way or another, she would know the truth soon.

* * *

The sound of hammering brought Judy striding around the side of the homestead. Blake was fixing the steps leading to the laundry, attacking each nail as if he had a personal grudge against it.

"Cade was going to do that," Judy said mildly.

Blake didn't look up. "I've saved him the trouble."

"Not if you reduce it to firewood. The timber's too old to take the full brunt of a man scorned."

The step shuddered as he pounded again, and said around a mouthful of nails, "No scorned men around here."

"Then Jo must be the wronged party."

"Why don't you ask her?"

"I did. She was no more forthcoming than you're being."

Blake took a nail from between his teeth and aimed the hammer. Crash. "Have you considered there's nothing to tell?"

"I considered it for all of five seconds. Last night, she was a happy woman. Today, she's a picture of misery. I'm not the most qualified person to comment, but I would hope you're not that lousy a lover."

"You're right, you're not qualified. And I've never had any complaints."

The hammer flew out of his hands and landed with a clang at Judy's feet. Without flinching she picked it up and returned it to him. "I'm glad we cleared that up."

Picking up a nail punch, he went to work on the last of the nails. "We had a difference of opinion over something her editor said. She went back to check it out. End of story."

"A difference of opinion over what?"

He could see Judy wasn't going to let this go. He set the tools down and wrapped his hands around the now-solid rail. Why shouldn't he tell her the truth? If he was right about Karen Prentiss, the whole family was entitled to know. "There's a chance her editor could be my birth mother."

Judy staggered back. "Karen Prentiss could be your—"

"You can say the word. If it's true, it's a biological fact. Not that it makes her into one in any other sense."

Judy collapsed onto the bottom step. "What tipped you off?"

He collected the tools, explaining about the editor's slip of the tongue.

Judy looked unconvinced. "She could have stumbled across the name in her research."

"I don't believe in coincidences that big. If Karen lived near the Baracchis at the time I was born, that's all the evidence I need."

"But if this couple were as sweet and child-loving as they were supposed to be, your mother might have tried to do the right thing in giving you to them."

His savage gesture dismissed the possibility. "She didn't give me to them. She left me on their blasted doorstep. The house could have been empty for all she cared."

"Assuming you're right, do you think Jo knew what Karen was up to?"

"She says she didn't."

Judy stood up. "Then she didn't."

"How can you be sure?"

"Jo is a person of integrity, you know that. And she cares about you. She wouldn't knowingly deceive you."

"I wanted to think so."

She placed a hand over his. "Keep thinking so. If you'd seen her face before she left, you'd have no doubts."

"She's gone?" His voice came out sounding ragged.

"On the noon flight to Perth. Obviously she thought there was nothing left for her here. Is she right, Blake?"

"The hell of it is, I don't know. I thought I was in love with her, but this morning when she knew about the Baracchis, I saw red."

"She didn't know. Karen did. There's a difference. You should be confronting the editor, not taking this out on Jo."

"It's too late."

Judy made a sound of annoyance. "Nothing's too late while you're still breathing. Go after her. Find out the truth."

"How? The next flight isn't for two days."

"Unless you have contacts at the airport. One of the flying instructors is returning a plane to Perth this afternoon. If I ask nicely, he'll give you a ride."

He swung her into the air as he'd done when she was a little girl. "I owe you one, little sister."

"Not so little, and you owe me big-time."

He hesitated. "Will Des be okay?"

"Cade and I are here if Dad needs anything. He's resting today after overdoing things at the muster camp, but when he hears why you've gone he'll support you one hundred percent. He knows where he fits into your life. That won't change no matter what you learn. But he'd want you to *know*. And besides, you can't tell me it isn't what you've wanted your whole life?"

"You know it is." He didn't have to tell Judy how his world had shaken on its foundations when he suspected who Karen Prentiss really was. Judy knew him too well not to understand. Or to figure out how devastated he'd been when he worked out why Karen had sent Jo to Diamond Downs.

She'd sent Jo. He hesitated. Did he want to see her again, knowing she could be part of the deception?

"You're still not sure how Jo fits into all this, are you? There's only one way to find out. If you let her walk out of your life and she's innocent, you'll regret it forever."

"Finished?" he asked when Judy drew breath.

"Do you want to keep arguing?"

"I want you to call your pilot friend. I told my team at Sawtooth Park I'd check in with them later today. While I'm there, I can pick up some gear and go on to the airport."

After the vast emptiness of the outback, Perth seemed uncomfortably big and bustling. Jo's apartment overlooking the Swan River should have been welcoming, but crazily, she'd felt more at home in a rough bush shelter beside Dingo Creek.

Why didn't she face facts? Her home was wherever Blake was. Somewhere between helping him build the shelter and spending the night together in a hidden valley, she'd fallen in love with him.

Nothing else explained why his lack of trust sliced so deeply.

Damn it, she wasn't part of whatever game Karen was playing. Why couldn't he give her the benefit of the doubt until they knew the whole truth? The answer was obvious. He wanted to make love to her, but he didn't love her. With his history, he might not be able to love. She hated to think so, but the possibility had to be considered.

She slowly moved around the familiar yet strange rooms of her home, doing laundry and ordering pizza even though she wasn't hungry. There wasn't any fresh food and she didn't feel like shopping. She debated calling Karen but if her husband answered, he'd want to know why Jo was calling Karen at home. What explanation could she give him? And if this was a misunderstanding, Jo didn't want to cause trouble between the couple.

Instead, she called Lauren, telling the other girl about her adventures and promising they'd get together as soon as she could. Lauren sounded distracted and Jo soon learned the reason. She had a boyfriend, Adam, who'd moved into the group home soon after Jo had left for the Kimberley. In her usual way, Lauren's whole attention was taken up with the new relationship.

Hanging up, Jo felt as if her world had shifted. In her own fashion, Lauren had grown up and didn't need Jo anymore, not in the way she'd always had. From the sound of things, she might well marry before Jo. The thought choked her and the tears she'd held back all day formed a leaden lump in her chest. She jumped up, denying them escape.

She might not be able to redeem herself with Blake, but she might be able to help his foster father. During the flight, a theory had formed in her mind, but she would need help proving it. Her parents might be out of the country, but her brothers weren't. What good was having brothers in specialized fields if she couldn't call on them for assistance?

She cancelled the pizza and grabbed her handbag.

He'd been mad to come, Blake told himself as he paced his hotel room, dodging the remains of a room service meal. City surroundings always made him uneasy, bringing back memories of miserable foster homes where love had been at a premium.

It was at a premium now and it was his fault. He should never have accused Jo of conspiring against him. Suddenly, his pacing faltered. Was he getting his licks in before someone had the chance to hurt him, pushing Jo away before she could do the same to him? He owed it to her to set the record straight. He snatched up the phone book.

Not giving himself a chance to change his mind, he headed down to the lobby and gave her address to a cab driver, then drummed his fingers on the seat the whole way to her apartment.

She wasn't home.

He actually debated waiting on her doorstep until she returned, but the lost-waif symbolism was too strong. He hailed another cab and went back to the hotel.

Jo made a point of arriving at the office of *Australian Scene Weekly* bright and early the next morning. Simon, the security man in the lobby, smiled in recognition, but Jo didn't stop to chat as she usually did. She wanted to catch Karen when she was likely to be alone in the magazine's offices. With no witnesses, she would have no reason not to be honest with Jo.

The editor was working and looked startled when Jo barged in. "This is a surprise."

She planted both palms on Karen's desk and leaned over it. "I want to know the real reason why you sent me to the Kimberley."

Jo couldn't recall Karen appearing so nervous before. "Because it's a great story. And it's working." Her hand fluttered over a thick wad of e-mails. "Reader response is amazing."

"Terrific. How did you know about the Baracchis?"

The editor stared at her for a long moment and then pulled in a deep breath. "You'd better sit down."

Before she did so, Jo had to ask, "Are you Blake's mother?"

"Go ahead, Karen. I can't wait to hear this, too."

Both women turned. Blake was angled against the door frame, his arms crossed over his broad chest. Seeing him out of his khaki bush clothes, Jo's breath caught at how amazing he looked in a cream polo shirt and navy pants. Under the grim set of his mouth, his chin was shadowed. The effect was edgy and inviting. She looked away before she betrayed herself by making eye contact.

Behind Blake, a uniformed man hovered. "Sorry for the intrusion, Ms. Prentiss. This man almost knocked me out of the way when I tried to stop him coming up. I'm about to call the police."

"There's no need. Thank you, Simon. He's expected. Come in, Blake."

He did so, shutting the door behind him. He kept his distance from her, Jo noted, her heart aching. She hadn't expected seeing him again, knowing he didn't love her, to hurt quite so much. She shoved aside her pain. This wasn't about her. It was about Blake.

Karen had linked her hands on the desk and was staring at them, avoiding Blake's intense scrutiny. "I'm not your mother. I didn't even know you existed until a year ago. Then I didn't know where to start looking until I heard about the Logan family and their foster son called Blake."

"You expect me to believe that?"

"It's the truth. Your mother was my older sister, Delia Rickard."

Sadness for Blake gripped Jo. "Was?"

"Delia died in hospital last year. I'm sorry, Blake."

Jo saw his hands clench into fists. So close, she thought. "What happened?" he asked tonelessly.

Karen rose. "I'll get us some coffee. This could take a while."

Jo motioned the editor to stay where she was. "I'll get it."

A coffeemaker was already bubbling on a side table across

the office. Jo came back with two cups, sugar sachets and a container of milk, putting them in front of Karen and Blake, and then getting a cup for herself. When he automatically murmured his thanks, she caught a glimpse of his eyes, so filled with pain that her heart turned over.

"How did she die?" he asked, sounding as if the question had been forced from him.

Karen added milk to her coffee and stirred it. "There's no easy way to say this. In her teens, she fell in with a bad crowd who encouraged her to experiment with dangerous drugs that resulted in her becoming mentally unstable. The family got treatment for her, but the harm was done. She probably died from an overdose of her medication, probably forgetting when or how much she'd taken. She'd been in and out of hospital from her early twenties. Sometimes she lived with our parents and managed her illness with medication. At other times she lived on the streets for months, completely out of touch with reality. You were most likely born during one of those episodes."

"She must have received medical care, at least during the birth."

Karen gave him a searing look. "Do you think I didn't check with the hospitals? They had no record of her giving birth under her real name, but she used many different ones depending on her moods. It was a miracle that she'd given the hospital where she died her real name, or we may never have known what happened to her."

"She was lucid enough to realize she couldn't take care of a baby," Jo contributed.

Karen nodded. "She could barely take care of herself. Our parents often found her wandering and brought her home. She'd be okay for a time, then disappear again."

Blake's stony expression gave no clue as to how he was taking the revelations. "How did you find out she'd had a baby?"

A faint smile lit Karen's face. "Delia had a habit of writing notes to herself on scraps of paper because she didn't trust her memory. Quite a few had her name written on them. She carried hundreds of the scraps with her everywhere she went. Among the papers the hospital gave us after she died was a thirty-year-old birth notice torn out of a newspaper and carefully kept in an old wallet. The original name had been crossed out and Blake Rickard written above it, with her name replacing the mother's. In the margin, she'd written Baracchi and a street name. My family lived down the street from them for several years. But nothing else made any sense until I read about Des Logan fostering an abandoned child named Blake."

"The name Baracchi was never connected with me in the media," Blake pointed out.

"Was that the slip of the tongue that brought you here? I suppose I had the name in my mind and it came out. Or perhaps I wanted it to come out. The reports did mention your name and the street where you were found. It seemed like too much of a coincidence for you not to be Delia's child."

"Why didn't you tell me what you suspected, instead of fabricating a story assignment?" Jo asked.

Karen fiddled with a sugar sachet. "I didn't want it to be true."

Blake looked as if he'd been slapped. "I can see how a bastard nephew could ruin your yuppie image."

"That's where you're wrong. Ron and I were unable to have a child. It killed me to think Delia had left you with strangers when I would have given anything to have had the chance to raise you."

Blake's tone had softened fractionally as he asked, "Why do you think she kept my birth a secret?"

"Ashamed, perhaps. Our parents were fairly straitlaced. Or, more probably, delusional. At the time, she simply might not have known what was happening to her, or where the baby came from. We'll never know. It might not mean much to you now, but I am truly sorry, Blake."

"It was hardly your fault," he said, earning a slightly sur-

prised look of gratitude from Karen. "From the sound of
things your family did all they could for—my mother."

The slight hesitation wasn't lost on Jo. She wished she
could reach out and touch him. Unsure of her welcome, she
held back. So much pain, so much loss. And nothing to be
done except endure it. Blake's mother hadn't been a horrible
person. She'd been a poor, tortured creature who, in all likelihood, hadn't known what she was doing. In what glimmer
of reality had remained to her, she'd tried to do what was best
for her son in her own, confused way. Jo hoped the knowledge
was some comfort to Blake.

"I can show you photos of Delia and your grandparents,"
Karen offered. "My parents would have given a lot to meet
you. Right to the end, they grieved for Delia, blaming themselves for what they could or should have done, when there
was nothing. We even tried tracing your natural father, but
didn't have anything to go on."

"Give me some time," he said.

"As much as you want. I realize this is a shock. For me,
too, when I learned that my sister could have had a child. For
the year since I found out about your birth, I've lain awake at
night thinking about you, and looked at men around the right
age in the street and wondered if we were related."

"What were you going to do once you were sure Blake was
your lost nephew?" Jo asked. She saw him rest his hands on
his thighs, his lean body angled forward, waiting.

Karen stared into her coffee cup and then lifted her head.
"Would you believe, I had no idea? I knew he'd—you'd—be
a grown man by now, independent. I didn't know if you'd want
to have anything to do with your mother's family."

He stood up, all restless energy. "I've lived with my history as I've known it for a long time. The Logans are the only
real family I've had in my life. I can't suddenly fit myself into
another family as if I belong there."

"Nor do I expect you to, not right away. The next move is
up to you."

In every way, Jo thought. There was one more doubt to be cleared up. "Karen, Blake thinks I knew why you gave me this assignment."

His head snapped around and he really looked at her although his expression gave Jo no clue to his thoughts. "I know you didn't," he said quietly.

But Jo wanted no doubts left in his mind. "Karen?"

"I don't know why it matters to you, Blake, but for the record, all Jo knew was that I wanted a series of survival-type articles written about her experience of roughing it in the Kimberley. I hoped you would agree to an interview, for my sake as much as for the magazine's, but I didn't tell anyone why it was important to me."

"I shouldn't have doubted you, Jo," Blake said, his tone rough. "This is one hell of a shock."

"To all of us," Karen put in. "Finding your sister had a child you never knew existed is a lot to take in. If it helps, she would have been proud of you."

"I have to take your word for that."

"There's a lot I can tell you about growing up with Delia, before she became ill. Will you let me share some of my memories with you?"

"In time." When he'd had a chance to absorb the full import of what he'd learned, Jo heard. When she'd recovered her repressed memories in the cave, he'd advised her to give herself time and to seek help if she needed it. She hoped he would take his own advice.

While they talked, she'd been aware of the magazine staff arriving to start their day and the floor outside Karen's office was gradually assuming its usual hum of frenetic activity. Jo felt strangely detached. Had her reality changed so much in a couple of weeks? Not only her reality had changed. She also had changed.

She would turn her back on this world, once offering everything she'd thought she needed, and return to the Kimberley with Blake without hesitation if he wanted her.

Karen's door flew open and a harried, middle-aged man stepped inside the office. "Our production manager," Karen said for Blake's benefit.

The man nodded to Jo and Blake. "Sorry to butt in, but if this story is to make next week's issue, you need to sign off on these ASAP." The man gave Jo a nod of recognition.

Karen's shoulders lifted in an apologetic shrug and she reached for the glossy proofs the production manager held out. Blake's photo jumped out at Jo. She stared at it in disbelief. "What's going on, Karen?"

Blake looked over Jo's shoulder. She could feel his anger radiating toward her as he read. "What the devil is this?"

The headline read Exclusive! Crocodile Man's Family Secret Revealed.

Karen gave a wan smile. "I was going to show it to you."

"When? The day after the magazine hit the newsstands?"

"Of course not. Al, leave this with me. I'll get back to you shortly."

Caught in the crossfire, the production man seemed more than happy to retreat. Jo didn't blame him. Blake's murderous glare raked her and he stabbed his finger at the page. "Tell me you didn't know about this."

"I can't deny some of the photos are mine." One was of him working on the shelter. "I never meant them to be used in this way."

"Jo knew nothing about this," Karen said. "It was my idea. Possibly not one of my better ones."

"Use any of this without my permission and I'll sue the magazine and everyone responsible for every cent you've got."

He didn't have to single out Jo. He might accept that she hadn't been part of Karen's original agenda, but expecting him to believe she wasn't behind the sensational headline was too much. "You can't use my photos, either," she said shakily.

"I'm afraid we can. Your contract gives the magazine the right to use anything you produce in the course of an assignment," Karen assured her.

Denial screamed through Jo with one stroke, Karen was destroying Jo's chance of having a future with Blake. "If you do this, I'll never write a word for the magazine again," she vowed.

Blake's palms came together in silent applause. "Quite a double act you two have going. The hard-boiled editor and the writer innocently duped into supplying her with headlines. Well, this time you chose the wrong target."

He took the proof and tore it in half, returning the pieces to Jo, the symbolism clear. "Blake, I didn't know," she repeated. If he chose not to believe her, there was nothing more she could say.

Looking unconvinced, he said, "Whether you did or not, both of you owe it to Delia Rickard's memory not to be a party to this sensationalized garbage."

Karen spread her hands wide in a defensive pose. "I won't run the story. Just don't disappear from my life, Blake."

Or from mine, Jo prayed. But the door had swung shut behind him.

Chapter 15

Karen sank back, her expression as much puzzled as hurt. "I wouldn't have used the story without checking with him first. If he'd given me the chance, I would have made it worth his while. I understand his foster father is ill and in need of funds."

Jo placed the torn pages on her boss's desk. "Some things aren't negotiable."

"Like integrity, I know," Karen said, sounding distant. "For all her problems, Delia had her own kind of integrity. She kept her little notes because she didn't want to hurt anyone. They were her way of keeping track of her life and the people in it. The doctored birth notice showed she was proud of Blake and wanted to make sure she didn't forget him, although she did anyway."

"She couldn't help herself."

The editor went on as if she hadn't heard. "He's right, you know. I was jealous of Delia—of her freedom to come and go as she pleased, leaving me to take care of our parents, although all their concern was for her. I was never more jealous than when I learned she'd had the baby I wanted so desperately."

"So Blake was also right about why you sent me to the Kimberley? You wanted me to spy on him for you."

Karen seemed to bring herself back from a long way away. "Not entirely. I wanted to know how he'd turned out, of course, but the survival story was attractive, too. I thought it would be exciting and different. You were just the writer to take the ball and run with it. The avalanche of response to your first article shows I was right."

"About everything except Blake. He might be your sister's child, but you have a lot to learn about him. He's a man of courage and compassion, but because of his experiences, he's also a very private person. Sensational headlines are the last thing he would want. I may not have much control over the situation, but if you run any of this, I mean what I said. I'll never write a word for you again."

"Are you in love with him?" When Jo didn't answer, the editor pressed on. "You are, aren't you?"

"Imagining the headlines already?" Jo asked, avoiding the question.

"I guess I deserve that. No, this time I'll wait until you're ready to write the story yourself, if you decide to." Still, Karen couldn't resist adding, "Provided *Australian Scene* gets an exclusive on the wedding pictures."

A wedding seemed like an impossibility after today. "You don't give up easily, do you?"

"Neither should you. From what I've seen of Blake and read in your first article, he's worth going after. And having you in the family would be one way to ensure I don't lose my best writer to another magazine."

She smiled to assure Jo she was teasing, although Jo suspected, at some level, her editor meant every word. What a surrogate mother-in-law she would make, she thought, and was amazed by her own thoughts. "Does that mean we have your approval?"

"Yes, although it wouldn't make any difference. You and Blake have more in common than you think."

Considering his refusal to believe her, Jo nodded. "He's a stubborn, hardheaded son of a…"

"As I said, two of a kind," Karen cut across her.

Was it possible? Then Jo remembered Blake's avowed habit of getting in first, before others had the chance to hurt him. Maybe she meant something to him after all. If his feelings for her were strong enough to make him push her away, there was hope for them yet.

"You could be right," she said, standing up. "Your nephew is about to find out that I can be every bit as stubborn as he can."

"He left here in quite a temper. How will you go about finding him?"

"I have a good idea where to look."

"Then what are you standing there for?"

From her research, Jo knew that Tiger Mountain Reserve outside Perth was one of only three centers in the world where visitors could interact with tigers. The second was on Queensland's Gold Coast, on the opposite side of Australia, and the third in San Francisco.

She was pleased when the ticket seller remembered her. "Planning to write another story about us? You'd be surprised how many visitors still mention your last article," she said.

"We're going to meet Jo's friends Bob and Blake, and see the tigers," Lauren promptly told the receptionist.

The woman processed Jo's credit card and returned it, together with two tickets bearing colored pictures of tigers. "If you're official guests, I probably shouldn't take your money. I can check with Bob, and let him and Blake know you're here."

"We're just visiting," Jo assured her. "I'm happy for the donation to go toward the reserve's conservation work." Her heart sped up. She'd read him right. Blake had come to the one place in the city where he would feel at home. Since Perth was short on crocodiles and rain forest, Tiger Mountain, where he'd first worked with animals, had seemed the obvious place to look for him.

Bringing Lauren along had seemed like a good idea when Jo thought of it. A chance to see her friend and give her a treat at the same time. And save Jo having to face Blake alone? Yes, that too, she acknowledged inwardly.

Striving to keep a tremor of anticipation out of her voice, she asked, "Where will we find Blake?"

"Either in the savanna area with Bob, or in the sanctuary, playing with Amulya. She's the tiger he helped to hand-raise, and now she has two cubs of her own. They're off display until the cubs are older, but I'm sure Bob will show them to you. Shall I let them know you've arrived?"

Aware of the line lengthening behind them, Jo smiled. "We'll surprise him, thanks."

Coward, she told herself. She didn't want to take the risk of Blake making some excuse to avoid her. She hoped he'd be kind to Lauren, if not to Jo herself. At twenty-two, Lauren had blossomed into a lovely young woman. Only her child-like behavior betrayed her, although Jo was amazed at the progress she'd made since moving into the special home. Or was it the result of having a young man take an interest in her?

They walked past a series of naturalistic enclosures where koalas drowsed after feasting on eucalyptus leaves. Lauren bounced excitedly at Jo's side, her long auburn hair swinging around her face. "I love animals."

"I know you do." Lauren's bedroom was crammed with cuddly toy animals, many given to her by Jo. "I should have brought you to Tiger Mountain a long time ago."

"You're always busy," Lauren said.

Jo gave her a sharp look but, as usual, Lauren wasn't complaining, merely stating a fact. "You're right, but being busy is no excuse for neglecting my friends."

"I'm still your friend. And I have Adam, as well, now."

They paused while Lauren leaned over a fence to pet a kangaroo and exclaim over a tiny joey poking its head out of the mother's pouch. "Look, she has a baby. Do you think Adam and me could have a baby?"

Concern gripped Jo. "Have you talked about this with Mrs. Richardson?" The Richardsons were Lauren's house parents.

Lauren's look was scathing. "I don't have to. I know we're not supposed to make babies until after we get married."

How easy it was to forget Lauren's natural candor. "How long have you known Adam?" Jo asked.

"Two weeks. I love him."

About to question whether Lauren could have fallen in love with Adam in such a short time, Jo choked back the words. Hadn't she done the same thing with Blake? And from the sound of things, Lauren had behaved with a lot more restraint than Jo herself. Who was the smart one? She felt herself color and looked away.

"You'll like Adam," Lauren went on, oblivious to Jo's turbulent state of mind.

"I'm sure I will. You don't have to marry someone just because you like them."

Lauren made an impatient sound. "I know that, too. But I will because I love him. He takes me out. Last week, we went for pizza. It was fun. He wanted us to go for pizza today but I told him we couldn't because you needed to see me. He said we can have pizza after."

Who was doing a favor for whom? Jo stopped beside a lake where a pair of black swans were herding a trio of fuzzy gray cygnets. "It's okay to tell me if you have other plans, Lauren."

The other girl scuffed her shoe on the gravel path. "You won't get angry?"

"Of course not. I'll be happy for you."

"I told Adam you wouldn't be angry. He said I should come because it would make you happy."

"Your Adam sounds like a good person."

"He makes me laugh."

High praise indeed, Jo thought, suppressing a twinge of envy at Lauren's uncomplicated view of the world. They went on to talk about the other girl's job at a supermarket near her home, while Jo kept her eye open for signs directing them to the tigers. The closer she got, the more she felt like turning and running. This was Blake, not a stranger, she reminded herself, although what they'd shared in the Kimberley seemed like a dream now. If there was the slightest chance of turning the dream into reality, she owed it to them both to take the chance.

Suddenly, Lauren pointed excitedly. "Look, there's a tiger."

Jo recognized the towering cutout of a Bengal tiger dominating the entrance to the tiger habitat. In this specially created environment, a sign proclaimed, the tigers could play, swim and live together with their handlers while visitors learned about these critically endangered animals.

The entrance opened onto a savanna edged by stands of rain forest, with a lake and waterfall on one side where the tigers could swim. A moat and low wall separated the visitors from the animals. Inside the enclosure two men lounged on the grass, talking as easily as if three full-grown Bengal tigers weren't climbing over and around them.

Common sense told Jo that Blake knew what he was doing. He had hand-raised some of these tigers and worked with them before opening his crocodile park. The assurance didn't prevent panic from fluttering through her. Tigers, no matter how well socialized, were still wild and unpredictable. She couldn't bear the thought of anything happening to him.

His distrust might have shaken her feelings for him, but they were still strong. He only had the power to hurt her because she cared for him so much. She could no more change her feelings than belay the sun from rising in the morning.

Leaning over the wall, Lauren asked, "Which man is your friend?"

Jo forced her fears aside. Both the handlers wore Tiger Mountain uniforms, she saw now. Not sure whether to be relieved or disappointed, she said, "He isn't there."

"Hello, Jo. Doreen at the gate told me you'd arrived."

Jo smiled as a tall, rangy man in khaki shirt and shorts and a battered leather bush hat joined them. He looked to be about fifty, although Jo knew he was closer to seventy. "Lauren, this is Bob Stirton, who owns Tiger Mountain."

The shy young woman and the older man exchanged greetings. Then Bob said, "It figures two beautiful woman aren't looking for an old codger like me. Doreen said you're hoping to surprise Blake."

Cold feet was more than a metaphor, Jo discovered. Her own felt suddenly icy, although the day was warm. "Is he around?"

"He's getting reacquainted with Amulya and her babies. This way."

He took them behind the scenes to another rain forest area separated by a high glass wall from a series of gravel walkways. Behind the wall, Blake was on the ground with one arm around a huge female Bengal tiger. In the other, he held a squirming cub. Jo's heart leaped into her mouth. "Is he safe in there?"

She was aware of Bob's speculative look. "They're old friends. He raised Amulya from two weeks old."

"But with the cubs…"

"Watch."

Hands pressed against the glass, she saw the mother tiger lift another cub gently in her mouth and place it onto Blake's lap. Jo felt her eyes mist. She had never seen such trust in her life. Was it too much to ask for the same deal between her and Blake?

"Would you like to meet Amulya?"

"You mean go in there?" She wasn't sure which scared her most—meeting the tiger or removing the last barrier between her and Blake. She didn't hesitate. "What do I have to do?"

Bob told her, adding, "We'll watch from out here. Okay with you, Lauren?"

The younger woman's apprehension was obvious. "The tiger won't eat Jo, will he?"

The older man shook his head. "Blake will take care of her."

If only the rest of their relationship were so clear-cut, Jo thought. Blake didn't seem surprised when he saw her with Bob in the small steel cage the handlers used to access the enclosure. Only when the outer gate was safely locked did Bob open the inner one, motioning for Jo to step through. Her heart was pumping with excitement at having no barriers between her and a full-grown tiger, and at Blake's apparent acceptance of her presence.

Step one accomplished, she thought.

Bob rejoined Lauren behind the glass wall and then the outside world ceased to exist for Jo. There was only Blake, the man she loved, and the magnificent animal lying trustingly beside him.

"Hello, Jo. Walk up quietly and sit down beside me," he instructed in a low, even tone. "This is Amulya. She's five years old, weighs nearly three hundred pounds, and these are her babies, Tara, Kiran and Mohini."

Wonder displaced fear as she followed his instructions. "Can I touch her?"

"You can stroke her flank but stay away from her head and paws. If she rolls over or gets up, stand up and move behind me."

She was touching a tiger, Jo thought, her mind spinning. Under her hand, the animal's flank felt firm like a horse's, the fur thick and more doglike than feline. "I can't believe I'm doing this."

"Why did you come?"

"To see you. I couldn't let it end like this."

One of the cubs sitting on his lap mewled and he passed it to the mother, where it immediately began to nurse. He placed the other two cubs alongside their sibling at the mother's flank. Tiny paws with needle-sharp claws kneaded the tiger's belly and the sweet smell of milk filled the air.

A maelstrom of sensations assailed Jo. She had never imagined herself as a mother, but seeing the cubs nursing stirred something deep inside her, primitive and irresistible. She wanted Blake's children.

"Nothing has ended unless you've made up your mind it should," he said.

She stared at him. "But I thought…you mean you believe I didn't know about those headlines?"

"I admit I was suspicious at first. Coming on top of Karen's revelations, I was so angry I could barely see straight. Heading for Tiger Mountain was reflex. Being around wild animals has a way of putting life into perspective. Going a few rounds with the tigers in the other enclosure worked off most of my frustration."

She could barely breathe. "And now?"

"I'm grateful to Karen for giving me answers about myself, but I won't let her turn my life into a circus."

"She knows. I told her if she runs the story, I'll never write another word for her again."

"What happened to editor at thirty-five, publisher at forty?"

Pleased he'd remembered, she set her mouth. "I'll find another way to get there."

The tiger made a moaning sound deep in her throat. "It's okay, she's talking to her babies," Blake said when Jo stirred in alarm.

"Does she purr like a cat?"

He shook his head. "Tigers are big cats, but the difference isn't only in size. Big cats like the tiger are able to roar. Only small cats can purr."

"You're a fountain of information. Amulya obviously remembers you."

"I take that as a compliment. I bottle-fed her from when she was the same size as these little guys, and I visit whenever I'm near Perth."

Jo had a hard time imagining the huge animal ever being small enough to be bottle-fed. Then she looked at the cubs and melted. "I'm surprised you didn't stay with the tigers."

He smiled. "If we'd had wild tigers in Australia, I might

have been tempted to go on working with them. But wonderful as Tiger Mountain is, the outback is where I feel most at home."

Because he'd felt caged as a boy, being handed from one family to another, she assumed, understanding the appeal the outback represented. Her only complaint was being overprotected by her family, but she had also felt the overpowering sense of freedom in the Kimberley.

"And odd as it might seem, I like crocodiles," he continued. "They may not be as endangered as tigers, or need as much help to make it in the modern world, but they've survived since the time of the dinosaurs. In my book, that makes them special."

"'Special in a way only a mother could appreciate,'" she quoted.

"Perhaps. Looks like this mother's done her duty for the moment. We'll leave the family to their nap."

Jo gave the magnificent tiger a last pat and then risked stroking the babies one at a time. Amulya kept a wary eye on her, but didn't seem to object. "How can you tell them apart?"

"Look at their faces. Every one has different markings. Hard to believe people still shoot them, isn't it?"

She released a breath. "These little guys don't know how fortunate they are being born here."

His brow furrowed. "They'd be more fortunate if they could return to the wild, but Tiger Mountain is their only chance of survival. Bob appreciated the story you wrote, by the way. The more people who come here, the more he can do to help conserve what remains of the wild tiger population."

"I'm going to ask Karen about doing a follow-up about Amulya and her babies," Jo promised.

"Won't that be difficult if you're never going to write a word for her again?"

His teasing tone tugged at her. Was it to be as simple as meeting him on his own ground? "The threat only applies if she messes with you."

Blake held out a hand to help her up. His gaze went to the tiger and her cubs. "You and Amulya have a lot in common."

Outside the enclosure, Lauren was chatting happily to Bob. As Blake and Jo left the confinement area and were brushing grass off their pants, Bob said, "Come on up to the office for coffee. Doreen says you might be interested in writing another story for us. I'm in the middle of setting up a photo exhibition of the park's history. Some of the pictures could interest you."

"I'd be happy to look at them, but I need to put Lauren in a cab first," Jo said. "She has a date."

The other girl colored shyly. "Adam's waiting for me. We're going out for pizza."

Bob nodded. "Sounds good to me. Thank you for visiting Tiger Mountain, Lauren. You bring your Adam here sometime and I'll personally give the two of you a guided tour."

Lauren's face flushed with pleasure. "Is it okay for us to come when you're not here, Jo?"

Another step in her friend's growth, she recognized, trying not to feel slighted. Enabling Lauren to be as independent as possible had been her goal, and the hope of Lauren's caregivers all along. "Of course it is. Just let Mrs. Richardson know where you're going. I'm sure Bob will take good care of you and Adam."

"Count on it."

Blake walked them back to the entrance, waiting while she saw Lauren into her cab and gave the driver the girl's address. Then Blake escorted Jo to Bob's office above the park's main restaurant overlooking the reserve.

"Up here, I feel like an eagle in his nest," Bob said. "Make yourselves comfortable while I do a couple of things in the office and rustle up some coffee. I haven't finished sorting the photos yet, but you're welcome to go through them. Most of them have a written description of the shot on the backs."

He set a box of photos on the desk between her and Blake. Jo waited until the door closed behind Bob. "Blake, I…"

"I'm the one who should apologize," he said, cutting her off. "I blew up when I should have waited to hear your side of the story."

"You've had an extraordinary day," she conceded. "It's not every day you discover a birth mother and a whole new family."

"And I took my shock out on you. I have a short fuse, Jo. I wish I could promise it won't happen again over something else, but it might."

"At least I'll know where to look for you—wherever there are tigers or crocodiles."

"You won't have to because from now on, I want us to be a team."

What was he suggesting? "You mean work together?"

"I mean *be* together. Working with the tigers gave me time to think things through and reach a decision I should probably have made long before. I want to ask you something but this isn't the right time or place, so you don't have to say anything until I ask you properly. And I would like to find the right place to ask you my question. Since this is your town, name the most romantic restaurant in Perth?"

She didn't hesitate. "My place."

She saw him expel a heavy breath. "All right, provided you let me send out for food. I don't want you cooking tonight."

"I'm sure we can arrange something." Already her pulse was double-timing. She didn't regret nominating her apartment over a fancy restaurant. For what she suspected he had in mind—a proposal of marriage—anywhere would be romantic. He had said he didn't want her answer yet, but she was tempted to blurt it out anyway. Only the thought of spoiling the anticipation held her back.

This was turning out to be an amazing day. First, the bombshell of discovering Blake's birth family, then almost losing him through mistrust, and now the prospect of a happy ending to beat the band. No wonder her emotions felt as if they were on a roller coaster.

To steady herself, she reached for the box of photographs. "Since Bob gave us access to these, the least we can do is look through them."

She took a handful and passed another lot to Blake. As Bob had said, they were mostly from the early days of Tiger Mountain. Comparing the barren setting he'd taken on with the lush and successful attraction spread out below them today was like a metaphor for her relationship with Blake, Jo thought.

"Hey, there are even a few from Diamond Downs," she said, recognizing some of the settings. "They look to be fairly old."

"Before I became part of the Logan family, Bob mounted an expedition to relocate a rogue crocodile from the river system below Cotton Tree Gorge," Blake explained. "For a long time, he kept up the crocodile activity to fund his development of Tiger Mountain. After I came to work for him, he took me along on some of those expeditions. These days, he concentrates on tigers and leaves the crocodile-chasing to me."

Thinking of Blake with Amulya and her cubs, Jo had a vision of him one day passing the baton to his child. Not that she wasn't daunted by the idea of her son or daughter being involved with wild animals, but if genes were any guide, she'd have little say in the matter.

On the other hand, they could inherit her genes and become writers rather than action types, she thought. Talk about getting ahead of yourself. Blake hadn't proposed yet, and already she was planning their children's futures.

Suddenly, her eye was caught by a fading photo she was sure she recognized. She held it out to show him. "Isn't this the river below the Uru cave?"

He looked at it thoughtfully. "Judging by the water level, this was taken in the wet season,.."

"What was Bob doing up there?"

"I can answer that," the older man said, coming in. "I'd finished capturing Des's rogue crocodile, and wanted to photograph some ancient rock art of a style I hadn't seen before."

"The paintings attributed to the Uru people," Blake speculated. "We found a gallery of them not far from where you took this photo."

Bob nodded. "I read about that. I never made it that far because The Wet was setting in, but I came across an old bark canoe wedged on a floating island in the lower reaches of the Bowen. There's a picture here somewhere. Ah, yes."

He pulled out a grainy, almost sepia-tinted shot of what looked to Jo like a tangle of undergrowth. Gradually she made out the bow of a canoe. "Why does it have *JV* written on it?"

Blake looked thunderstruck. "Let me see. My God, it isn't *JV*, it's *J* for Jack, and the *V* is the bottom half of the diamond shape Jack Logan used as his mark. The top part probably weathered away. This was the canoe belonging to Des's grandfather."

Bob massaged his chin. "I've had that photo for twenty-five years and never connected it with your great-grandfather's disappearance. Too bad there'd be nothing left of that old canoe by now."

"Probably not, but if we can identify the location, we might get closer to finding out what happened to him," Blake said.

"Can we get a copy of this photo?" Jo asked.

"I'll have my assistant scan it for you when she brings the coffee. Does this mean you'll be too busy solving a mystery to write about Amulya's cubs?"

On impulse, Jo jumped up and kissed him on the cheek. "If you've given us the key to Jack Logan and his lost mine, your tigers can have the front page."

A flush sprang to the older man's cheeks. "You really think an old photo could be that important?"

Blake nodded. "We won't know until we get back to Diamond Downs and check it out."

Chapter 16

"**I** thought you'd be itching to catch the first plane back to the Kimberley," Jo said in the cab as they drove to her apartment. Copies of Bob's precious photos were safely tucked in her bag.

"The first plane isn't until tomorrow and, unlike Judy, I don't have a friend handy with his own plane."

"So that's the only reason you're staying in Perth tonight?"

He leaned across and kissed her. "What do you think?"

With his mouth on hers, she could barely think at all. "Karen wants to tell you more about your mother. Wouldn't you rather spend time with her?"

"I've waited over thirty years. I can wait a little longer. For now, I'm happy knowing who she was and why she did what she did."

"Does it help?"

He nodded. "It helps."

She couldn't begin to imagine how much. All his life he'd

believed he'd been unwanted, never guessing that his mother had tried to leave him with people she thought would take better care of him than she could.

They pulled up outside a handsome art deco building. Hers was one of the top two of four apartments with a balcony overlooking the Swan River, the reason she'd fallen in love with the place. Stairs just outside her own back door leading down to a garden was another.

Inside, Blake looked around. He had imagined modern, functional furniture piled with a writer's paraphernalia. The richness of black lacquer furniture and burgundy Chinese carpets; a squat porcelain planter, topped with glass and serving as a coffee table; and framed calligraphy on the walls revealed yet another side of her personality. "You like oriental design?"

She put her bag on a side table. "Mad about it."

"You'd love shopping in Broome, especially Chinatown. The shops date back over a century." He saw himself fastening a strand of Broome's famous pearls around her neck. The furnishings in his home at Sawtooth Park would also have to change to suit her taste, he decided, finding the idea appealing. The idea of *her* in his home appealed even more.

"Can I get you a drink? I have sake, beer or wine."

"Beer's fine, thanks."

"You can take the man out of the outback," she said as she went into the kitchen. Through the open door, he saw more oriental touches and a gleaming stainless steel stove. A shelf of well-thumbed cookbooks explained her deft touch with the bush bread.

In an alcove off the living room a computer sat on a lacquered desk. When she returned with two beers, he was inspecting the calligraphy above it. "What does this say?"

"'Beware of the dog.'"

"You're kidding?"

She shook her head. "A friend I interviewed did it for me for fun. I should have her do one about crocodiles."

He sipped the beer. "Do all your story subjects become friends?"

He saw her breath hitch. "A rare few become more than friends."

He put the glass down and moved toward her. Before he could do more, the doorbell rang. The oriental curse springing to his lips was a long way from "Beware of the dog."

"Who can that be? Only a few people know I'm back in Perth." She put her own drink down and went to the door.

Blake leaned against the desk, irritated at recognizing Nigel's voice. Didn't the man know when to quit?

Nigel didn't look any happier to see Blake, giving a nod in token greeting and then ignoring him. "I went into the magazine today and Karen told me you were in town, Jo. I was hoping we could spend the evening together."

Not in this lifetime, Blake wanted to say, preferably as he escorted Wylie out. Jo's glare warned him she preferred to handle this herself. "I'll see about organizing dinner—for two," he said pointedly and took his cell phone into the kitchen.

A dial-up service put him through to a local Chinese restaurant that delivered and could be encouraged to include a bottle of champagne after he volunteered his credit card number. He didn't particularly care what they ate, but he wanted to do this right. So he hunted around the kitchen until he found wineglasses, candles and matches, woven straw place mats, bowls and chopsticks.

Murmurs were still coming from the living room, so he called Diamond Downs. Cade answered. Blake brushed aside discussion about his birth mother for the moment, although he wasn't surprised that Judy had already spread the news of his quest. He would rather share the details with his family— the people he still thought of as his real family—face-to-face. Instead, he filled Cade in on the discovery of the photo.

"That's interesting," Cade said. "When I was updating Des's bookkeeping, I came across some old family photos in a file in his office. I'll hunt them out. I'm sure I saw something about Jack and a canoe in there."

"How is Des?" Blake asked.

"You can't slow him down with an ax."

Not good, but refusing to take things easy, Blake translated. What else was new? He told his foster brother he and Jo would be returning on the next day's flight and hung up before Cade could ask about Blake's plans for tonight.

Turning his attention back to Jo, Blake tried not to eavesdrop on her conversation, but Nigel's voice carried from the other room. The man was practically pleading for a second chance. Hearing her firmly reject her ex, Blake smiled. *Kiss, kiss, goodbye*, he said in his head. *No, forget the kiss part. Just goodbye*.

He got his wish. The front door slammed. When he returned to the living room Jo was sitting on the sofa looking shaken.

"Shall I go after him and punch his lights out for you?" he offered.

Her smile bloomed wanly. Better. "My hero."

"I've ordered dinner and champagne to arrive in another thirty minutes," he said in an attempt to change the subject.

She shook off Nigel's visit like a dog shedding water. "What will we do in the meantime?"

Blake completed the move he'd started before they were interrupted. "We could pick up where we left off."

"Half an hour isn't much time."

He brushed a hand over her hair. "You'd be surprised what's possible in half an hour."

And he proceeded to show her.

The time constraint meant their clothes ended up strewn over the floor; the bedroom seemed too far to go. The sofa was more than adequate, being the width of a bed when he pushed the cushions together at one end. And he made sure they used the space wisely by taking turns being on top.

They'd reached Jo's turn when the doorbell rang. She muffled her laughter against his chest. "What should we do now?"

"Answer it together?" he suggested.

She lifted her head. "We'd get arrested."

He buried his face in her hair and thrust his hips upwards. The doorbell rang again more insistently.

"Coming," she called and shook with laughter again. "If that poor delivery person only knew."

How she had any energy left to talk, far less move, Blake didn't know. Too sated to stir, he watched her roll to her feet. A fringed silk throw was draped over a chair. She wound the fabric sarong-style around herself, tucking the ends in under one arm.

Moments later, she came back with a fragrant carrier bag she placed on the coffee table. Hands on hips, she surveyed him. "Just as well the delivery boy couldn't see into this room. You look like an emperor after an orgy."

"As long as you're the empress, subject to my whim," he said. "Come here, woman."

She laughed. "Being subject to your whim isn't much good if I faint from hunger. In case you haven't noticed, the coffee and pastries we had in Bob's office were the only food between me and breakfast. I'm sure his tigers get better fed than that."

Resignedly Blake swung his legs to the floor. He was hungry, but not for food. "You're wrong. They only feed the tigers five days out of seven."

Poking through the containers, she asked, "Economy measure?"

"Imitating their natural diet in the wild."

"Well, mine is to eat seven days out of seven, preferably three times a day."

Admiring her trim behind outlined by the delicate silk, with the fringes brushing the backs of her legs, he wondered where the food went. Definitely not to her slender hips.

On the table, she set out the place mats, chopsticks and bowls he'd rounded up earlier, and lit the candles, casting a pleasant glow over the room although it was still daylight. By that time he'd dressed, even though he'd convinced her to stay in the sarong. "You look gorgeous," he said, kissing the top of her head.

"And convenient," she said, not sounding too put out.

The champagne was chilled and of a reasonable vintage. He handed her a glass and took one, linking wrists with her while holding the glass. "To us."

Keeping her wrist curved around his, she brought the glass to her lips, her gaze meeting his over the rim. "To us."

He drank and lowered the glass. "I think you know what I want to ask you."

"Yes."

"That sounds like an answer."

"It is. I love you, Blake. I want us to be together always."

"In spite of my short fuse and convoluted family history?"

She pressed a kiss to his mouth, her tongue darting out to catch a droplet of champagne at the corner. "If you had a different history, you wouldn't be the man I've come to love."

"Then you'll marry me?"

"Provided we don't have to share our honeymoon with crocodiles."

He pretended dismay. "Darn. I had the expedition all planned. Now we'll have to stay at home in bed."

Her eyes sparkled with amusement. "Poor baby."

He sipped champagne. "Speaking of babies, how many shall we have?"

"One," she said.

"But I thought…"

"At a time," she added. "If you want, we can keep up the Logan family tradition and become foster parents, as well. My parents have been nagging me about marrying and providing them with grandchildren. They will be thrilled when I contact them and tell them our news."

"From the moment we met, I knew you were a woman after my own heart."

She finished her champagne and put it down. "I like to get what I'm after."

Liking the sound of that, he nevertheless felt a frown settle. "What about working your way up to publisher?"

"Karen won't want to lose touch with you, and she's already said she doesn't want to lose me. For starters, I can telecommute. Later, I might do what I've always dreamed of doing, and write a book. The Logan family alone should keep me in material for years."

"Now the truth comes out. You're marrying me for my material."

"Can I help being shameless?"

To prove it, she untied the sarong and let the silk pool at her feet. He drained his glass and put it aside, regretting the time he'd wasted dressing as he hastily reversed the process.

Then her feverish mouth was on his and he felt himself stirring again, although moments before, he'd have sworn it was impossible.

She made the impossible possible, he thought, lifting her against him. She hooked her legs around his hips and linked her hands behind his neck. He carried her across the room to the sofa. His last coherent thought was that he should make a note of the brand of champagne they were drinking. The maker should patent whatever was in it.

A considerable time later, she said, "I think the food's cold."

"Unlike the two of us." He kissed her along the inviting angle between her neck and shoulder. "Why do you think microwaves were invented?"

"For lovers," she said and then dissolved into silvery laughter.

He propped himself up on one arm, studying her. "What's so funny?"

"I was wondering what we'll tell our children when they ask how you proposed marriage to their mother."

"We'll say we were practicing to have them. By then, they'll probably have toddler picture books on the subject and be telling us how it's done."

"I think they do now."

He grinned. "See, I'm perfect father material. Already a fuddy-duddy."

Running a hand across his muscular flank, she said, "You'll never be a fuddy-duddy. But you are perfect."

His grin faded. "Hardly, after learning the truth about my mother. It's not the legacy I hoped to hand on to my kids."

"Not knowing doesn't change the reality. Would you rather have gone on wondering?"

"Do you need to ask?"

She wriggled out from under him and reached for the sarong. "Then let's reheat and eat. My energy level's practically zero."

He pulled on his pants, but didn't bother with the rest of his clothes this time. Wishful thinking? Learning from experience, he told himself. Barefoot, he padded to the table and was surprised at how hungry he was.

Sitting across the table from Blake, Jo made an effort to marshal her thoughts. Difficult when every move he made reminded her of how they had spent the last few hours. How they would spend many more, now that she had accepted his proposal. She had a vision of them sitting across from each other like this years into the future, and knew without doubt it was what she wanted.

She pulled her thoughts back to the present. "Yesterday, I went to see my brother Curt, the investment banker."

Helping himself to Mongolian beef, he asked, "Is Karen paying you too much?"

"Very funny. I wanted to check out Max Horvath's finances."

"I hope your brother is on the right side of the law."

"Curt knows a lot of people, including some of Max's main creditors."

Reaching for the fried rice, Blake paused. "And?"

"It's worse than you suspected. Curt says Max has been given a bit over a month to come up with the money he owes, before his creditors move in on his assets."

"Including the mortgage over Diamond Downs." Blake gestured with his chopsticks. "That doesn't leave us much time."

"We'd better hope the canoe photo leads us closer to the diamonds."

Jo knew she should get up and clear away the remains of their belated feast and then get ready for the flight to the Kimberley. But she felt good lying in the crook of Blake's arm and she should enjoy the feelings.

After they were married, she wouldn't have the luxury of lying abed, far less leaving last night's dishes for the morning. She'd have her work to do and if the children didn't attend school in Halls Creek, she'd have to supervise their lessons by computer.

Was she ready to turn her whole life upside down? It was one thing to spend a few weeks in the outback, roughing it with frills, to use Blake's expression. It was quite another to commit to a lifetime on an isolated property with limited shopping and cultural facilities.

She turned her head to watch Blake sleeping. One arm was under her shoulder and the other was flung over his head. The covers had slid down to his waist and his chest rose and fell rhythmically. The hypnotic sight banished any misgivings. If need be, she could be back in Perth in half a day, or touch down in one of the exotic Asian ports that were closer to the Kimberley than most Australian cities.

And she would have Blake.

Did anything else really matter?

He opened his eyes and gave her a lazy, sexy smile that turned her heart to mush. "You're thinking again."

She traced a finger down his chest. "Only good thoughts."

"I prefer naughty ones."

"Those, too."

He rolled over. "Keep that up and we'll never make our flight."

They did, anyway. And the cleanup and phone calls to his aunt and Lauren, as well as a snack at the airport. As Blake said, it was amazing what could be done in a short time if you had sufficient incentive.

And what an incentive he provided.

What a difference a couple of days made, she thought as they checked in at the Great Western terminal. On the flight to Perth, she'd been devastated because Blake had believed she'd been conspiring against him. Now, he not only knew the truth, he also knew Jo hadn't willingly deceived him.

In her wildest dreams she'd never imagined returning to the Kimberley as Blake's fiancée. He'd said they would go to Broome to choose an engagement ring as soon as she finished her story. Seeing the old pearling port through his eyes would be an adventure, but the need for a ring paled beside the love and trust she now felt for him.

"When shall we tell your family about us?" she asked as the twin-engine Beechcraft taxied out to the runway. She had the uncanny sensation of going home.

"Judy's already guessed, which means the whole clan probably knows by now. She practically ordered me to get my butt down here and not let you slip through my fingers."

"Now there's a provocative metaphor."

He groaned. "And nothing to be done about it for hours."

"Never heard of the mile-high club?"

He looked around the compact cabin seating less than twenty people. "Not a chance."

Aching from last night and this morning, she would have been horrified if he'd treated her suggestion as anything but the joke she'd intended, but she couldn't resist asking, "What happened to 'Where there's a will'?"

"I was referring to finding the lost mine. While you fare-welled Wylie last night, I called Cade. He thinks he might have come across some more photos linking the canoe in Bob's pictures with Jack Logan."

Although inwardly pleased with his progress, she made a face. "Should I be shattered to discover I wasn't the only thing on your mind last night?"

He grinned. "I guarantee I didn't think about the mine for long. And purely in the interests of providing for you and our future family."

"In that case, you're forgiven."

He leaned over and kissed her, making her wonder if her reference to the mile-high club had been as frivolous as she'd thought.

Judy was waiting for them at the airport, her expression telling them immediately that something was wrong. "It's Cade," she said before Blake could voice a question.

Blake hefted their cases into Judy's car. "He was fine when we spoke last night."

"He isn't fine now. Last night, he was in Des's office going through some files when someone broke in and knocked him cold."

Blake swore under his breath, his body going rigid. "Is he okay?"

"He spent the night in the hospital with a nasty lump and a few hours missing from his memory. A few minutes ago, he called to say he's being discharged. He's waiting for us to give him a ride home."

"Thank God," Jo said a heartbeat before Blake did. "Did you see whoever did this?" she asked.

"Dad and I were watching *Pearl Harbor* at full volume. We didn't hear a thing, and Cade can't remember anything from when he went into the office until he came to on the floor."

"Was much taken?"

Judy wrinkled her brow. "That's the strange part. Nothing, as far as we could tell. The safe and computer equipment weren't touched."

"How's Des handling this?"

"About as badly as you'd expect. He's convinced Max Horvath is behind the attack. Left alone, he'd ride over there and challenge Max if it killed him, and it probably would."

A trace of a smile haunted Blake's features. "What do you think?"

"I think I'm a damned fool for giving Max an excuse to hang around the homestead."

Jo knew as well as Blake that nothing he could say would assuage Judy's feeling of guilt, and she might very well be justified. "Was he with you last night?" Blake asked.

"He tried to invite himself to dinner but I told him I had female problems. He couldn't get away fast enough. He looked so embarrassed that wild horses wouldn't have dragged him back."

Blake gripped the car door frame. "Could Eddy Gilgai be responsible for the attack on Cade?"

Judy looked thoughtful. "Do you think he'd be that stupid?"

Blake smacked a hand to his forehead. "I'm the stupid one. I'm pretty sure I know what Cade's attacker was looking for."

"The canoe photos," Jo contributed, making the connection at the same moment. She got into the back seat, leaving the front for Blake and Judy.

"What canoe photos?" Judy asked as she drove toward the hospital.

Blake explained about finding the photos in Bob Stirton's collection. "Cade thought he'd found some more in a file in Des's office."

"After Cade was taken to the hospital, the police asked me to check to see what was missing. I don't remember seeing any file of old photos."

Blake swore. "Whoever hit Cade must have taken them."

Jo leaned on the seat between them. "We think Max is getting desperate. In Perth, I learned that his creditors have given him a little over a month to meet their demands."

Judy's hands tightened around the wheel. "Oh, God, I didn't know. The embarrassment could have been an act. He could have sneaked back last night."

"Or he could have sent one of his henchmen. You weren't to know."

Judy slammed her palms against the wheel, making the car shudder. "I should have known. I was so busy playing Jane Bond, thinking I could get under his guard, that I never dreamed he would get under mine."

"He's had more practice at this than you have," Jo reminded her. "The only way he could have known about the file was if he overheard the phone call between Blake and Cade."

In the driving mirror, Jo saw Judy's face pale. "I'm beginning to wish we'd never heard of the wretched diamond mine. What if Max finds it before we do?"

Blake's mouth thinned. "We still have Bob's photos. And there's no way Max can know about Jo's hidden valley. That gives us an edge."

Judy shot him a hopeful glance before returning her gaze to the road. "Do you think it's enough?"

"It has to be. I owe Des too much to let Max Horvath destroy him."

"You know Dad doesn't think like that."

"No, but I do."

Hearing the steely ring in his voice, Jo felt a surge of renewed hope. If he believed the landmarks in Bob's photos would lead them to a fortune that had been lost for decades, she would keep the faith, too. They were in this together.

"I need some good news," Judy said as they approached the hospital building. "Tell me you two have worked things out."

Blake blew out a breath. "We've worked things out."

"Woo-hoo! This will make Dad's day, as well." She pulled up outside the main entrance. "Hold the details till we collect Cade, then you won't have to say everything twice."

"There's something else," Blake said, putting a hand out to keep his foster sister in the car. "In Perth, we found out who my birth mother was, and why she abandoned me."

Judy looked stunned. "I know you said it was a possibility, but to know for sure? Are you okay?"

"As okay as you'd expect. I'll fill you and Cade in on the way home."

Tension vibrated through his foster sister. "Do you still think of Diamond Downs as home?"

"It always will be."

Jo saw Judy's eyes brim. "All my life I've dreamed you'd find your natural family, but I was also scared that if you did, we'd lose you."

"Now you know that isn't going to happen." His voice sounded rough with emotion. "Finding out where I came from has made me even more thankful for everything Des and you guys did for me, and more determined than ever to keep Diamond Downs safe for the next generation."

His fingers gripped Jo's. "Max Horvath has no idea what he's taken on. If he wants a war, he's got one."

Chapter 17

Jo awoke to an unfamiliar sound and took a moment to identify it. Suddenly, it hit her. For the first time in her experience, it was raining at Diamond Downs.

Judy had put her and Blake in the same connecting rooms they'd used before. Jo stretched and smiled. Two beds still hadn't been needed. She'd woken up beside him this morning. But he was already up, so she padded to the window and watched the fat droplets of water pelt the glass and stream down the dust-caked surface.

She had never seen rain like it. Sheets of water bounced off the parched earth out of a sullen sky. Miserable-looking working dogs huddled in their kennels in the dusty yard. The air felt too oppressive to breathe. This must be the start of the north's famous wet season when monsoon rain fell for months at a time, filling the empty riverbeds and spreading in shallow lakes across the plains as far as the eye could see.

Then she remembered the tide marks high overhead in the

hidden valley. If The Wet had indeed arrived, what chance did she and Blake have of reaching the diamond mine before Max's creditors moved in?

On edge with worry, she showered and dressed in T-shirt and jeans, and tied her hair into a high ponytail for coolness. When she went into the kitchen, Judy was cooking breakfast. Cade sat at the table, an impressive white bandage bound around his head.

Judy good-humoredly refused Jo's offer to help, so she poured herself some coffee and sat down beside Cade. "How do you feel?"

"Foolish." He touched the bandage and winced in pain. "If it wasn't for the pounding in my head, I'd think I imagined being clobbered. I can't remember a thing after dinner yesterday until I surfaced in the hospital."

"The pounding is the reason you can't remember," Judy said, placing a plate of eggs and bacon in front of him. Evidently the injury hadn't lessened his appetite. "You're only upset because you can't keep joshing Blake about being caught with his pants down."

Jo knew Cade and the others had enjoyed teasing Blake about being caught unawares at the overhang, letting Eddy Gilgai sneak up on him. Now the score was even.

Jo refused Judy's offer of a cooked breakfast and reached for a container of cold cereal. "I can't think of eating hot food in this weather." As she ate, she asked, "Do you think the rain is here to stay?"

Seated across from her, Judy shrugged. "Hard to tell. We usually have a few warm-up downpours before The Wet really sets in."

Jo's sigh of relief was audible. "I was afraid we'd lost our chance to explore the hidden valley."

"Probably why Blake wanted to get over there so early this morning," Judy said.

"He what? We were supposed to go together."

Judy toyed with her food. "Maybe he had an attack of chivalry and decided against dragging you out in the rain."

"Surely the decision should be mine?"

Cade cupped his hands around his coffee mug. "When it comes to women, Blake has a strong, protective urge."

"Don't I know it," Judy agreed.

Thinking of how often her own brothers had driven her crazy trying to baby her, Jo shook her head. "He knows I don't want a protector."

Judy lifted her hands, palms outward. "You'll have to work that out with Blake."

Jo set her jaw. "I intend to, just as soon as he gets back."

Her future sister-in-law grinned. "From the look of you, I wouldn't want to be in his shoes when he does."

Was what he had done so terrible? Jo asked herself as she returned to the bedroom. Through the connecting door, Blake's unused bed mocked her. By taking the decision to accompany him out of her hands, Blake had made her feel less like a full partner in their relationship.

Needing to pace, she wandered into the other room, coming up short at the sight of one of Bob's copied photos propped on Blake's desk. She turned it over. "Join me at Cotton Tree Gorge after breakfast."

Sweet relief washed over her. Had he understood her feelings after all? The note looked as if he'd written it in the dark to avoid waking her. Even so, he still had explaining to do. Such as what was so all-fired urgent that he couldn't wait and take her with him?

Judy looked concerned when Jo explained where she was going. "We've had enough rain to make the land look different. You should take me or Cade with you."

"Cade's in no shape to go anywhere, and you should be here in case Des needs you." She listened for a moment. "The rain sounds like it's easing off. I'll be fine."

Judy spun a bunch of keys across the table. "You'll be safer if you take the pickup."

Jo pocketed the keys. "Thanks. I'll call you when I catch up with Blake."

The rain had indeed eased off and patches of blue showed through the leaden sky. Her heart lightened with the weather as she drove.

She was still mad as hell.

Since her abduction, her family had tried to make decisions for her and protect her from everything remotely risky. Her early boyfriends had had to run the gauntlet of two testosterone-charged inquisitors, and she'd had chaperones to everything other than church. They'd probably have accompanied her there, but she'd joined the choir to thwart them.

Coming of age hadn't made much difference. Her brothers had vetted her apartment before she bought it, conducting a house-to-house of the neighbors for her safety, they'd said. She believed it was to check for single male tenants. Just as well chastity belts had gone out of fashion or she'd be locked away in a tower somewhere, a frustrated virgin.

Blake knew perfectly well how she felt about making her own choices. He had no right to leave her behind for her own good. They needed to start as they meant to go on, she resolved. If she let him treat her like fragile china now, their marriage wouldn't stand a chance. If he acted like this now, imagine how he'd behave if she became pregnant?

Distracted, Jo had to slow down while she got her bearings. True to Judy's prediction, the downpour had filled the creeks and started to carve new ones. Rock walls glistened with newly revealed layers of color. The landscape looked freshly minted. And different.

Apart from the usual bush sounds of insects and distant animals, she was alone, but her nerves prickled as if she were being watched.

Get a grip, she ordered herself. No sense letting the bush get to her. The adversaries she really needed to worry about were all too human, and she was the only one for miles.

Retracing Blake's route to the gorge was tougher than she'd

expected. But giving up and returning to the homestead in defeat wasn't an option. She could do this, she repeated to herself as she hunched over the wheel, the sound of her engine reverberating around the ochre cliffs.

At last, the track widened to a familiar stretch of land along the lower reaches of the Bowen River. She stared in amazement. The rock terraces edging the river were now lapped by a widening ribbon of dun-colored water. The smell of mud, mangroves and tropical blossoms wafted up to her.

Blake's Jeep stood well away from the water, under a tree. Feeling her heart leap, she parked beside it and lifted out her hat and water bottle. Backing out of the car, she gave a shriek as a pair of arms closed around her.

"Blake, if this is your idea of a joke…"

"I'm not Blake."

She struggled in the strong, masculine grip, managing to turn sufficiently to recognize Eddy Gilgai. At his belt swung a formidable knife and a boomerang. She fought the fear threatening to swamp her. "You're Eddy, aren't you? My name's Jo Francis. I'm not trespassing. I'm a guest of the Logan family, so you can let me go."

"I know who you are."

He started to pull her backward, toward the river flats. Oh, God, was he going to throw her to a crocodile? Terrified, she started to struggle and then stopped. This wasn't going to help. She needed to keep her wits about her to get out of this in one piece.

"This won't do you any good. Blake is waiting for me."

"He don't know you're here."

"Yes he does. He left me a note."

Eddy laughed, a disturbingly unhinged sound that chilled her blood. "Blake didn't leave no note. I did."

Suddenly, the messy handwriting made sense. She shuddered, imagining Eddy sneaking into the homestead and into her bedroom. He must have come in after Blake left, while she and the others were at breakfast. Blake would surely have stirred otherwise.

"How did you get hold of the photo?" she demanded. And found she could answer that, too. "It wasn't Blake's copy. It was a similar one from the file you stole from the office after you attacked Cade."

"Didn't think you'd spot the switch. Pretty smart, huh?"

"Smart enough to get you killed when Blake catches up with you."

"He's gonna have to wait his turn. A lot of people want to kill Eddy Gilgai, starting with Max if I don't tell him what he wants to know."

"You work for Max. Why would he want to kill you?"

"His patience is runnin' out. If I don't take him to old Jack's diamond mine soon, I'll be crocodile bait for sure."

He wasn't making any sense. "Your people already know where the mine is. You've kept the secret for decades."

"My people, not me. They don't trust me with secret business."

With good reason, she thought. "You've been stringing Max along all this time?"

"I was following you people, hopin' you'd show me where the mine is. Pretty neat trick to feed the big croc in Dingo Creek so you'd think that's why I was hangin' round your camp."

They'd fallen for it, too. Neither she nor Blake had realized Eddy's activity was a cover for what he really wanted. "What have you done to Blake?" she demanded, striving to keep the fear out of her voice.

"I took care of him. Wasn't hard after I left some of your stuff in Cotton Tree Gorge to make him think you went in there."

"Blake wouldn't be fooled by such an obvious trick," she said, hoping it was true. "He'll come looking for me here."

"Before then, you and me will have them diamonds."

"I don't know where they are, any more than you do."

"You can show me the place where you disappeared."

"What are you talking about?" She knew he meant the place where she'd tumbled into the hidden valley. Blake must have recovered and come looking for her before Eddy could investigate the overhang. Why hadn't he gone back there later, and found his own way into the valley?

"Those rock paintings on the walls near where I disappeared are taboo to you, aren't they?" she asked on a hunch.

"None of your business," he growled.

"They are," she persisted. "What happens to you if you see them?"

"I get rich," he swaggered.

From Shara, she'd learned that there were serious penalties for people who viewed rock art against traditional law and custom. She decided to try bluffing her way through. "Even if I tell you where the diamonds are, they won't do you any good. If you look at the rock art protecting it, your people will kill you."

"They say they gonna kill me anyway. If I get him the diamonds, Max'll protect me."

She let herself slump in his hold. "How can I take you to the mine when I don't know where it is?"

He shook her viciously. "You better remember real quick if you want to see your fella again."

"He isn't my fella. I was looking for him to tell him so." Close enough to the truth, she thought. She had intended to give Blake a piece of her mind.

"He's your fella all right. You show me the mine or you and him be goin' for a nice swim in the river down there."

He forced her around so she could glimpse a great horned head and yellow eyes showing above the caramel water. "After I show you, you'll throw me to the crocodile anyway," she said, proud that her voice shook only a little.

"It be so quick, you never know about it."

She almost laughed. He sounded as if he was doing her a favor. Memories of an old lady promising to send her to the angels came crashing down on her. But she was no longer six years old. She had the power to act. With all her strength, she jabbed her elbow backward into her captor's stomach.

Braced to run the second his grip slackened, she took off, ignoring his curses and the light glinting off the blade in his hand. Something whistled past her head and a killer boomerang Blake had called a nulla nulla lodged in a tree trunk inches away.

Sobs caught in her throat as she grabbed the boomerang. Frantically she wrestled the weapon out of the tree and spun around, holding it like the club Blake had told her it was.

"Is this the weapon you used on Blake and Cade?" she demanded, keeping her eyes wide open although terror urged her to squeeze them shut.

He danced the knife blade in the air close to her face. "You give me that."

"If you insist." She ignored the mad pounding of her heart and the blood singing in her head, and swung the club in a savage arc. At the last minute, he ducked and the heavy weapon slammed into his shoulder, doing enough damage to make him swear volubly, but not disabling him as completely as she'd hoped.

Sweat made the club spin out of her hand and go tumbling down the muddy bank, where she heard it hit the water with a splash.

Recovering his balance, Eddy stalked her with the blade. "You better show me that mine now. Big croc's gettin' hungry."

She backed away. She didn't dare look to see where she was putting her feet, trusting the squelching sensation underfoot to guide her, and praying she wouldn't lose her footing. This close to the water, the crocodile could easily lunge for them. The mud was a dance floor to its broad, webbed claws. At any moment fate could decree either she or Eddy become the creature's dance partner.

It wouldn't be her if she could prevent it, she resolved. Blake was still in the gorge somewhere, perhaps injured at

Eddy's hands. The thought gave her the strength to act. "Help me, I'm slipping," she screamed, making a convincing show of sliding sideways in the mud. At least she hoped it was a show.

Reflex—or the awareness that he could lose his meal ticket—made Eddy lunge for her. Using her joined hands as a club, she swung against his body with all her strength and sent him stumbling and slipping down the bank.

Her momentum meant she had to throw herself backward into the mud to stop from following him. By the time she had righted herself, Eddie was standing waist deep in the river.

No, not waist deep. Something had hold of him around the chest. His arms flailed in the air and his mouth gaped, but no sound came out.

Rigid with horror, Jo was unable to move or scream. The threat seemed unreal in such a beautiful place but the humped, threatening shape of the crocodile's body was unmistakable. Then the crocodile started to drag Eddy down into the murk.

Oh, God, she hadn't wanted this. Whatever he'd done, this was too appalling an end for anyone. She wrenched herself free of the clinging mud and grabbed the first thing at hand, a fallen tree branch longer than her body.

It took almost more courage than she possessed to approach the water and look death in the face. She hefted the sapling so it was half in and half out the water, the bushy branches within reach of Eddy's flailing arms and hideous, soundless scream.

"Grab the branch, grab hold," she screamed. "Dear God, grab the branch."

But there was no one to hear her terrified plea or her sobs when she realized the water had closed over the crocodile and its burden. All she saw were bubbles rising to the surface. There was no trace of anything, not even blood. Around her, birds shrieked in alarm.

Then she was slipping, too, faster and faster toward that terrible murky graveyard, her fingers clawing at the branch in the effort to save herself, but it was no good. She and the branch were carried into the water.

Time froze, taking on the quality of a bad dream. As she struggled to the surface, spitting mud, she expected to see the crocodile's blazing yellow eyes fix on her at any moment. Then the dragon body would come up like a submarine surfacing. With a powerful sweep of its tail, it would be on her.

She saw nothing.

A current had caught the branch and she was being swept along. She had no idea how she'd managed to retain her death grip on the sapling, but it was tangled around her like a barrier of safety. An illusion, she knew. The big crocodile was probably lord of this stretch of river, but there might be others.

Blake had told her that after a kill, a crocodile stayed around, keeping watch over its prey. With a meal in its underwater larder, it might not be looking for another yet.

An image of Eddy in the great beast's jaws made the gorge rise in her throat until she forced it down. She was alive for now. Somehow she had to get out of this river. Eddy was beyond her help, she had no doubt, but Blake was out there somewhere, possibly injured. He needed her.

And heaven knew, she needed him. Fighting for her precious independence seemed so pointless now. What good was freedom of choice, if the one choice that mattered was denied to her?

Staying in the middle of the tangled branch, she kicked out with all her strength for the bank, struggling to get out of the current, and make it to shore. Weakened from the fight with Eddy, she had few resources left to fight the current but she drew on some unseen force deep inside her and knew that it came from Blake.

He would never allow her to give up. How could she demand less from herself?

"Hold on, I'm coming."

A sob burst from her throat. She must have conjured

Blake's voice out of her desperate longing. But the figure swimming strongly toward her was no fantasy. He was also fighting the swirling water, but his greater strength saw him make more headway.

She dragged air into her aching lungs. "There's a crocodile. Go back." She was still sobbing, "Go back," when he reached her.

"Too late, I'm here," he said grimly, then saved his strength to grab the branch and do what she'd been unable to do for herself, tow it out of the current by brute force. But to her confusion, he didn't steer for the bank as she'd tried to do. Instead, he aimed for a floating island and beached them on a refuge of tropical greenery in the middle of the river.

Feeling the current release her, she sagged, but immediately understood the need to get farther away from the water. Hauling herself to her feet she staggered another thirty feet before collapsing.

Blake's hands came under her arms. "Only a little farther, then you can rest."

"Sadist," she grumbled but let him help her put a few more yards between them and the water.

Nor did she object when he stripped off his shirt and wadded it to provide a cushion for her on the matted ground. Bare to the waist he had never looked more magnificent. "I thought I'd never see you again," she said when she regained the energy to speak.

His arm, already tight around her, became a steel band. "When I saw you in the water…" He coughed as if to clear his throat, but she'd heard the betraying emotion.

"It's okay. I'm okay," she said, slightly astonished that it was true. "How did you know it was safe to dive in?"

"I didn't care. You were in the water."

Love for him welled through her, almost more than she could bear. "Thank you."

His lips grazed her forehead, her nose, her mouth. Light,

possessive kisses she would have resisted only hours before. Now, she accepted them for the homage he intended. For the love.

Sorely tempted to retreat into the sanctuary of his love and banish all memory of tragedy, she resisted, knowing it would not be banished for long.

She squared her shoulders and moved a little away from him. "Did you see what happened? How the crocodile took Eddy."

Blake's jaw firmed. "I saw. I was on the escarpment, following the wild goose chase he'd set out for me, when I heard you scream. I couldn't get down to you any faster."

"There's no chance he's alive?"

"None."

"He didn't make a sound, just flailed his arms, and then the crocodile took him under."

Blake seemed to understand her need to go over the details. He didn't try to hush her or comfort her until she'd haltingly recounted the event, but held her strongly, reassuringly.

When her words faltered at last, he pulled her against him, stroking her back and hair. "Horvath will pay for luring you here and putting you through this."

She had explained about being drawn to the gorge under false pretenses. "Eddy said he wrote the message. There's nothing to tie it to Max."

He hurled a lump of driftwood far out into the river. "That man has more lives than a cat. There must be some way to link him to these attacks."

"If there is you'll find it. Once we get off this island."

He gave a wry smile. "I was hoping you wouldn't bring that up so soon."

A chill gusted through her. "There's no way off except to swim, is there?"

She saw him weigh up his answer and then lift his shoulders. "No."

A plunge into ice water couldn't have shocked her more

but she faced him unflinchingly. "Then we swim. We did it once, we can do it again."

He cupped her chin and pressed his mouth against hers. "You're one hell of a woman, Joanne Francis."

As he'd no doubt intended, she pulled down the corners of her mouth. "I warned you about the consequences of using that name."

"Then try this one for size, Mrs. Stirton."

She played along. Anything to banish the fear lurking at the fringes of her mind. "What makes you think I intend to be Mrs. Anybody?"

"It's your call. After this morning, I won't impose anything on you that you don't want, not even my protection if it makes you feel smothered."

She nestled into his arm. "At this moment, I welcome all the smothering I can get."

"Only at this moment?"

How well he knew her. "Okay, it probably won't last. But I'll try to keep my independent streak from getting us into any more trouble."

"Can't ask for more than that." He got up and started uphill.

"Where are you going?"

"Before we swim for it, I want to be sure it's our only alternative."

Her relief was ill-disguised. "I'm with you there."

Scrambling through the tangled undergrowth and stumbling over the raft of river debris was no picnic, but she wasn't anxious to brave the river again just yet.

The island was obviously home to large numbers of birds. Remains of nests and broken eggs littered the high ground. "In spring, this place must be alive with chicks," she observed.

"It's the reason no one ever comes here, to preserve the breeding ground as a sanctuary," he explained.

She almost fell over a massive mound. "Wow, I'd hate to see the bird that belongs to."

"Not a bird, a crocodile," he said.

Jo shivered and glanced around uneasily. "Now I see why you found my survival project so amusing. This is the real thing, isn't it?"

"Don't worry, you're handling it like a veteran. No regrets?"

"About staying in the Kimberley? Never." How could she when everything necessary for *her* survival was right here in front of her?

"I have to go to the ladies' room," she said with a glance at the crocodile mound. "Could you—um—stand guard?"

"My pleasure." Chivalrously, he turned his back while she found a relatively clear place among the screening bushes. Never had she dreamed of a crocodile nest for a bathroom, she thought.

A few minutes later, she rejoined him to find his gaze fixed on a tangle of branches a few yards away. "It's okay, you can look now," she teased.

He pressed his hands to her shoulders and turned her so she faced the direction of his gaze. "I am looking. Tell me what you see there."

Something familiar about the scene nagged at her. "Twigs, branches—oh, my heavens! It's the place in Bob's photo."

"If the canoe washed up here, no wonder it wasn't found."

Almost reverently he knelt at the cluster, parting the twigs carefully, although he knew as well as she did that little would remain of a dugout canoe after twenty-five years.

There was always hope. "Anything?"

He let the branches fall back and stood up. In his hand was a curving piece of wood the size of a saucer. If they hadn't been looking for fragments of a canoe, she might never have recognized it. He turned it over. Long ago something had been burned into the wood, the actual letters lost to time.

Blake held the remnant almost reverently. "This confirms our guess that the underground creek in Francis Valley is part of the Bowen system."

"The Bowen goes all the way to the Uru cave, where Max Horvath found traces of diamonds. We must be getting close to the mine."

"Not close enough. With The Wet coming, we're running out of time."

"One hurdle at a time," she said firmly. "Feel like a swim?"

Her light tone didn't fool Blake. He knew she was scared to death and after what she'd witnessed today, she was entitled. He wished he could spare her the ordeal ahead.

Damn, but this independence thing of hers was going to be tough to respect, when his every instinct urged him to guard her with his life.

There was one thing he could give her. "Crocodiles only feed once or twice a week. The one that took Eddy won't be interested in us for a few days."

She nodded in appreciation of his attempt. "Let's get this over with."

He read the river carefully, watching the movement of debris on the water, before choosing where he judged the current to be weakest.

Reaching shore was still a battle, made more nightmarish by knowing what might lurk beneath them. Blake helped her fight the current but could do nothing about the fear except stay close to her, knowing that by swimming close together, they made a more formidable target and reduced the risk of an attack.

By the time they reached the mud flats, she could barely drag herself ashore but she staggered to higher ground with him before collapsing. He had never loved or admired her more.

Words were all he had the strength to offer. "I love you, Jo."

She lifted her head. "I love you, too." Then she laughed huskily.

The warm sound thrilled him. "Now what?"

"In all the best love stories, this would be the moment when we throw ourselves into each other's arms and make passionate love."

"We'll take a rain check," he promised. "But not for long. I like the feel of you in my arms too much."

"About as much as I like being there," she assured him.

"I never thought I'd find a woman like you."

"One who swims crocodile-infested rivers and fights off bad guys?" she asked.

He summoned the energy to roll closer, draping an arm across her. "Not to mention looking sensational in a wet T-shirt."

His mouth found hers and Jo gave herself up to the joy of being alive and being loved. Coming close to losing both today, she knew she would never take such blessings for granted again.

He let her take as long as she needed to recover and then helped her to her feet. He didn't have to tell her that Eddy's death would have to be reported to the police and an investigation started. She shrank from going over the events again and again for the authorities, but recognized the necessity. And Blake would be with her.

They would be there for each other for the rest of their lives, she knew, her spirits starting to lift.

On the way to the cars, she stumbled and he took her hand, reinforcing the thought. "If we can survive a day like today, we can survive anything," she said as much to herself as to him.

His grip tightened. "Survival is for wimps. Together, you and I are going to live and thrive, and take the world by storm."

She remembered something she'd said to him before in jest. Now she said in all sincerity, "My hero."

He was and always would be, she knew. Today, she had

learned perhaps the most valuable lesson of her life. It wasn't a weakness to need someone, as long as the feeling was mutual.

Of that, she had not the slightest doubt.

Epilogue

"What do you like best about the Kimberley so far, Lauren?"

The young woman looked thoughtful. "I like Perth better, Mr. Logan. But the kangaroos are nice, and the colored birds are pretty."

Des grinned. "I appreciate an honest woman. Would you like anything else to eat or drink, Lauren or Adam?"

"No thank you," they chorused and smiled at each other.

Enjoying coffee on the homestead veranda after dinner had become a pleasant routine during Lauren's and Adam's visit to Diamond Downs. Jo had proposed the trip to celebrate the ending of the threat to their group home. Jo's editor had kept her word and pleaded their case with her developer husband. Ron Prentiss agreed immediately. Anything to keep his gorgeous wife and her new relatives happy, he'd said.

Jo's concern that her friend might find the Kimberley

frightening had proved unfounded, although she suspected Adam's presence had a lot to do with the changes in Lauren. Attentive and gentlemanly, he was good for her.

He encouraged Lauren to take risks within her capabilities, making Jo wonder if she should have done more over the years. When it came to her friend, she'd been the overprotective one, Jo thought, sneaking a glance at Blake. At least they'd put that issue to bed now. Was it almost two weeks since Eddy was taken by the crocodile? It felt like years.

Blake was deep in conversation with Ryan Smith, the last of the Logan foster family for Jo to meet. To support the family while Eddy's death was investigated, Ryan had flown in the day before from Broome. By now, Jo had stopped looking for family resemblances between the boys, but she was starting to recognize the shared core of strength and decency that was Des's legacy to them all.

Ryan was as tall as the other men, but leaner although no less muscular. His red hair was a distinction among his foster brothers. Jo had liked him at first sight, and also hadn't missed the chemistry vibrating between him and Judy Logan. According to Judy, Ryan had spent the least amount of time with the Logans and had had the most difficulty adjusting, although she hadn't gone into details. Judy also hadn't mentioned that she was attracted to Ryan, but Jo sensed it immediately, perhaps because of her own heightened feelings for Blake.

With Cade, they were discussing the discovery of the site where Jack Logan's canoe had washed up. A map was spread between them, and Blake's finger stabbed it as he made a point. It was a shame he couldn't get back to the Bowen and trace it to its conjunction with the underground creek. Somewhere in between lay a fortune in diamonds.

But he'd neglected his crocodile park for too long because of her, she thought with a twinge of conscience. He hadn't done anything he hadn't wanted to do—she knew him well enough now to be certain. But the breeding ponds at Sawtooth

Park had developed technical problems requiring urgent attention, and he'd had no choice but to go back to his work.

Not that the search for the mine would be neglected. Judy had assured them that she and Ryan would continue the quest. In fact, she'd insisted on it, saying it was time she did more to help.

An excuse to spend time with Ryan? Jo wondered. How well she understood the craving. She had moved with Blake into his rambling house at Sawtooth Park and, between his work and her writing, they spent every hour they could together. It was barely enough.

In two months, they would be married. Jo had suggested the date to give Judy and Ryan time to learn what they could before The Wet set in, knowing that their foster father's security and well-being were the best wedding presents Blake could receive.

A commotion at the door heralded Judy bearing a huge cake.

Blake's handsome features were reflected in the dancing candles. "What's this for?"

"Karen Prentiss thinks the date your mother wrote on the birth notice she kept with her must be your real birthday. In case you hadn't noticed, it's today. So make a wish and blow out your candles."

Looking uncomfortable with the attention, Blake was sporting about it. As he blew the candles out, his gaze met Jo's across the cake. There was no need for Blake to wish for their happiness. Two people couldn't possibly be happier than she and Blake, his tender gaze telling her more eloquently than words.

Her glance went to Ryan Smith, standing with his hand on Judy's shoulder. Maybe part of the wish might be for them to work out their future as happily as her and Blake.

She didn't have to ask what else Blake had wished for. She knew. For his foster father to have the heart transplant he needed to restore him to health, and for the mine to be found so Diamond Downs could remain in Logan hands. Although with The Wet Season fast approaching, Jo feared that was going to take a lot more than a wish.

* * * * *

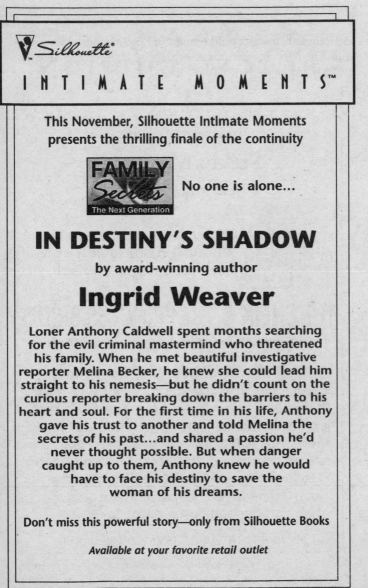

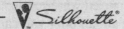

If you enjoyed what you just read,
then we've got an offer you can't resist!

Take 2 bestselling love stories FREE!

Plus get a FREE surprise gift!

Clip this page and mail it to Silhouette Reader Service™

IN U.S.A.	IN CANADA
3010 Walden Ave.	P.O. Box 609
P.O. Box 1867	Fort Erie, Ontario
Buffalo, N.Y. 14240-1867	L2A 5X3

YES! Please send me 2 free Silhouette Intimate Moments® novels and my free surprise gift. After receiving them, if I don't wish to receive anymore, I can return the shipping statement marked cancel. If I don't cancel, I will receive 6 brand-new novels every month, before they're available in stores! In the U.S.A., bill me at the bargain price of $4.24 plus 25¢ shipping and handling per book and applicable sales tax, if any*. In Canada, bill me at the bargain price of $4.99 plus 25¢ shipping and handling per book and applicable taxes**. That's the complete price and a savings of at least 10% off the cover prices—what a great deal! I understand that accepting the 2 free books and gift places me under no obligation ever to buy any books. I can always return a shipment and cancel at any time. Even if I never buy another book from Silhouette, the 2 free books and gift are mine to keep forever.

245 SDN DZ9A
345 SDN DZ9C

Name _____ (PLEASE PRINT)

Address _____ Apt.#

City _____ State/Prov. _____ Zip/Postal Code

Not valid to current Silhouette Intimate Moments® subscribers.

Want to try two free books from another series?
Call 1-800-873-8635 or visit www.morefreebooks.com.

* Terms and prices subject to change without notice. Sales tax applicable in N.Y.
** Canadian residents will be charged applicable provincial taxes and GST.
All orders subject to approval. Offer limited to one per household].
® are registered trademarks owned and used by the trademark owner and or its licensee.

INMOM04R   ©2004 Harlequin Enterprises Limited

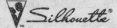

SPECIAL EDITION™

Coming in November to
Silhouette Special Edition
The fifth book in the exciting continuity

DARK SECRETS. OLD LIES. NEW LOVES.

THE MARRIAGE ACT

(Silhouette Special Edition #1646)

by

Elissa Ambrose

Plain-Jane accountant Linda Mailer had never done anything shocking in her life—until she had a one-night stand with a sexy detective and found herself pregnant! *Then* she discovered that her anonymous Romeo was none other than Tyler Carlton, the man spearheading the investigation of her beleaguered boss, Walter Parks. Tyler wanted to give his child a real family, and convinced Linda to marry him. Their passion sparked in close quarters, but Linda was wary of Tyler's motives and afraid of losing her heart. Was he using her to get to Walter—or had they found the true love they'd both longed for?

Available at your favorite retail outlet.

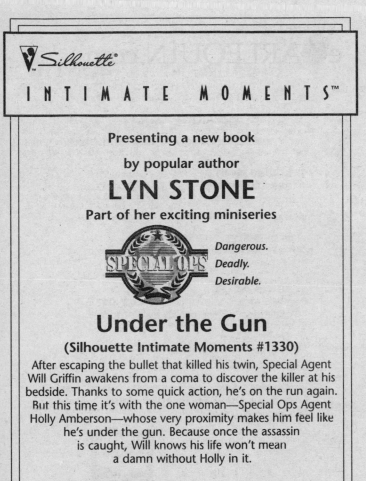

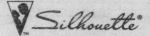
Silhouette®

COMING NEXT MONTH

#1327 ALONE IN THE DARK—Marie Ferrarella
Cavanaugh Justice

Patience Cavanaugh felt relieved when detective Brady Coltrane agreed to find the man stalking her. But there was just one problem. Brady was irresistibly sexy—and he wanted more than a working relationship. Even though she'd vowed never to date cops, he was the type of man to make her break her own rules....

#1328 EVERYBODY'S HERO—Karen Templeton
The Men of Mayes County

It was an all-out war between the sexes—and Joe Salazar was losing the battle. Taylor McIntyre tempted him to yearn for things he'd given up long ago. Would their need to be together withstand the secret he carried?

#1329 IN DESTINY'S SHADOW—Ingrid Weaver
Family Secrets: The Next Generation

Reporter Melina Becker was 100 percent sure Anthony Benedict was too potent and secretive for his own good. His psychic ability had saved her from a criminal who was determined to see her—and her story—dead. They were hunting for that same criminal, but Melina knew that Anthony had his own risky agenda. And she *had* to uncover his secrets—before danger caught up to them!

#1330 UNDER THE GUN—Lyn Stone
Special Ops

He could see things before they happened...but that hadn't saved soldier Will Griffin from the bullet that had killed his brother. Now he and fellow operative Holly Amberson were under the gun. With his life—and hers—on the line, Will would risk everything to stop a terrorist attack and protect the woman he was falling in love with....

#1331 NOT A MOMENT TOO SOON—Linda O. Johnston

Shauna O'Leary's ability to write stories that somehow became reality had driven a wedge into her relationship with private investigator Hunter Strahm. But after a madman kidnapped his daughter, he could no longer deny Shauna's ability could save his child. Yet how could he expect her to trust and love him again when he was putting her in jeopardy for the sake of his child?

#1332 VIRGIN IN DISGUISE—Rosemary Heim

Bounty hunter Angel Donovan was a driven woman—driven to distraction by her latest quarry. Personal involvement was not an option in her life—until she captured Frank Cabrini, and suddenly the tables were turned. The closer she came to understanding her sexy captive, the less certain she was of who had captured whom... and whether the real culprit was within her grasp.

SIMCNM1004